Grasping for Grace

Never Grow Up

D. PICHARDO-JOHANSSON

Acknowledgment

Special thanks to Mary Frame, for her constant encouragement over the past months, and to Savannah Jezowski, for being an amazing cheerleader in addition to an awesome developmental editor.

Dedication

To my husband David (again), the man who inspired this novel. He's the best play-buddy in the world with whom I rediscover childhood every day.

About This Book

This novel is Book 4 in the Sunshine Series. Reading previous books is not necessary to enjoy the plot. It contains brief references to characters and events from previous books just as an extra treat to readers of the series.

All books in this series are stand alone, with no cliffhangers and can be read out of order. But I usually recommend reading Book 2 first, (Just for Joy: Beyond Achievement), in order to maximize excitement and minimize spoilers for that book's mystery portion. If you haven't yet read Just for Joy and would like to read it first, send me an email (pichardojohanssonmd@gmail.com) and I'll direct you to how to get it discounted or free.

Prologue

(Five years ago)

HE FELT LIKE HE'D JUMPED IN A TIME MACHINE AND traveled back two decades.

Oh my God, it's Grace! It has to be!

Sitting at an end of the long conference table, Jacob Wetzel's heart pounded as he stared at the blond woman leading the meeting. She was beautiful, no doubt about it, but that wasn't what made his pulse race. It was the way she scrunched her nose every time she sneezed. The way she pursed her lips when she concentrated. And especially the little scar under her chin—which he remembered happened when she fell off a sleigh.

She must have changed her name, but it has to be her.

An avalanche of memories from childhood flooded his mind. He could hear the sound of her laughter as he pushed her on the tire swing. He felt the summer wind on his skin as they ran together to jump into Lake Michigan. He could see the green fireflies float around them as they lay in the tall grass at night, watching stars.

He made no effort to follow her words as she talked. The anger he'd carried into that office evaporated. He no longer cared that his father had dragged him into this small, coastal Florida town he'd never heard of, and forced him into this meeting.

Slow down. It's not the first time you've thought you found her.

She made no attempt to look at him from across the table—for which he felt thankful. For the first time, he realized how much he'd let himself go. He felt self-conscious about the weight he'd gained, his wrinkled shirt, his unkempt hair, and ungroomed beard.

But also, for the first time in years, he felt a semblance of joy and hope in his soul.

But how can I ever approach her looking like this?

Chapter 1

"**I**'M SORRY, BUT IF I SEE ONE MORE COUPLE KISSING THIS week, I'll throw up."

Allison Connors unloaded her armful of folders and handouts onto the passenger seat of her gray Mercedes. She placed her phone in the dashboard holder and took the driver's seat while continuing her FaceTime call. "Emery, it's no fun being the last sane woman standing, surrounded by lobotomized, syrupy couples." After unbuttoning her sky-blue jacket that matched her skirt and eyes, she fastened her seatbelt and drove away from the Fort Sunshine Women's Shelter. "But also, I never attend weddings as a matter of principle. I won't partake in a ritual that forces women to become the property of men."

On the screen, Dr. Emery Love's narrow green eyes glistened, and her full lips trembled. "But, Allison! You can't miss Fe's wedding! It's bad enough that you skipped the rehearsal dinner and refused to be a bridesmaid."

Only the Botox immobilizing her face prevented Allison from cringing. She clutched the steering wheel and kept calculated coldness in her voice. "Bridesmaid duty is a sadomasochistic practice. The same goes for weddings—and the oppressive institution of marriage."

"Please, Allison," Emery begged. "All the girlfriends are here, helping Fe get ready. She'll be devastated if you don't come wish her luck on her big day."

The ethical dilemma—principle versus sisterhood love—was

killing Allison. And she felt exhausted after her intense group session with abuse survivors at the women's shelter. It didn't help that her volunteer work had to be squeezed in later in the day when she was tired from her day job as a psychotherapist and her side job as a feminist activist and self-help writer.

But she couldn't disappoint her girlfriends.

With a groan, she turned the car and headed to the Beachfront Crowne Plaza. "All right! I'm on my way. But I'll just wish Fe good luck and then I'm out of there."

Emery cheered and clapped with delight, telling Allison about all the fun they'd have together. Taking advantage of a red light, Allison shot her a warning look. "I'm *not* staying for the wedding, so don't even dream of introducing me to one of the groom's—and your—two hundred cousins."

Disappointment flashed on Emery's face. Newer in the group of friends, she still hadn't lost hope of pairing Allison off. But if Allison knew anything about her, it was two things: Emery was stubborn, and she thought life was a soap opera.

"Allison, it's modern times; there's no shame in admitting it, so tell me the truth." Emery leaned closer to the screen and her lustrous auburn waves curtained her face. "You're gay, aren't you?"

"Unfortunately not," Allison mumbled, continuing on at the green light.

"Then why?" Emery threw her free hand in the air. "Why do you dislike men so much?"

Approaching the beachside, Allison lowered the window to let the fresh ocean breeze play with her golden hair. "Why do I hate men? Because they did nothing to deserve their good luck. Winning the genetic lottery of a Y chromosome was all it took for them to get world supremacy, freedom from the period, and the good side of all double standards."

"Aaaand..." A voice sounded in the background. "... you can tell she's never met a man who knows what he's doing in bed." Wearing only lacy black lingerie, their friend Hope joined the screen with foam curlers in her caramel-highlighted hair. "Don't bother, Emery. If the perfect man fell from the sky and landed on Allison's windshield, she'd turn on the windshield wipers to get him off her car."

The girls tittered and Allison's lips twitched, resisting the urge to curve. Too late, she realized she'd missed the hotel entrance. She kept driving down the A1A highway, admiring the hints of ocean between hotel and condo buildings, while looking for a place to make a U-turn.

As Allison pulled into a parking lot, Hope teased, "If the perfect man fell from the sky in front of Allison's car, she'd make sure to run him over with her Mercedes, flattening him on the pavement..." They giggled again. Hope gestured to move an imaginary shift stick. "And then she'd hit reverse to run him over again, backward."

"Are you guys done torturing me?" Allison asked, steering the car around. "Contrary to you I don't need to spend my life glued to some guy, smooching, giggling, and whispering secrets like third-graders."

Hearing a clicking noise from the phone, she glanced down and saw Emery tapping the screen. "No, miss! You're not off the hook until you admit that your refusal to be part of Fe's wedding is nothing but sour grapes. Deep inside, you want to find love too."

Allison was outraged. How dare Emery insinuate she wasn't happy by herself? She'd written a bestseller, teaching women that they could be!

As she drove off, she opened her mouth to protest, but something held her back.

Emery had a point.

Now that all her friends were pairing up and having less time, being single wasn't that fun anymore. She felt left behind.

Ouch.

"And I totally get that a woman may choose to remain single on behalf of freedom. But what good is freedom for in your case?" Emery insisted. "You never travel, you never date, you don't even go out unless we drag you… all you do is work."

Ouch again.

Clearing her throat, Allison straightened her shoulders. "I teach my clients to walk away from energy-draining situations. So I won't waste more time in this pointless chat. See you soon."

The darn phone refused to disconnect the call and Allison had to tap on the screen repeatedly. As she finally succeeded, a distant yell startled her.

"HEY! STOP!"

Whipping her head up, she caught a glimpse of a skateboarder speeding across the street.

She stomped on the brakes and the tires screeched. The seatbelt pulled against her chest and the pile of folders flew from the passenger seat onto the car floor.

It was too late.

She heard a thump against her car hood and, simultaneously, the sound of something cracking under the tires. The blue-and-red shadow of a human figure collided briefly with her windshield; then, in an acrobatic-like move, bounced off, and jumped away to the road shoulder, rolling on the ground before stopping.

As the car jerked to a halt, her heart stopped for a second, then raced.

Oh God! I killed someone!

She turned on the emergency lights. As she hurried out of the car, thousands of terrifying scenarios flashed through her mind. The victim could be dead or paralyzed. And it was all her fault for being on her cell while driving. She saw herself in jail, her career finished, her life plagued by guilt.

The first thing she noticed was the cracked skateboard under the car tires.

Oh no! I hit a kid!

As she rushed to the figure lying facedown on the side of the road, her brain registered that the victim was too tall and muscular to be a kid. The person shifted. *At least he's alive!* "Don't move!" she snapped, "I'll call nine-one-one and—"

The figure rolled over and the next words died on her lips.

That was not a kid. That was a man.

And what a man!

Chapter 2

ALLISON'S GAZE SLOWLY SLID UP FROM RED SNEAKERS TO firm calves, then muscular thighs partially covered by black spandex shorts. For a few seconds her eyes remained glued to the generous bulge under those shorts until she managed to peel them away to take in a royal blue jersey stretched over a flat abdomen, an expansive chest, and bulky arms. Under wrap-around sunglasses and a red helmet, she could guess at an attractive, tan face, set off by an angular jaw covered in fine stubble.

"Can you hear me talking?"

His clear, deep voice startled her and for a moment she couldn't understand. "Excuse me?"

"Can you hear me talking?" he repeated the question.

She hesitated. "Yes, I can hear you."

"Good!" He exhaled. "That must mean I'm still alive."

She was still making sense of his strange words when he made an attempt to get up. Quickly, she knelt next to him, not minding her expensive pencil skirt.

"Wait, don't move! I have to call an ambulance!"

He took off his glasses, and she met a pair of dark, thick eyebrows and green-hazel eyes, which widened when meeting her face. "Oh, my God! I *am* dead! I'm in heaven!"

Before she processed his words, his hands reached out to her, touching her face, shoulders, and her chest through her white silk blouse. Surprise gave way to the strangest feeling of arousal, quickly replaced by anger.

"Hey!" She slapped his hands.

He gasped. "You're not a hallucination! You *are* real!"

She opened her mouth to reply when his next words startled her. "Allison Connors!"

Taken aback, she studied his face. "I'm sorry. Have we met?"

He didn't answer immediately. His eyes flicked to her hands, then came back to her face. "I work with your boyfriend."

Confused, she stared at him. "What boyfriend?"

Briefly closing his eyes, he pumped a fist in the air. "Yes! You don't have one!" A grin lit up his face. "Would you have dinner with me tonight?"

Before she could shake off her astonishment, he jumped up from the ground with amazing agility.

"Wait! What are you doing?" She stood up, surprised that he didn't seem injured. "You might have a concussion! You could get permanent brain damage!"

He stopped brushing the dust off his jersey and looked up to her with a blank face. "Is that a bad thing?"

She was stunned. Was he really such an idiot? Before she could answer, his grin returned and he laughed.

"Come on!" he said between chuckles, opening his arms. "I don't even get a smile out of that joke? God, you are wound tight!"

She was about to answer coldly when he shouted, "*Shit*! I'm bleeding!"

"Oh no! You're really hurt!" She took a hand to her chest, noticing for the first time the blood covering his left elbow.

He reached for the hem of his jersey to take it off and she resisted the urge to roll her eyes. *Oh, please. What's up with men wanting to show off their—*

The next words died on her brain. In a flash, his shirt was off, and she was facing the most beautiful torso she'd ever seen.

There was nothing over- or underdeveloped in the gorgeous

male specimen before her. He had perfectly defined chest muscles, a flat, strong, ridged abdomen, and beautifully rounded shoulders to go with his bulging arms. Only the faint, dark body hair covering his chest, getting thicker near the waistband of the shorts, made him look real and not like an airbrushed picture. Allison felt something twinge in her lower pelvis and sudden heat spread through her body like a hot flash.

What on earth is happening to me? She was the woman who found men nearly disgusting. Why was she finding this stranger so attractive?

The man was using his saliva to wipe the blood from his elbow, trying to assess the source of the bleeding. The view of his tongue licking his own hand again and again threw her into another hot flash. She forgot her initial wonder about how he'd survived a crash like that.

"It's only a scrape," he said. The way he flexed his arm to bring the elbow to his eyesight contracted his arm muscles, making them bulge even more. "But it's already getting swollen. Ow. That's gonna hurt when I cool down."

Making an effort to keep her eyes on his face and not his torso, she exclaimed, "Are you trying to kill yourself?"

Holding his elbow, he squinted and tilted his head, as if trying to recall. "Not *recently.*"

She pressed her temples with a growl. "I mean, what kind of grown-up man runs around on a skateboard?"

"One who's in touch with his inner child." He smirked.

She glowered at him. "Well, someone better tell your inner child that this is a highway and not a skating rink."

His eyes moved from his elbow to her and ran slowly from her eyes to her lips, to her breasts, and down the rest of her body, then returned to meet hers. His voice was silky. "Maybe someone should volunteer to give my inner child a spanking."

His gaze was so intense Allison's words stuck in her throat and refused to come out.

His voice snapped her out of her trance. "I think I blew my ankle and I'm not sure I can walk," he said. "Would you help me try?"

With a nod, she rushed to his side.

He wrapped his arm around her shoulders and, before she knew it, her arm whipped back, elbowing him in the chest.

"Ow!" he complained, rubbing his sternum.

"Sorry! It's a reflex," she apologized. "I don't like to be hugged."

She positioned her left arm around his waist and offered her right hand for him to hold, serving as a cane. Limping, he took a few steps. She felt his solid body weighing her down and suppressed a grunt. She was a tall woman, and it was unusual for her to run into a man tall enough to make her feel small.

She was deeply aware of the strong naked torso under her arm. A vision of that torso rubbing against her breasts in bed took her completely by surprise. There was something highly enticing about this man's smell and her body was betraying her with all types of strange, primal reactions.

In the midst of her confusing feelings, her psychologist's brain was fascinated. *So, is this what people call physical chemistry?*

"Should I drive you to the emergency room?"

"I'd rather not; I'm between health insurances right now. If I can get some ice and ibuprofen, I'll be fine."

"Can you drive if I take you to your car?"

"I got here on the skateboard."

"Can I get you a taxi or an Uber?"

"I could call one myself, I have my—" He stopped mid-sentence. "My cell! Where is it? I had it in my hand when—" He turned abruptly, gazing at the highway and cussed.

His cussing startled her. She followed the direction of his eyes to a flattened silver rectangle lying on the middle of the highway, being run over again and again by the speeding cars.

"My phone!" He sprang out of her arms and dashed into the

middle of the street, to pick up the phone before running back. "Damn it! It's pulverized!"

"I'm so sorry!" she mumbled. "I'll be happy to refund—" She stopped. "Wait a minute! You can run? Why were you making me help you?"

With a soft smile, he looked at her from under his eyelashes. "Because your arm around me felt so good."

Anger rose inside Allison like an erupting volcano. She held it in and kept her voice cold. "Well, since you've proven that you're perfectly fine, I'm out of here."

She spun on her heels and strode away, heading for her car.

"Wait!" he called out. "Are you seriously leaving me in the middle of the highway, injured and without a cell phone to call for help?"

She stopped in her tracks and turned around slowly.

He seemed exhausted and overwhelmed, holding his broken cell phone in one hand and his jersey in the other one. Pressing his lips together, he fluttered his eyelashes, as if begging for mercy.

She exhaled sharply. "Fine! I'll drive you home!"

His grin returned and his chest shook with laughter. "That was easy! I thought therapists were immune to guilt trips!"

Before she could process his words, he ran to her car and got in the passenger seat.

* * *

At the first red light, Allison texted her friend Joy—Hope's sister—that she'd been in a "minor car accident" and couldn't make it to the wedding. With Joy being a psychiatrist, and more grounded than Hope and Emery, Allison trusted she'd manage to deliver the news without spoiling Fe's night.

Luckily for Allison's driving abilities, the man's shirt was back on and he was silent. The farther she drove, the more surprised she was that he'd gotten so far on his skateboard.

"About how long until we get to your house?"

He was distracted, absorbed in the window view. "Actually, I'm homeless."

She slammed on the brakes and pulled over, then gawked at him.

Is he serious? His helmet now off, she studied his shaggy, dark-brown hair in need of a haircut, then slid to his angular face to take in his stubble and the small scar over his right eyebrow. She examined his clothes before crossing her arms and narrowing her eyes. "You're messing with me. Your workout clothes and your shoes are a high-end brand. That broken cell phone is the latest iPhone-plus. There's no way a homeless guy could afford that."

His lips twitched before curving into a devilish smirk. "You're a smart lady!"

She scoffed. "Sir, I have a PhD and five published books! But we're digressing. Am I supposed to be driving you somewhere, yes or no?"

"Yes. To my hotel."

Okay. He's from out of town.

That explained a lot. She definitely would've remembered running into a man like this in this small town. She took off again.

They'd driven in silence for a few more minutes when her phone chimed with a text from Joy's cell. At the next red light, she glanced at the message. *"This is Richard. Joy forgot her phone. Are you okay, Connors? Do you need help?"*

Allison cringed internally. If she had a low opinion of all men in the world, Special Agent Richard Fields, Joy's fiancé, deserved a *special* prize. She still couldn't believe that a bright psychiatrist like Joy had paired up with a Neanderthal like him.

She texted back. *"I'm fine. Just make sure Joy gets my message."*

As she silenced her phone before he could finish ruining her evening, she became aware of a gaze on her. The man on the passenger seat stared at her with an unsettling intensity.

"You never answered my question about whether you'd have

dinner with me tonight," he said.

She stopped at a crosswalk to let a group of surfers cross, then turned to face his relentless scrutiny. "You didn't answer *my* question about where you know me from. And I asked first."

He surveyed her face. "You really don't remember me? Huh." His expression softened and his generous lips parted. The fantasy of that mouth kissing hers jumped into her mind, taking her breath away.

What on earth is happening to me? "I'm sorry. I need help here."

"I'm Jay."

That did nothing. "Would you please refresh my memory?"

In a deep, silky voice, he said, "You don't remember us dancing together that night, and then kissing? You really don't remember how I helped you out of your fancy dress, and how it got stuck over your head, and how we laughed as I freed you from it and we fell in bed?"

His words planted all kinds of images in her mind. The sound of horns blowing brought her back to reality, and she realized the crossing surfers were long gone. She returned her attention to driving.

She refused to give him the pleasure of seeing her agitated, so she kept her voice neutral. "You're trying to gaslight me, but it's not going to work. I know that didn't happen because I *never* go home with men I just met."

"Oh, but we *did* meet before. Can I dream I stand a chance tonight?"

She stomped on the breaks and pulled over again. Glaring at him, she kept her voice icy. "Listen to me, Jay, or whoever you think you are. You're being disrespectful and I will *not* tolerate that."

He raised his hands as if surrendering. "I'm sorry. Jeez! I was just being funny." He lowered his hands. "You're a tough audience. When was the last time you laughed out loud?"

His question caught her off guard. She honestly couldn't remember. "Are you going to behave appropriately or should I take off and leave you right here on the street?"

He gasped. "You can't leave me here!"

"Your guilt trip won't work this time. I know you're fine now."

Brows knitted together, he narrowed his eyes. "No, you don't. My back is hurting; I could have a herniated disc. Or worse, I could have something life-threatening like an internal hemorrhage or a cranial hematoma."

She hadn't expected all those big words. Maybe he was smarter than she thought at first. "Are you a doctor?"

"God, no!" He chortled. "But don't change the subject. How do you know you won't get a nasty letter from a lawyer next month, saying you were driving recklessly, neglected to tend to my serious injuries and are now responsible for my million-dollar hospital bill?"

She froze, terrified. He had a point. "I didn't really hit you with the car," she said cautiously. "I saw you; you jumped off the skateboard and used my car hood to propel yourself out of the way."

Subtle smugness filled his face. "You have no proof of that."

When she didn't answer, he said, "This is my proposal. Let me take you out for dinner. Spend a few hours with me; then, I'll sign a blank page that your lawyer can fill out with legal jargon saying I release you from all liability. It's a win-win. You'll also be soothing your conscience by making sure I'm fine." He extended his hand.

She considered it. "I'll give you *one* hour."

He left his hand extended without deviating his eyes from hers. "Three is my final offer. If you remember who I am, you're free early; if I make you laugh, I get an extra half an hour."

The negotiations were getting more complicated by the minute, so maybe it was better to take the offer. She extended her hand but stopped an inch away from his. "You're not planning to tickle me, are you?"

Snickering, he closed the gap to take her hand. "That sounds tempting!"

Chapter 3

Allison had to admit that crazy Jay knew how to wow a woman. The dinner venue he chose was at the Sebastian Inlet—a point where the Indian River met the Atlantic Ocean. With the ocean on one side and the bridges going over the river on the other side, they had 270 degrees of breathtaking water view—the most amazing place to watch a sunset. Even the clouds over the ocean toward the east reflected the colors of the dying sun for a wrap-around effect of pink and orange sky.

During the drive there he'd proposed to pass the time playing a game, asking each other questions. She'd used her "veto card" to block his questions about her childhood—she had no intention of revisiting those times. He'd then asked simpler questions, such as her favorite foods, drinks, and movies. She'd used her turns to get hints about whether they'd really met before. Apparently, he was a personal trainer in town only temporarily and had an early flight to Atlanta to catch the next day.

While they waited for their food, she asked, "So, you're here on a business trip?"

"No, I'm here to pay my last respects to a friend."

She placed a hand on her chest. "Oh, I'm sorry. A friend died?"

"Worse." He snorted. "He's *getting married*."

She suppressed a giggle. "Yikes! I agree, that's worse!" She tasted the pomegranate-berry smoothie he'd recommended to her; it was delicious. "So, you had to suffer through the wedding?"

"Nah, I only came to organize his bachelor party and attend the rehearsal dinner." He took a sip from his own smoothie. "Don't get me wrong; I really like his girl, and they seem happy, but I refuse to attend weddings on principle. In my opinion, weddings should be classified as sadomasochistic activity."

If it hadn't been for the Botox, Allison's eyebrows would've risen to her hairline. She nodded emphatically. "Yes! That's what I always say!"

"Ugh! And that's only weddings!" he added. "Don't get me started on the obsolete and tyrannical custom of marriage!"

She wanted to hear more, but he changed the subject. "My turn again. I get to ask you two questions in a row. Question number one. Which is your favorite sense?"

She considered it. "Well, I can't say taste, because everything good to eat is fattening. I can't say smell, because my allergies don't let me smell much. I love music, so maybe hearing, but I also love visual arts." She gazed at the pink clouds on the horizon. "If I had to choose, I guess I'd choose sight."

"Ah." There was a tone of disappointment in his voice, making her wonder if she had failed a test.

"What do you mean by 'ah'?"

"Nothing. I just notice you didn't even mention touch. That's my favorite."

She shook her head. "Touch is my least favorite sense."

His face turned more pensive than she'd yet seen. "I'll have to do something about that."

Wait. What?

Before she could react, he continued. "My second question. If you could have any superpower in the world, what would it be?"

The questions were a stretch from usual conversation. "Well, I don't know. The power to heal all the traumas in the world? Bring the world peace?"

"Come on, darling." He chuckled. "This isn't a beauty pageant.

You can tell the truth. Jumping so high you can get to the moon? Shooting lava from your hands? Changing to gas or liquid form?"

The conversation was progressing from pointless to ridiculous. "Can I get back to you on that one?"

"Sure, take your time. You don't want to end up with the wrong superpower if you make the wrong choice."

His expression was dead serious as if he truly believed superpowers were possible. Was he messing with her again? Or was she putting her life in danger, hanging out with a mental patient?

She studied his face. "Are you under any type of psychiatric care?"

"Not *currently*," he answered with a candid smile.

Allison pondered the evasive answer. "Have you *ever* been on antipsychotic medication?"

"Only recreationally." His eyes sparkled.

She stiffened in her seat. "That's nonsense. Antipsychotic medications can't be used recreationally. There's no high from them and they have pretty nasty side effects."

With a grave expression, he nodded. "That's exactly what I found out. After the second time I got horrible nausea from haloperidol and chlorpromazine, I decided they were not for me."

"The *second* time?" She stared at him in disbelief.

"I try everything twice before I decide if I like it or not," he explained. "Bungee jumping, skydiving, electroshock therapy…"

Her smoothie went down the wrong pipe, making her cough. She knew electroshock therapy was reserved as a last resort for the most severe cases of mental illnesses. "Have you ever had electroshock therapy?"

He glanced over his shoulder and lowered his voice. "Only recreationally. Now *that's* more fun than antipsychotic medication."

Her heart speeding up, she was considering pushing him off the restaurant deck and running away at top speed when she noticed the light shaking of his body, followed by laughter.

She sighed deeply in relief. "You almost got me there! You're just messing with me!"

He changed his expression to serious again, but his mouth twitched as if resisting to curve. "Are you sure?"

She searched his eyes for a hint of whether he was as insane as she suspected. He held her gaze.

What have I gotten myself into?

* * *

Once she got the hang of his strange humor—saying outrageous statements with a straight face—Jay turned out to be quite fun company over dinner. He almost cracked her up talking about childhood games and cartoons she'd completely forgotten about. She was surprised to hear his childhood interests had so much in common with hers, suggesting he was from her same generation; she'd assumed he was younger. His stamina was such that if it hadn't been for the sexy laugh lines framing his hazel eyes, she would've guessed he was in his early twenties.

When darkness thickened, he produced a credit card from his broken cellphone case and insisted on paying for their dinner—one more piece of evidence against him being homeless. They returned to the car, and he guided her to his hotel, one of the most expensive on the beachside.

Impressed, she stopped the car in front of the entrance and peeked at the luxurious lobby through the glass doors. "So... here's where you're staying?"

"Yes, but don't get any ideas. I'm not a multi-millionaire or anything. My work is paying for it." He got out of the car, walked around to open the door for her and offered his hand.

She cleared her throat. "No, thank you. We say goodbye here."

"I'm aware that I don't look that smart, but I know how to read the analog clock in your Mercedes. I still have fifty minutes left of my time." He extended his hand again.

She didn't move. "I'm not going to your hotel room."

Even in the partial darkness, she could see his amusement. "All I want is to take a walk on the beach behind the hotel. But now that you mention my room, should I have invited you in?"

She blushed—she didn't know she was capable of blushing. She discreetly grabbed the pepper spray from her purse and slid it into her jacket pocket, then exited the car, ignoring the hand he offered.

The staff from valet parking arrived and greeted Jay by his first name with giant grins. The doormen beamed and waved from the entrance with shiny eyes, asking if they needed help. He was either an important guest or a great tipper—at least that was a point against him being a psych hospital fugitive.

They strolled past the hotel entrance and headed to the beach. They had walked in silence for a while when she asked, "Why do you insist on holding me to the full three hours, Jay? I already told you: I don't sleep with men I just met." *Or any man in the past three years.*

"I'm still hoping you'll remember me," he replied, something hopeful in his soft smile.

She sized him up. "I think you're bluffing and we've never met before. My guess is that you know me from the back cover of one of my books, or one of my recent TV appearances."

Narrowing his eyes, he leaned closer. "Or maybe I know more about you than you think. Maybe I've been stalking you for years. Maybe *I* planned our encounter today."

Fear paralyzed her for an instant, then she realized the absurdity of what he said. "It was unexpected that I drove to the beachside today. There was no way you could've planned that encounter. Stop trying to confuse me!" She took a hand to her forehead.

Breathing out her frustration, she decided it was time to regain control. He was unsettling her so much she'd almost forgotten her best weapon.

She shot him her most professional therapist look. "Behind

every funny guy hides someone who's been repressing dark feelings. My analysis is that you have chronic, unprocessed anger."

His smile died away, and he stiffened in place.

"And behind every man-child who refuses to grow up, there's someone conflicted about becoming his dad. I bet you have father issues."

His expression transformed into shock.

A-ha. I'm on to something.

Her inner celebration didn't last. He scowled and puffed his chest out. She suddenly became aware of how much weaker than him she was, and that they were on a dark beach where no one would hear her if she screamed for help. Determined not to show fear, she held his gaze.

He finally spoke. "Maybe the answer is simpler than that, and all I have is unprocessed anger against *you*. Maybe it bothers me that a woman claims a man can be replaced with a vibrator, a triple-A membership, and a handyman service."

A light went on in Allison's mind as she heard her own words quoted. "So that's how you knew me, from my books! All the nonsense about knowing me from before is bull crap."

Guilt flashed across his face. "Maybe I was curious to find out if you really are the man-hater you come across as in your interviews."

"This is unbelievable!" She looked heavenwards. "I've been wasting my time being polite to you!"

"Well, I'm glad we met up today so I had a chance to tell you this." His eyes fixed on her. "If you really believe what you say about men in your books, I'll assume you've never met one who's worth a rotten potato or who has any idea what he's doing in bed."

The realization that she'd made him lose his cool helped her regain some sense of control. Why was she letting this man upset her? She was the one teaching her clients to walk away from codependent relationships.

She glanced at her watch. "To hell with it. I'm not sticking around. Have your lawyer contact mine."

His arm clasping hers kept her in place, reminding her brain of his strength and her body of his animal magnetism. He seemed exasperated. "Why are you making this so difficult? I'm nothing but a good guy, trying to be nice to a beautiful woman who got his attention. Why do you have to push me away, when I can tell you like me?"

She tensed, not knowing how to reply.

He exhaled a sigh of despair. "You women seem to believe that we men are these... powerful, evil creatures, always scheming against you. And that if you lower your guard for just one second, we'll use you and then throw you away. Well, has it ever occurred to you that maybe men are just teenage boys trapped in adult bodies? Boys who blush, and get sweaty-palmed when we see a girl we like? Has it ever occurred to you that we may be putting up a show of self-confidence around you, but deep inside we're just human beings, terrified of rejection and heartbreak?"

She was taken aback by the passion in his voice and the pain in his eyes, but she gathered herself. "Who are you trying to fool? Am I going to believe that *you*,"—she waved a hand in front of his chest— "this mass of muscles, hot lips, and flirty eyes, have *ever* been rejected by a woman, let alone had your heart broken?"

"Oh, so now you know everything about me just because you've seen how I look?" He brought his face right up to hers and the invasion of her personal space felt strangely exciting. "That's disappointing coming from a woman who's ranted so much against body objectification and obsession about looks—chapter twelve of your last book ring a bell?"

She used a hand to shove his chest away and felt weirdly aroused by the feeling—darn it, those muscles were so hard it was ridiculous. "What? Are you going to make a display of testosterone-driven aggression now? If you dare touch me, I'll hit you with my pepper spray and shock you with my stun gun."

"Oh, please! Save your energy!" He got one step closer. "I'd need to be crazy for real to want to touch a cold-blooded... control-obsessed woman like you. I bet your heart wouldn't race if—"

Allison never knew what happened; suddenly, he was kissing her. His arms wrapped around her waist, he ravished her mouth with so much passion she already felt her lips swelling.

But the strangest thing was that she was doing nothing to stop him.

What are you doing? The fierce feminist writer in her raged. *Use your pepper spray, push him away. Get a grip on yourself, woman!*

But that voice got smaller and fainter until it became a whisper and then disappeared. The exquisite feeling of his mouth on hers and his large, silken hands stroking her back bypassed her brain and went straight to her core, shaking her with thunderbolts of desire. A savage, non-intellectual woman in lust she'd never known before responded ardently, wrapping her arms around his neck and pulling him toward her, deepening the kiss.

Against her will, he slowed down the frantic pace of his kiss, and his mouth slowly teased and tortured hers, savoring her. With every gentle thrust of his tongue, electric charges pierced her.

His hands moved down her waist to her hips to pull them against his, and she felt fire between her legs. He kissed her neck, then followed its curve up to her earlobe. His warm breath caressed her ear when he whispered, "Are you sure you don't want to come to my hotel room?"

The words permeated her ears and then skipped her brain and went straight to her lower pelvis.

Could she let go of her tight control for one night to enjoy this beautiful stranger? Even the therapist in her argued she could pass it off as a statement of "feminist sexual empowerment"—or something like that; her mind wasn't working well.

Shaking herself, she stepped back, getting out of his arms. "Are you out of your mind?" her voice sounded weak to herself. "There's no way I'm—"

The following words died on her lips. Jay slowly lifted his jersey, pulling it over his head.

He stood in front of her, in all his glorious physical perfection, shirtless and in spandex shorts leaving little to the imagination, a soft smile on his lips.

Allison felt the rumbling of an earthquake inside her. Everything was a blur after that.

Chapter 4

Six months later.

THE APARTMENT WAS FULL OF PACKED CARDBOARD BOXES and empty of furniture—except for exercise equipment in the living room. Lying down on the weight-lifting bench, a bald young man used his scrawny arms to bench-press the weight bar on top of him. In spite of the oxygen cannula on his nose, his breathing was labored.

"Come on, Ethan. Ten more!" Jay cheered his friend on. "This is fun!"

Ethan shot Jay a murderous look. "This is just as fun as my last bone marrow biopsy."

"Come on! You're the strongest man I know!" Jay meant that.

Panting, Ethan returned the empty barbell to its holder and sat up. "I'm strong in character—not muscles." He mopped his hairless head with the hem of his sleeveless shirt. "Don't get me wrong, man. I'm deeply thankful you do this for free—I could never afford your rates. But… are you trying to kill me?"

Jay *tsked.* "If aggressive lymphoma and chemotherapy didn't kill you, a little weight lifting won't hurt."

"I used to find your manic tendencies endearing—but not anymore. I'm done for today. I'm going to shower."

"I'll make you work extra hard tomorrow," Jay threatened, faking a scowl.

Ethan took off his oxygen, reached for his walker and paced

away. "I can't even remember where we packed the towels."

"Check the boxes on the kitchen counter."

Watching his friend push his walker into the kitchen, Jay thanked his lucky stars Ethan was alive and in remission, and felt glad his friend had fallen for his plan. He didn't really need Ethan's help to pack for this move—but that excuse had worked to bring him to Atlanta and get a second oncology evaluation. He didn't really need to become Ethan's roommate in Fort Sunshine—but it was a discreet way to help his friend financially until he could return to work.

As Jay sprayed and wiped down the bench, Ethan reviewed the boxes on the quartz kitchen counter. "What's in this taped box? I don't remember seeing it."

Jay walked to the modern kitchen, finished in white quartz and stainless-steel. "Childhood relics. When I visited my hometown in Wisconsin a few years back I rescued some things from my grand-ma's attic."

Ethan moved to a different box and removed a book. "*Manless and Happy*, by Allison Connors."

Jay felt a surge of the same frustration he'd experienced every day for the past six months as Allison refused to return his messages.

"Why would you read feminist self-help?" Ethan commented, scanning the summary.

"I find the author's dry sense of humor quite funny. Listen to this." He searched for a marked page on the book. "Marriage is the ultimate happy ending: *It ends your happy.*" Jay guffawed.

Ethan stared at him blankly. "I don't find that funny."

"Well, I do." Hoping Ethan would drop the subject, he put the book down, returned to the bench and added weights to the barbell.

Ethan extracted more books from the box. "Is she the only au-thor you read?" Digging deeper, he pulled out DVDs, a stack of pic-tures, and printouts of Internet articles. "Man, are you obsessed with this woman?"

Jay rolled his eyes. "You'll have the moral authority to criticize my obsessions whenever you stop fixating on your doctor."

"I'm not fixated on my doctor!" Ethan protested. Crossing his arms, he cleared his throat and looked away. "She's just the future mother of my children and she doesn't know it yet."

Jay adjusted his knee brace, memories of Allison's soft skin flashing through his mind. "I'm not obsessed with Allison Connors. I just buy her books, print out her Internet articles, and DVR her TV appearances."

"Really?" Arms crossed, Ethan shot Jay a skeptical once-over.

"And read her blog, listen to her podcasts, watch her YouTube videos, and follow her on Twitter, Facebook, and Instagram." Feeling restless, Jay positioned himself on the bench and launched into bench-pressing. "And I may have sent her an occasional fan message using a pseudonym."

Ethan's hairless brows drew together. "So… you cyberstalk her."

"No, I *follow* her. Like a fan. A love-hate kind of fan. Half her misguided feminist statements give me an ulcer. Yet I just can't stop reading her."

"And that's not obsession. *At all.*" Ethan had mastered the art of being cynical with a smile.

Jay put down the barbell. "She's like a train wreck; *you can't not look.* Come on! Like that has never happened to you! Haven't you ever followed sensationalist news? Reality TV?"

While removing a towel from a nearby box, Ethan shot Jay a sideways glance. "No. I've been close to dying four times in the past year. I'm more selective than you about what I spend my time on." Ethan had walked a few steps, supported by his walker when he stopped in his tracks. "Wait a minute! Is this the same Allison you hooked up with when you went to Dr. McDevitt's wedding six months ago?"

Damn it. Jay'd hoped that Ethan's self-diagnosed chemo brain would prevent him from remembering. Pausing his workout, he gave a reluctant nod.

Clicking his tongue, Ethan walked back to Jay. "My friend, we both know you have a tendency to develop unhealthy attachments to women."

"You sound like my last shrink." With a grunt, Jay resumed bench-pressing the weights.

"You can't seem to get a balance with women. You either screw them for a weekend and never call them again, or you get all psycho with them."

Jay kept pumping the barbell, barely losing his breath. "For the hundredth time: I don't get psycho with women."

"Excuse me?" Ethan cleared his throat. "What about your first girlfriend?"

Jay didn't answer for a moment. *But I think Allison is my childhood girlfriend. I think this time I finally found Grace.* "Come on, you know the saying, 'You never forget your first love.' I repeat: I don't have 'unhealthy attachments' to women."

"Then, how about your sister?"

Jay put down the weight and teased, "That's not unhealthy attachment. I just want to feed her to the sharks."

Groaning, Ethan pulled Jay's arm to make him stand up from the bench. "For the thousandth time, Jay, a man as tall and strong as you are can not joke about things like that. Look at you!" He made Jay face himself in the floor-length mirror on the wall. At six foot five, Jay was usually unaware of his uncommon height and the bulk of his muscles; but next to Ethan, frail and of average height, the difference was glaring.

Ethan continued, "You're a friendly Labrador trapped in the body of a pit bull. But people take one look at you and assume you're a 'roid-rage' time bomb. You have to be more careful with your crazy sense of humor; that's how you get in trouble."

"You don't have to tell me. Hello. Court-mandated therapy anyone?"

Ethan walked away from the mirror. "Jay, you're an incredibly intelligent man, very successful; you have a heart of gold. Why do you get so much pleasure out of acting weird and making people believe you're crazy?"

Feeling suddenly tired, Jay paced away. "My last shrink said I refuse to mold to the world because Conan tried so hard to mold me to himself."

Ethan's deep blue eyes widened. "I'm shocked. You're mentioning your father's name? *The unpronounceable*?"

Jay didn't answer. *Damn it.* He'd been doing so well until six months ago. Allison's comment on the beach had unleashed a load of unwanted memories.

"Conan's not going to live forever, you know," Ethan remarked. "It wouldn't kill you to at least shake hands once before he dies."

Jay snorted. "He's going to outlive me, just to spite me."

Ethan shook his head with a sigh but wisely changed the subject. "Back to this Allison. Man, I don't endorse your creepy tendencies. But you're a great guy and deserve the best. Instead of cyber-stalking this woman, why don't you just ask her out? You know, like a normal, *sane* man would?" Without waiting for an answer, he nudged his walker away.

Jay's phone rang, showing a call from Miranda. Assuming it was his niece again, he sat on the carpeted floor, getting comfortable. "Hi, munchkin, ready for Wednesday?"

"Jake?" The low voice was not that of his niece, but Miranda Baker—the nanny who'd taken care of him since he was eight. Who would've imagined she'd still work for the same family almost three decades later?

"What's up, Mimi?" he asked.

Miranda's Midwest accent thickened, hinting her worry. "Jake, remember how you made me promise I'd call you if I thought our girl wasn't safe?"

Jay's chest tightened. "What are my crazy sister and brother-in-law doing now?" Jay's younger sister was a former child actress, with all the instability and entitlement that came with it. But her latest husband, a former teen band singer, was worse.

"The tone and the language of their fights are escalating," Miranda mumbled. "I think they're on drugs again."

"But you're keeping my munchkin isolated from all that, aren't you?" he asked, tense.

"I do my best. But if Mr. Blanche takes that job in Japan and they move away, I won't be there to protect her."

Restless, Jay got up and paced around the room. His only peace of mind was that the little girl rarely saw her mother and spent her days with her nanny.

"Hey, Jake. Did you ever talk to your lawyers about those guardianship papers?" Anxiety oozed under Miranda's casual question.

"They told me it's probably a lost cause," he replied with a sigh. "Unless my sister dies or becomes incompetent, the guardianship papers don't apply."

"Their marriage is hanging by a thread," Miranda whispered. "Maybe, if you delay her plans, she'll end up changing her mind about moving."

Or things could go the other way. Jay wouldn't be surprised if his sister decided to stick with her latest husband and bulldoze her way to a new continent just to fight him. One thing she deserved credit for was that she never discriminated against him for being their father's illegitimate son. She treated him the same way she treated her other siblings—dragging him into her tantrums and making his life difficult.

"Are you really sure it's a lost cause?" Miranda wondered. "I know my girl would be so much happier with you."

A wave of nausea hit Jay, and a fine mist of sweat formed on his forehead. He had no doubt he was great company for his niece one day a week, but twenty-four seven? "I—it's not that easy, Mimi. I... I travel a lot. Sometimes I work long hours." *And I've never been able to stick with anyone for long.*

"I know, I know." The woman's tone turned apologetic. "But if you ever consider having her for real, you know you can count on me to take care of her." Generous Miranda would never admit it, but in addition to losing the little girl she loved, she also dreaded the prospect of losing her job.

A childish voice sounded in the background and Miranda rushed to say goodbye. "I have to go. But please, think about it."

Jay felt the uncontrollable urge to go run twenty miles, swim five, or push his weight-lifting limits until every fiber of his body hurt.

But that little girl was the thing he loved most in his life. "I'll see what I can do, Miranda."

Chapter 5

THE AFTER-HOURS PHONE-THERAPY SESSION HAD LASTED one hour and forty minutes. Unable to slide in a single reassuring word, Allison had showered, slipped on her aqua wrap dress, and driven to Emery's bachelorette party while listening on speakerphone.

Tiffany Wetzel-Donovan-Carlson-Blanche—she collected ex-husbands' last names like a magpie collects shiny objects—ended the recount of her heartbreaks with a sob. "Jordan is the same as all the others. Why do I have such bad luck with men?"

Poor little rich girl. During the past five years, Allison had seen her endlessly seek the love she didn't get from her workaholic father. If there were an emotionally unavailable man in a fifty-mile radius, Tiffany would magnetize to him. "Sorry, I have to go now," Allison said while pacing the restaurant lobby with the phone on her ear. "But you'll be fine. You'll come out of this split a stronger, wiser woman, and you'll learn from your mistakes. Take some time for yourself, to rediscover self-love. You don't need a man if you decide to become your own best friend."

On the other end of the call, Tiffany cleared her throat. "But, you know… a hot guy at my gym asked me out for drinks Friday and I said yes."

Allison felt like throwing the phone in the nearest trashcan. And she'd thought that leaving family therapy to become a counselor to single women would be easier work! Her job was still like herding horses to water and seeing them refuse to drink. She wished she could choke the horses and yell at them to make them react.

Fe appeared behind Allison and snatched the phone. "Sorry, Ms. Tiffany, you'll have to finish this during your regular appointment. Allison has a bachelorette party to go to. Bye-bye now!" She disconnected the call.

On a normal day, Allison would've been enraged at Fe's lack of professionalism. But she had to admit she felt relieved. Also, she still felt in debt to Fe for having disappeared the day of her wedding.

As Fe dragged her by the arm to their table, Allison admired the burgundy cocktail dress that clung to her friend's generous curves. A chunky amber necklace brought out her honey-colored eyes and hair. As usual, the girl had overdone the glamour. "How do you know Tiffany?" Allison asked.

"She's called you so many times when we're together I almost feel like we should invite her to join us."

From their table, clad in a ladylike cobalt dress, Joy waved at them and pointed at an iPad. "Look, Allison! Your interview from Nash's show is available!"

Allison sat next to Joy. Wayne Nash was a local talk-show host who'd recently begun airing on a streaming network.

"Isn't he too old to wear his hair that long?" Hope asked, adjusting the plunging neckline of her little black dress as she leaned forward.

Allison huffed. "He thinks he's the new Howard Stern—but I think he's more like a Jerry Springer wannabe."

On the screen, Nash whipped his head, making his salt-and-pepper curls bounce. "So, Allison, in your book, *Manless and Happy*, you say that men are disposable."

The Allison on the iPad gave a cold smile. "Wayne, I never said that men are disposable. I said that men are *dispensable*. Meaning that if a woman chooses to have a man in her life, it should be because she wants to, not because she needs to."

Noticing how much flatter Nash's curls were on the next image, Allison rolled her eyes. "He cut out a whole segment to skip my most clever answers!"

"Let's talk about your gay ex-husband," Nash said in the show.

Please, not again. Allison had never considered her arranged "beard" marriage to her colleague Ryan a real thing.

"I have a theory." Nash smirked. "Since your ex-husband left you for another man, could it be that, in revenge, you're trying to turn all women into misandrist lesbians?"

"Ugh, that man loathes me!" Fuming inwardly, Allison turned off the iPad. "Did you know that he and his cameramen refer to me behind my back as 'The Triple-B,' the Ball-Busting-Biatch? He portrays me like a man-hating radical feminist."

Her friends' long silence was suspicious.

Slowly, Fe covered Allison's hand with hers. "Honey, you kind of *are* that, but that's okay. That's what makes you unique."

Allison wasn't sure if she should cry or laugh at Fe's usual frankness.

Twirling her long brunette hair, Joy cleared her throat. "Sweetie, why do you bother going on Nash's show? He'd do anything to torture his guests. Especially you, since you've rejected his advances."

"It's hard to get invited onto decent shows. I'm so jealous of my frenemy Karen Knight, who just got called for *The Carrie O'Brian Show*!" Sighing, she laid her arms on the table and rested her head on them. "I desperately need the publicity. My books are my best hope of transitioning into professional speaking, so I can quit this dead-end therapy business that's draining my soul."

Another call from Tiffany lit up her phone.

Speaking of draining my soul.

In response to the warning looks of her friends, Allison sent the automatic text, "Sorry, can't talk now." And rejected the call.

"On another topic, Allison," Joy commented, returning the iPad to her pristinely organized purse. "Please, promise that you'll cut

Emery some slack when she gets here. I hear you; I also don't like Ken—*at all*. But we have to be supportive of our friend."

"That's precisely why I shouldn't be here," Allison mumbled. "Because I care about Emery and I'm afraid I might say something to stop her from getting married."

Her friends' guilty expressions reassured Allison they felt the same way. With a groan, she continued, "I saw through Ken Carter's bullshit long before we ever shook hands. Marrying a skunk like that is the worst thing a woman can do. As if marrying *anybody* isn't a delusional act."

Stirring her margarita, Hope snickered. "Aaaand this is the part where she bursts into a gloomy song about divorce statistics."

Allison considered quoting some of those statistics, but it was a lost cause. The three women at the table with her were long-goners, unable to see relationships objectively. Hope, a previously free spirit who'd fallen flat on her face for a single father and had now become a stepmother of three. Fe, the woman who'd broken all her promises to herself by marrying a workaholic physician. And of course, Joy, who still hadn't learned that her FBI agent fiancé was a sublimating sociopath.

Fe, Joy, and Hope were examples of the eternal story: the moment a woman fell in love, she lost herself, her independence. Her power.

Not me. Allison would never fall for a man if that was the price to be paid. It didn't matter how gorgeous he was, or how he'd blown her mind in bed, or how many times he'd left his number with her secretary.

Allison straightened her three-quarter sleeves to cover her subtle hand tremor. Resisting the temptation to return Jay's calls after he'd left all those messages at her office had been difficult. Luckily, he seemed to have given up, judging by his silence for the past several weeks.

"What's wrong with women in the world?" Allison ranted, trying to drown out her own thoughts. "They'd rather be with a jerk than risk their own company. Emery isn't even fooling herself! She's nothing but a ticking biological clock agreeing to become Ken Carter's arm candy. Willing to look the other way when he puts her down or when he flirts with other women right in front of her."

"Hello, my favorite girls!"

Allison's brain still hadn't recognized the singsong voice when a pair of arms wrapped her shoulders in a hug from the back. A rush of claustrophobia overtook her, and before she realized what happened, she sprang out of her seat and threw her elbow behind her, hitting the hugger in the face.

The scream entered Allison's ears at the same time her brain identified the voice as Emery's.

"Ow!" Emery cried in pain.

Fe rushed to rub Emery's back while Joy examined the injured eye. Hope gathered ice in a fabric napkin and offered it to Emery.

"I'm so sorry!" Allison apologized, mortified.

Wearing a veil, a lit-up plastic tiara and a T-shirt reading "Bride to be" over her mint-colored hospital scrubs, Emery rubbed her face. "If you gave me a black eye one week before my wedding, I'm going to kill you, Allison!"

Allison sat back in her chair, bracing herself. "I'm sorry, it's a reflex. Everybody knows that I don't like hugs. Especially not by surprise."

"Come on, honey." Fe held Emery's hand. "I may have some arnica gel in my purse. If we use it right away, we might stop the bruising."

"I refuse to have a bruised face in my wedding pictures!" Emery protested, holding the ice on her eye as they walked away.

"Gee, Allison," Hope joked while gathering more ice. "Is this part of a secret plan to stop Emery's wedding?" She followed the two other women to the restroom.

Joy tapped Allison's hand reassuringly. "I know you didn't do it on purpose."

As Allison mumbled a thank you, she heard someone call her name, "Allison Connors? Ms. Allison Connors?"

Her eyes darted to the young waiter pacing the restaurant holding a tray. She raised a hand. "It's *Doctor* Allison Connors."

The waiter approached her table and set a tall glass in front of her. "A gentleman bought you this drink."

"Then send it right back to his table and tell him I'm not interested in being picked up," Allison replied, eyeing the young man coldly.

He shook his head. "I can't; he's not in the restaurant. This gentleman called from Atlanta, paid with his credit card over the phone and left a generous tip insisting that I deliver this message to you. He directed that if you refused to take it, I should read it out loud." He extended her a folded paper. "Going once…"

Allison was taken aback. She could tell Joy was too, by the way her dark brown eyes had widened.

"Wait, how would someone from out of state know where you are, Allison? Is your social media advertising your location?"

"I don't know. I better check that."

"Going twice," the waiter said.

Allison examined the drink and it suddenly hit her. It was the same pomegranate-berry smoothie she'd enjoyed six months ago at the Sebastian Inlet.

Her pulse raced, her palms turned to ice. She didn't need to read the note to know where it had come from.

It was from Jay.

"Three times." The waiter unfolded the paper and read it out loud. "I haven't stopped thinking about you since our night together. I want to see you again, and this time I'm not taking no for an answer."

Chapter 6

THE MINUTE THEY FINISHED THE LAST TASK OF THE bachelorette party—the obligatory male strip club—Joy dragged Allison to her counseling office. Gosh, Joy only *looked* sweet and shy. The woman had an iron character and was determined to have Allison confess what the deal was with the mysterious man.

In a way, it was a relief for Allison to finally say what she'd been hiding for months. Thirty minutes into venting, sitting on Joy's recliner, Allison concluded her story. "And when I woke up the next morning, he had already gone to the airport. He left the signed page for my lawyer on the bed, along with an effusive letter saying how much he'd enjoyed our night, sharing his contact information and begging me to call him. I tore up that letter and threw it away immediately." She held her forehead. "I still haven't forgiven myself. Never in my life did I imagine I'd be so irresponsible as to go home with a man I'd just met—as if I were a brainless, hormonal teenager who melted away at the sight of a good-looking chest. What would my clients think of me if they knew I lost control like that? I'm supposed to be an example for them, teaching them to take control over their lives."

Joy remained quiet for the longest time. Then, Allison noticed the twitch in her full lips and the way her delicate hands trembled as her breathing sped up. "I… I can't believe it! Allison Connors likes a guy! Never in a million years—"

"Stop!" Allison raised a warning hand and shot Joy her harshest glare, speaking in a cold, stern voice. "Listen to me, Joy Clayton. If I wanted a crazy girl-gone-wild telling me to throw caution to the wind and go screw this man like there's no tomorrow, I would've called your sister, Hope. I need you to be impartial to help me organize my thoughts. So, please, put down those cheerleader pompoms and put on your big-girl psychiatrist panties. Are we clear?"

Joy took a long, deep breath and joined her hands together as if aiming to summon the nonjudgmental counselor. "Okay, I'll be professional and give my unbiased opinion. Let me see if I've got this right." Narrowing her dark eyes, Joy grabbed her chin. Allison had the unpleasant feeling that she was mocking her. "Your awful problem is that you met a guy who you find incredibly attractive. You had a great time with him on an impromptu date. And then you went ahead and—here I paraphrase your words—had *the best sex of your life*. And now he's calling you, and wanting to get together again. That is *your problem*. Did I get it all?"

Allison gaped at Joy. When she put it like that it sounded ridiculously simple.

"No, you did *not* get it all. You're missing the most important part. Yes, I liked the guy, but I'm afraid he… he's not very well in the head."

Joy fluttered her dark eyelashes. "Elaborate, please."

"I suspect he's a pathological liar." Allison fiddled with her bracelet watch. "And I think he's either fully manic or a bipolar patient going through a manic phase."

Leaning forward, Joy made a *T* with her hands, asking permission to take a time-out from the therapist role. "Allison, that's almost exactly what you said about my Richard a couple of years ago. I'm starting to like this guy."

"No. It's more serious than that." Allison shook her head with zeal. "This guy is freaking crazy and I mean it! Someone's-going-to-find-my-lifeless-body-floating-somewhere type of crazy."

Joy repeated the "time out" sign. "Allison, you also said something like that about Richard once."

"He's arrested at a developmental stage—"

"My point, sweetie," Joy interrupted her, "is that you're a little harsh when judging men." She laced her fingers together. "And you seem to be missing a critical detail that has *me* in shock. Have you realized this is the first time since I've known you—since college—that you went to bed with a man... and actually enjoyed it?"

Allison didn't answer. Of course, she'd noticed that "detail." She'd given up on sex long ago. Fiasco after fiasco had led her to conclude men were not worth the trouble.

"I wish Hope were here to ask the big question I'm almost too shy to ask." Joy said. "Gosh! What did he do to you?"

Allison was surprised not to feel uncomfortable talking about it. "There wasn't any magical move or any out-of-this-world thing. He just... took his time. It was like he had nowhere else better to go and didn't mind if it took him all night to please me." She stopped to think about it. "Honestly, I feel vindicated. More than one ego-bruised guy in the past accused me of being the problem and called me a cold fish. For the first time, I realized that maybe the problem wasn't me—it was them."

"You have to give this guy a chance!" Joy blurted out.

Grumbling, Allison crossed her arms. "What if he's dangerous?"

Joy rotated her wrist forward. "Search public records and confirm he's not a felon. It's not called privacy invasion anymore, you know. It's called dating in the age of the Internet."

"I tried once; it was useless." Allison denied with her head. "He has a very common last name and I have no clue about his date of birth. Do you have any idea how many Jay Johnsons I found online?"

"Wait. Did you say Jay Johnson?" Joy grabbed her phone and searched for something. Within seconds she turned the screen around. "Is this him?"

For an instant, Allison had trouble recognizing the attractive man in the picture, wearing a business jacket without a tie. But the mischievous air and the sparkling eyes were unmistakable. "Yes! How do you know Jay?"

Joy trembled slightly. "If I weren't wearing my big-girl psychiatrist panties, I'd be jumping on the couch, cheering. Do I know Jay? I LOVE Jay! I was a consultant for his company when it was still in early development."

Allison was confused. "Company? He told me he's a personal trainer."

"His more accurate title is 'Life Coach,' but he enjoys making people think he's crazy." Joy's eyes got lost for a moment. "Or maybe I should say *crazier* than he really is." She shuddered briefly as if to shake a thought. "I strongly recommend you talk to him about his career path. He may have the advice you need to make it into the world of professional speaking."

Allison was still processing those words when Joy opened a Google search on her laptop. "You have to search for him using his nickname, 'Triple J.'"

Within seconds, Joy had found his official website.

J. J. Johnson or "Triple J" was the founder of Legendary Heroes, an up-and-coming chain of personal training services offering the money-back guarantee of making clients look forward to exercising, instead of dreading it. He'd jumped to fame a few years back when one of his YouTube videos relating his weight loss journey had gone viral.

"The company slogan is 'Work Out Your Inner Child,'" Joy explained. "They get you to associate exercise with pleasure by connecting it to your best childhood memories. For example, they use virtual headgear on treadmills, so clients can pretend they're racing through video-game adventures." Joy grew more animated as she shared. "Their signature service is mixed martial arts training sessions while dressed up as your favorite historical or sci-fi characters. That service is getting all kinds of attention from the millionaires of

Silicon Valley, who are filling up Jay's nutrition and fitness seminars."

The website was packed with testimonials of clients who'd lost unbelievable amounts of weight and recovered fitness after injuries, despite a poor prognosis from their physicians. That included a video testimonial from a famous, senior-aged Hollywood actor calling Jay, "The best life coach I've ever had."

"If I can do it, so can you," Jay said on an introductory video. "I'm a pleasure-seeking hedonist. Nobody can make me do something I don't want to do, and I'd never stick to a program that wasn't fun." He leaned toward the camera. "But by reconnecting with our inner child—that playful, joyful, energetic person we once were—we can rediscover the passion for fitness and healthy living."

* * *

Allison waited a full twenty-four hours before contacting Jay, so as not to seem too eager.

I'm only doing this to boost my career. All I want is to interview him about his trajectory. Nothing more.

She'd stared at the piece of paper in her hand for an hour before she finally decided to enter his number in her contacts. Then it took her half an hour to type and edit her message to him.

She reviewed it now. *"Hi. It's Allison. Thanks for the drink. Your website impressed me. I'd love to ask you some questions about your career trajectory next time you're in town."*

She took a deep breath and hit the send button.

It was done. It had been sent. She felt both relieved and terrified.

Mere seconds had passed when her phone rang with a call from him.

Allison's heart sprinted. Her face flushed, her hands turned to ice, and she felt like a fifteen-year-old girl getting a call from her crush.

She picked up the phone. "Hello."

"What are you wearing?" Jay's husky voice was almost a whisper.

"Excuse me?"

There was a silence on the other line. "Oh! So when you said *career trajectory* you *really* meant career trajectory?" He cleared his throat and the sound of mattress springs hinted that he was moving around in bed. She could hear his smile in his next words. "Uh… okay. How can I help you?"

Chapter 7

SATURDAY MORNING, ALLISON ARRIVED AT THE OUTDOOR restaurant of the hotel where Jay was speaking that weekend. When he saw her arrive, his face lit up and he got up to greet her.

She almost tripped and fell, taking in his fresh haircut and clean-shaven face. If he'd sizzled in his workout gear, he was stunning in formal clothes.

He greeted her with a kiss on the cheek so quick and casual she had no chance to stop it. The kiss was done before she became aware of the heat it had caused on her face. When she'd proposed to meet over brunch instead of dinner, she did it thinking it was "safer," yet she didn't feel safe anymore.

"I need to make one thing clear first," she said as she took a seat facing the pool.

"Yes?"

His relaxed tone made her feel at a disadvantage, so she made an effort to sound calm. "I'm only here to interview you about your career path. There will be absolutely no physical contact and I have no intention of seeing you outside of business after this. Are we clear?" She spoke more to herself than to him.

"If you say so." He seemed unaffected by her words. She had the unpleasant feeling that he suppressed a smirk.

The waitress arrived and took their brunch orders. He ordered an egg-white omelet that sounded so healthy she felt self-conscious about ordering her usual eggs benedict and hash browns.

"So, you said you had questions about my career?" he asked over coffee as they waited for their food.

She exhaled in relief to hear his friendly tone. "Maybe I'll start by asking why you lied to me."

He chuckled. "I never lied to you!"

She faintly raised her eyebrows and tilted her head. "You told me, and I quote, 'I'm not a multimillionaire or anything.' Well, based on what I gathered from the web, you do own a multimillion-dollar company."

"You know how it is with web presence." He shrugged. "You have to toot your own horn and make it look like a big deal. It's all marketing." His eyes crinkled as he confided, "The last time I checked my personal bank account it had twenty-seven dollars in it." He tapped an app on his phone and his eyes widened. "Never mind! The last wire went through. It's twenty-seven thousand now." He rose from his chair and yelled. "Hey everybody! Payday! You all get a tip!"

As if used to the routine, the waiters and waitresses at the restaurant clapped and hooted.

As he re-took his seat, she covered her eyes with a hand and shook her head. "Jay, you either have a case of excess humility or complete cluelessness. You're practically a celebrity! Matthew Hester, the Hollywood actor, appears there in a video, raving about you."

He waved her off. "Matt is a personal friend more than a client now. We clicked ever since his first session."

"Whatever title you want to call yourself," she insisted, "your career is exactly what I'm trying to transition into. Conferences, web seminars, video courses… How is that going for you?"

His face was unusually serious as he considered her words, giving him another level of attractiveness. "You have to be ready to give up some security. Being an entrepreneur means you never know for sure where your next paycheck will come from—and some days you don't even know if you'll make payroll." He paused. "But in my case, it has been absolutely worth it."

He took a sip of his coffee and reclined in his chair. She noticed how his white button-down shirt played up his tan and hugged his muscles and forced her eyes to focus on the scar over his right eyebrow. "Allison, I rent an office at the Riverside building, just to have a physical address and a place to go if I have trouble focusing. But most of the time my office is the beach, the top of a mountain I've just climbed, or the airport on my way to my next trip. As long as I have my cell, my laptop and a chance to connect to Wi-Fi later, I don't need anything else. And that may not suit everyone, but it suits *me*. Because the biggest value in my life is freedom."

She bobbed her head, impressed by his words. "Mine too."

They held eye contact, and she had the strange feeling that they had more in common than appearances showed.

"That's why I want this career change," she said. "Not to mention I'd be able to reach and help so many more people, without feeling I'm pouring my soul into each case. One-on-one work with therapy clients is emotionally draining."

His attentive gaze enveloped her, and she felt warm and weakened at once. "I'm sure you can do that," he commented.

"It has been done." She forced her eyes away. "Take my nemesis, Karen Knight, for example. I am twice as smart as she is, and way better looking. Yet one day she decides she's no longer a therapist and instead is a life coach for successful professional women and she's everywhere."

"Why is she your nemesis?" he asked, amusement dancing on his face.

"She's actually kind of a friend," she corrected herself. "But she writes about the same feminism topics I do, so she's my competition in the field right now. But that's not important. My question is: how do you do it? How do you raise your sticker price overnight and get people to buy that you're above the rest of your class?"

He pondered in silence for a moment. "I'm not sure how it

happened, even less how to explain it. I'd practically have to tell you the story of my life."

She retrieved a notebook and pen from her purse, ready to take notes. "I have all day."

* * *

Jay turned out to be an amazing storyteller. Over coffee, he talked about his childhood passions and described his little hometown so vividly she got chills, remembering her own in rural Wisconsin. During brunch, he puzzled her while recounting his eclectic job history, and enthralled her sharing his life adventures—from rock-climbing, to sky gliding, to diving in shark-infested waters.

"You weren't joking when you said you've done it all twice," she remarked, ripping a coffee-stained page from her notebook.

He drummed his fingers on the table. "I've done everything except commit a felony, sleep with another dude, or sleep with someone from a different species." His eyes glazed. "At least not that I can remember. There's a college spring break that vanished from my memory after a tequila-shot drinking contest." After glancing around, he signaled her to lean closer and whispered. "Which is also my answer if someone asks if I've ever been kidnapped by aliens."

Used to his sense of humor by now, she rolled her lips between her teeth, suppressing a smile. "So, how does that side story relate to you becoming CEO of your father's company?"

"Oh, yes. The CEO job." He took the notebook page she'd discarded and folded it. "After so many adventures, you can only imagine how much I detested that job of never-ending indoor meetings, business suits, and suffocating ties—I still refuse to wear ties, except at funerals." He kept folding the page. "But I couldn't quit and disappoint my father, and none of my siblings wanted to take over. That was what triggered my weight gain. Fighting stress and depression through overeating and drinking too much, I gained eighty pounds."

Unbelievable. The image of his perfect naked body flashed in her mind. She fixed her eyes on his long fingers, folding the page, and memories of his touch that night flooded her.

His voice snapped her out of her trance. "So, one day my friend Luke and I brainstormed ideas on how to make exercise enjoyable, and he asked me the question that saved my life, 'What did you enjoy doing when you were little?'" His face became radiant. "Remembering our childhood passions was the turning point. Mine had been martial arts, outdoor hiking, and Greek and Roman legends—from my nerd days. Luke's passions had been computers, video games, and sci-fi characters."

She smiled too, understanding the thread of the story.

He turned the folded page over. "Everyone thought we'd gone crazy when we started building playground-inspired exercise equipment and dressing up in costumes. Back then, we had no idea it would become our new way of earning a living." He finished folding the page into a paper plane. "During my nights of insomnia, I started a video-blog. The video I posted when I reached my weight-loss goal—with time-lapse photos from beginning to end—went viral. And the rest is history." He threw the paper plane, and it gracefully flew across the swimming pool, landing on the other end.

Fascinated, she nodded. "So that's how your company grew so much in only five years. Did you keep your dreaded day job for a while before your new business took off?"

For a moment, his golden-green eyes lost their usual sparkle. "Actually, by then my father and I'd had a fight and I'd quit." He hesitated. "Taking that CEO job was my last attempt to mend our relationship. It has always been… conflicted."

"What do you mean by conflicted? Love-hate?"

He gave a mirthless chuckle. "That's an understatement." To her inquiring gaze, he explained. "I didn't know he existed until I was eight. My mother had told me my father was dead, to hide that she'd gotten pregnant by a married man."

The psychologist in her perked up. "How did you meet him?"

"After my mother died in an accident, he showed up to get me and took me to live with him and his family." He seemed reluctant before adding, "We never talked about where he had been during my early years."

She could sense the tension in his body, signaling that the topic was painful to discuss. She closed her notebook. "I always thought it was a cliché, but you proved it's truth: you followed your passions and they became a new career."

Seeming relieved, he grabbed a sugar packet to fold it into a tiny paper football. "The point of this long story, darling, is: when your inner compass tells you you're in the right place, don't question it— even if it doesn't make sense at first. Keep doing what brings you joy, and it will make sense in time."

Maybe he wasn't as crazy as he liked to present himself.

"Now, about *your* career change," he added looking at her. "I'll ask you the same question Luke asked me back then. 'What did you enjoy doing when you were a kid?'"

Allison had to think for a long time before she could find an enjoyable memory from childhood. "I'm afraid my answer is nothing useful. My favorite thing to do was play with dolls."

He gestured at her with an open hand. "Then go buy yourself a doll."

She almost laughed. "How is that supposed to help me?"

Amusement and apology mixed on his face as he shrugged. "I didn't know how dressing up as a space ninja to practice taekwondo would help me. Just do it to reconnect with your inner child."

Allison's eyes got lost for a moment. "I used to beg my mother to buy me a Barbie, but she never did. Sometimes I see those collectible Barbie dolls wearing designer clothes, and I confess I feel tempted to buy one."

She studied him as he played with the sugar packet. What was it about this man that made her remember her forgotten childhood?

Chapter 8

J AY CONVINCED ALLISON TO CONTINUE THE CONVERSATION while taking a walk on the beach behind the hotel. The afternoon sun made the waves sparkle and warmed them up against the cool March breeze. With the crashing waves as background noise, he answered her questions.

"So the company grew so much we had to split it. Luke focused on selling the virtual reality programs and apps online and I became the face of Legendary Heroes." He noticed she struggled to keep her balance in her wedge sandals, so he held her arm to help steady her.

Her eyes moved from his hand touching her arm to his face, shooting him a warning glare. Understanding the message, he let go immediately. *So much for hoping this interview was an excuse to see me.*

And that was fine. He didn't need to fall in bed with her again.

Ugh! Who was he kidding? Of course, he did.

As Allison quoted numbers about Legendary Heroes he didn't even know—she must've done a lot of research on his company—his eyes drank her in.

Look at that amazing porcelain skin. It was the softest thing he'd touched in his life. *Look at that gorgeous golden hair, tousled by the ocean breeze.* He so clearly remembered that hair falling over his face as she climbed on top of him that night. And how about the curve of those gorgeous breasts, stretching the fabric of her turquoise silk dress. He remembered their glorious texture so clearly.

But the whole purpose of seeking her out had been to end this obsession. Maybe if he got a good dose of her harshness, he could finally stop fixating on whether or not she was Grace and leave the past behind him.

Yet, every so often, that cold woman would hint at something different underneath. A deadpan joke, a crooked smile, a residue of a lisp that made her mispronounce some words. For a flash here and there, it was like seeing his childhood girlfriend again.

"You're doing it again. You're staring at me like I turned purple." Allison's flat voice brought him back from his musings.

A lonely seagull flew over them against the wind and seemed to suspend itself in the air for a moment, floating without advancing.

He considered his next words. Hoping to see a hint of recognition in her eyes, he'd shared way too much about his childhood today—yet she'd made no effort to reciprocate. "Do you remember the game we played in the car the day we met?"

"The questions game?"

He flashed her his best swoon-worthy beam. "You must've asked me a hundred questions today. When will it be my turn? I want to hear everything about *your* childhood."

She stopped walking and lifted a hand. "I'm sorry. It's my rule that I don't talk about the past. I have nothing pleasant to remember from my early years."

He was taken aback, flashes of his idyllic childhood games with Grace entering his mind. *She can't be my Grace, then.*

Still, he'd practically shared his life story today and he wasn't walking away without learning something about her. He simpered. "But you'll show your appreciation for my time by allowing me some questions, won't you?"

She seemed to debate inwardly for a moment. "You have one question. Choose it carefully."

Shit. Only one question.

Jay's brain flooded with options. Should he ask her something only Grace would know? Probe about her real intentions when she called him? Ask the question that was still killing him six months after their night together—*Was that as good for you as it was for me?*

His eyes fixed on her face and, on an impulse, he blurted, "What's the deal with the Botox?"

She eyed him with caution. "What about it?"

"I've seen footage of you from ten years ago where you already have the frozen face. Who uses Botox in their twenties?"

She hesitated, but then seemed to give in. "The truth is that the left side of my face is affected by something called facial palsy; it doesn't move as well as the other side."

He wasn't expecting that. In silence, he continued listening.

"I tried Botox once to get some symmetry, and someone commented that it made me look older—because instead of a twenty-something-year-old woman, I looked like a woman in her forties who just appeared younger because of the Botox. I liked it. I was just starting out as a family therapist, and it made me seem older and more experienced than I was." She paused, as if reluctant to share the last piece. "And I admit it also became a shield against the world. If people couldn't see what I was feeling, then I had an advantage over them—it was the ultimate poker face."

For a moment her blue eyes softened and he understood that her coldness was just a façade. She needed the protection of the motionless face not because she had no feelings, but because she had too many.

"How did the facial paralysis happen?" he asked.

Her expression darkened. "You had your question. Let's get back to your interview."

He sensed there was more to that story, but he decided to let it go for now.

The conversation continued as they made their way back to the poolside restaurant. Jay had given up on getting Allison to talk about her personal life and listened to her relate her frustrations trying to get publicity and being bullied by the moronic Wayne Nash.

"Nash's only advantage over me is that he gets to edit his show. He has no wits off-camera when there's no script to guide him." She huffed. "Some day I'll get to confront him on even ground."

"Well, now I'm even more glad I turned him down. Besides, if I turned down Carrie O'Brian's show, why would I go on his?"

Allison stopped walking and her mouth fell open; her usually blank face eloquently showed her stupefaction. Her voice climbed to a higher pitch than usual. "You got invited to go on *The Carrie O'Brian Show* and you said no?"

He suppressed his amusement at her shocked expression. "Carrie's husband attended my Warriors Boot Camp, lost a bunch of weight, and they're delighted with the results. She wanted me to go on her show—but I didn't feel like it."

Allison's words seemed to be strangling her. "*You didn't feel like it*? I would kill to go to Carrie's show! She's the Oprah of Florida!"

He dropped himself in one of the pool area chairs. "Meh, she's okay."

Allison emitted a guttural sound and her eyes seemed about to protrude out of their orbits. Jay loved it. "Do you have any more questions for me?"

With a shudder, she cleared her throat and ran her fingers through her hair. "What's next for Legendary Heroes?" she asked.

Jay's cheerfulness vanished. "I'm exploring a proposal. But I'm almost sure I'll reject it."

"What is it?"

"My friend Matt wants to partner with me."

Her hand halted on her hair. "You mean Matthew Hester, the Hollywood actor?"

He assented. "He's obsessed with the idea that we have to open a chain of Legendary Heroes gyms all around California. He says that, besides the Silicon Valley guys, plenty of Hollywood actors would also like to train with my team before their action movies. But I'm not sure."

She made the amusing shock-face again. "What? Why on Earth not? Legendary Heroes would become a billion-dollar company. Not to mention the fame and other sources of income that would bring you. Companies will chase you, begging you to endorse their fitness products."

"My point exactly." He shuddered like she'd suggested a root canal. "Who wants that? I don't want to complicate my life that much." He reclined on his chair. "What's the point of having a gazillion dollars if you never have time to enjoy them? If I say yes, I'll have to work like a slave. Right now I work only the hours I want when I want."

Allison held her breath for so long, her face started to turn blue. He debated whether to shake her when she finally exhaled. "Jay, look at you. Turning down an invitation from Carrie O'Brian. Turning down a partnership with a Hollywood celebrity. You know what a professional therapist would have to say about that, don't you?" She leaned forward and pierced him with her cerulean eyes. "You're trying to sabotage your career. You feel threatened by fame and success and are trying to get rid of them."

He felt like she'd slapped him in the face.

How dare she psychoanalyze me?

And even worse, how dare she make so much sense?

"That's not true."

"I read somewhere that your most lucrative service is your Warriors Boot Camp. The waiting list to enroll is gigantic—yet you refuse to hold them more than twice a year."

He frowned at her. She was right. Men paid ridiculous amounts of money for two weeks of personalized training with his team. If he agreed to host those events more often, he wouldn't have to worry about finances anymore. "Those boot camps are intense for *me*. I don't need that stress more than every six months. Besides, they're expensive. If I hold them more often, they won't fill up."

"They would if you opened them to women too. Right now, by

holding them only for men you're alienating fifty percent of potential costumers."

Her solid logic was irritating. "The activities at that boot camp are designed for men; a woman wouldn't enjoy them."

"Okay, no need to get flustered." She lifted her hands with a chuckle, and only then did he realize he'd raised his voice. "But I always say, if it weren't true, it wouldn't hurt you to hear it."

She winked at him. The playful gesture surprised him and dissipated his frustration. He gave a reluctant smile. "Sorry. It's not fun to feel I can be *predictable*. I've spent my life trying not to be."

She twinkled. "Don't take it personally. My gift and my curse are reading through people's bullshit."

Even as the Botox restrained it, there was something different about the way she smiled. Her face was flushed, her eyes shone with warmth.

Damn it. When she wasn't trying to bust the balls of every man on the planet, she wasn't that bad.

A text from Calvin, his events coordinator, brought Jay back from his trance. *"Ten minutes."*

He couldn't believe it was this late. "I guess I'm due on stage."

Allison seemed startled as she consulted her watch. "Wow. We've been chatting for hours." She rose from her chair and picked up her purse. "I'd better let you go."

"We can continue tonight," he blurted out, surprising himself. Her eyes rose to meet his and her immobile face gave no hint of what she thought.

He cleared his throat and forced a casual tone. "Maybe we can meet again after my last lecture for a late dinner?"

There. He'd done it. He'd extended his jugular and made himself a target for her contempt for men. He held his breath, bracing himself for her rejection.

"Actually, tonight it's impossible. I already have dinner plans."

… And there it was. The Ice-Queen had proved she always held the control.

"But—" she added. "What time is your last lecture tomorrow?"

Jay studied her face. Her calculated indifference hid a hint of shyness. The flutter in her eyelashes suggested… eagerness. Anticipation.

Slowly, his lips curved. It took all of his self-control not to grin. He had to restrain himself from climbing on the table, clapping and cheering as if his football team had scored a touchdown.

Chapter 9

EMERY'S BIRTHDAY WAS IN SIX DAYS, THE SAME DAY AS HER wedding. Allison strongly suspected Emery's fiancé, Ken, had chosen that date to get away with one annual birthday-anniversary combined present for his future wife. Fe had proposed taking Emery out for an early birthday dinner and they'd all agreed on tonight, when "unfortunately" Ken's friends were throwing him a bachelor's party and he couldn't attend.

But even more unfortunately, he'd sent his cousin Karen Knight to represent his side of the family.

Wearing her usual baggy pants, shapeless shirt, and brunette pixie cut, Karen babbled and bragged nonstop about her appearance on *The Carrie O'Brian Show*, as if rubbing her success in Allison's face. "And the minute the segment is released I plan to post a link on my website. That's going to do wonders for my search optimization!"

Big deal. It was only two minutes, answering a question, Allison sulked.

At the end of the table, Fe used her fingers to style her husband Shawn's auburn hair. "Karen, you're such a man-hater you make Allison look sweet in comparison. I disagree with your answer to Carrie; not all men are obsessed with the female body."

Welcoming the opportunity to change the subject away from Karen's bragging, Allison chimed in. "Really? Let's take a poll." She turned to Fe's husband—who also happened to be Emery's cousin and physician partner. "Shawn, what was the first thing you noticed about Fe?"

Shawn McDevitt reached for the hand sanitizer travel bottle in the pocket of his blue-green scrubs that matched his eyes. "Her smile, of course," he answered. To Allison's tilted head and raised eyebrows, he cleared his throat and averted his gaze. "And her butt."

"Thank you. And you, T.J.," she addressed Hope's husband, sitting next to Shawn. "What was the first thing you noticed about Hope?"

With a twinkle in his baby-blue eyes, T.J. Wagner slicked his blond hair. "A part of me wants to answer that it was her musical talent." He blushed and looked away. "But the truth is that it was her breasts."

"Which we all know are fake!" Hope raised her glass with a proud grin then pecked her husband on the lips.

Allison turned to Joy's fiancé, sprawled in his chair on the other end of the table. She'd rather not address that obnoxious man, but it was socially expected. "And you, Agent Fields, what attracted you to Joy?"

Without moving a muscle, he fixed his hazel eyes on Allison and deadpanned. "Her radiant aura and beautiful soul."

She shot him her infamous "anti-bull" glare. "And now the truth."

"That *is* the truth." He sustained her gaze with a hint of a smirk.

Oh, please! Allison couldn't stand that professional liar who'd once broken Joy's heart so badly. The girls said he'd proven himself by now, but for Allison, the jury was still out.

Richard Fields rose from his seat, threading a hand through his dark hair, sprinkled with gray. "Come on, guys. Let's go watch the game at the bar and give the girls some space to rant about us," he suggested to Shawn and T.J.

Tall and broad-shouldered, he seemed like a giant compared to petite Joy as he leaned down to kiss her cheek and whisper something in her ear, making her giggle. He then turned to Allison. "Plus,

Twitter tells me I'm persona non grata at this table."

Allison fought the smug grin threatening to spread over her face. She might've "accidentally" tagged Richard in her most recent post on Twitter—an article about how guns were phallic symbols meant to compensate for small penises.

"You're actually growing on me, Agent Fields. Like—"

"I know," he interrupted, lifting a large hand. "Like a skin fungus and a malignant tumor rolled into one."

"Mycosis Fungoides?" Shawn offered.

"There you go!" Allison snickered. "You're my Mycosis Fungoides, Agent Fields. Who doesn't love that?"

A spark of amusement crossed Richard's tan face. He flashed her one crooked smile that enhanced his laugh lines, then left the table with the other men.

Allison's phone lit up with another call from her client, Tiffany. It must be number twelve that day, in spite of Allison having warned her she'd be unavailable. As she rejected the call, she thought about the contrast between Emery and Joy, both high-functioning physicians, and Tiffany, the eternal child. The three women were so different, yet they all showed horrible judgment in men.

That was so wrong. A woman should never entrust her happiness to a man. It didn't matter how good he looked, or how great he was in bed.

Or how amazing he was turning out to be, or how much he blew her mind with his wise words.

Darn it. Now I can't stop thinking about Jay.

Emery returned to the table after stepping out to answer a call from the hospital's ICU. Between the black eye threatening her pictures and the stress of wedding preparations, the friends were tiptoeing around her like a psychiatric patient about to snap. "Allison, why do you hate Richard so m—?"

"Long story! Let's move on," Joy rushed to say. She then turned to Fe. "So, Shawn mentioned he's meeting a friend after this?"

"One of his best friends is in town teaching a seminar," Fe explained.

"Teaching a medical seminar?" Karen asked.

Fe shook her head. "No, a fitness seminar. I doubt you know this guy. His name is Jay Johnson. They call him Triple J."

Shrinking in her chair, Joy shot Allison a panicky look. *Darn it.* Allison hoped no one asked her anything—Joy was the worst liar in the world.

Karen tensed every muscle in her body. One of her eyes twitched and her voice turned icy. "Oh. Yes, I know that so-called life coach. He's insufferable! A complete prima donna. And he's also a total misogynist."

Fe threw her hands in the air so abruptly she almost knocked off her water glass. "What are you talking about? Jay is the coolest, most low-maintenance guy in the world! And he's a proud self-proclaimed feminist."

Hope slanted her eyes between them. "Are you guys sure you're talking about the same person?"

Twirling a hand, Fe squinted at Karen and offered, "Tall, dark, and ripped? Hot as hell… crazy as hell?"

Yup, that's him. Allison faked a sip from her mojito to hide her agitation.

Karen turned to Emery. "His company has a blatant discriminatory policy against women. Women and men are segregated in his group classes and not allowed to exercise in the same rooms. And, women are not allowed into his most famous jumpstart boot camp."

Fe placed a hand on her waist and thrust out her chest. "He says women distract his male customers and make them self-conscious. Don't forget these are grown men dressed up in costumes, staging fights. And the Warriors Boot Camp is geared toward men practicing martial arts. It would be too strenuous for women."

"That perpetuates the fallacy that women are weak and need to be protected. He's the ultimate example of what's wrong with men."

Karen counted with her fingers. "He's obsessed with the body; he's the incarnation of promiscuity; and he is an eternal child, refusing to grow up."

Fe, the ultimate defender of the underdog, had embraced the argument as personal. "What's wrong with being an eternal child?"

Allison felt as if she, Hope, and Emery were watching a Ping-Pong match, their eyeballs bouncing back and forth between the opposite ends of the table.

"Have you seen his website?" Karen grunted. "He dresses up in indecent costumes!"

Fe drew wide circles in the air with her index finger. "Have you paid attention to what young women wear nowadays? So now we have a double standard for showing skin?"

"Have you watched his YouTube videos? He's a grown man who collects action figures!"

"So what? My aunt Rosa collects antique teacups."

"He's crazy!"

Joy came out of her stupor and lifted a finger. "Uh… excuse me. As a psychiatrist, I have to disagree. The DSM V clearly states that for atypical behavior to be considered mental illness 'it needs to interfere with ability to relate and function.' Even if Jay doesn't behave in the most typical ways, he's a highly productive member of society. By definition that makes him eccentric, not crazy."

Allison gaped at Joy. "If in order to describe him you need to examine the fine print of the psychiatry manual, that's worrisome."

Her eye twitching, Karen turned to Allison, as if sensing an ally. "There's something sketchy about him!" She lowered her voice. "Every Wednesday he disappears and doesn't even answer calls." She made her voice a whisper. "I think he sees a parole officer those days. He must be an ex-con."

Fe grabbed Allison's arm. "Ignore her, girls! Jay doesn't see a parole officer on Wednesdays!" She half-shrugged. "He sees a woman."

The girls turned their attention to Fe. She bobbed her head. "I heard him talk to Shawn once. He told him, and I quote, '*She's not exactly a girlfriend, but a girl who's more than a friend.*'"

Allison felt as if the air in the room got heavier. She'd sworn to herself she had no intentions with this man outside a casual relationship. Yet the idea that he might be involved with someone else disturbed her.

"A weekly secret rendezvous?" Karen scrunched her small, pointy nose. "I smell something dirty there!"

"What do you know?" Fe asked, flicking her wrist. "Shawn says the guy is an incurable romantic who never forgot his first girlfriend. For all we know, it could be a cool love story."

"Romantic? Please!" Karen splurted, then pursed her thin, pale lips. "This is the man who has been quoted saying that 'sex is play' and that he doesn't believe in one-night stands—because he makes sure to try everything *twice.*"

Allison felt a punch in her stomach.

So, that's what this is all about? He needs to try me one more time before he dumps me?

Feeling nauseated, Allison barely listened to the conversation after that. Only then did she admit to herself she'd been truly looking forward to seeing Jay tomorrow.

* * *

That night, before going to bed, Allison browsed Jay's website. He had an extensive collection of video blog posts where he shared fitness and nutrition advice, but occasionally answered questions from subscribers' emails.

After a while searching, she found the video Karen had referred to, "Sex is play."

Jay was answering a letter from a fan asking about his take on casual sex. "Why do we make such a big deal about sex, trying to demonize it?" Jay answered. "Sex is like play. Remember when you were six years old and playing was everything? If you were lucky, you'd find a little best friend who became your play buddy, and you knew you could always reach for them when you wanted to play. That's wonderful. But not everybody had that luck." His eyes turned sad. "If we didn't have a best friend —or if we'd lost them—the next best thing we could do was keep going to the park and hope to find other little kids there, willing to play with us—even if after that we'd never see them again." He paused, giving a half-shrug. "It's the same with adults. Inside, we're just little kids looking for a play buddy."

Oh, please! Allison felt like gagging.

Why did she even care? It wasn't like there was any chance this guy would be more than a hookup. Maybe she wasn't the modern, open-minded woman she'd made herself out to be.

And to think that for even a brief moment, he'd made her doubt that what she preached to her clients was true.

Allison had a flashback of her stepfather yelling at her mother. And next, she saw a large oak tree and a tire swing hanging from it. She couldn't remember what that memory was about, but it caused her so much pain, she pushed it away.

Men are scum.

She grabbed her phone and texted Jay, *"I'm going to have to pass on the dinner invitation."*

The reply popped up almost immediately, *"Everything okay?"*

Bracing herself, she typed. *"Nothing personal. I think we've seen enough of each other for a while. I'm going to give you some space now and I hope you do the same for me."*

She sent the text, and within seconds her phone rang with a call from him. She rejected the incoming call and blocked his number.

Feeling the unreasonable desire to cry, she closed her laptop and crawled into bed.

Chapter 10

ON THE FLOOR OF HIS THERAPIST'S OFFICE, JAY VENTED AND did pushups at the same time without losing his breath. "I can't believe she rejected me! For the first time in... ever, I made sure to do everything right on a date. I was a gentleman; I didn't pressure her; I answered all her questions. I told her deep details about my personal life—heck, I even talked about Conan. And she *passed* on me?"

Sitting on a chair next to Shawn, dark circles under his eyes, Ethan pointed at Jay with his open hand. "And that has been my life for the past three days, Dr. Hazenberg. That's why I staged this intervention."

The therapist stroked his gray beard, smiling. "Well, Jay, if this Allison was the instrument to bring you back to therapy, she already has my seal of approval."

With a grunt of frustration, Jay rolled onto his back and began sit-ups.

Chuckling, Shawn tugged at the neckline of his blue-green scrubs. "I actually think this is progress. At least this time he's obsessed with a real, flesh-and-blood woman and not with that unreachable first girlfriend."

Jay halted mid sit-up. "Well... This is what it's all about, guys. I—" He stopped, knowing the doctor and his friends would drill him about this. He rolled and sprang to his feet, then faced Ethan and Shawn. "Do you remember how I told you that I ran into one of

62

Allison's books and developed a love-hate interest in her anti-men theories? Well, that's not exactly true. I didn't 'run' into anything. I searched her by name and started learning everything about her five years ago, after I met her in person."

Ethan frowned. "You'd met her before you hooked up?"

Jay nodded, then sat on the remaining chair in front of the therapist. "She doesn't remember me because it was before I broke off my relationship with my father. I was still using his last name—she met Jacob Wetzel, not Jay Johnson. Back then I was eighty pounds heavier—more, if you consider the weight I've added in muscle mass. I had a beard, dressed differently, and I was the most depressed I've ever been in my life."

Shawn slid his chair closer. "What happened then?"

"We shook hands briefly and she looked right through me—like most women used to do. And then for the next hour we sat at opposite ends of this conference room while she barely acknowledged my existence. I never said a word. I just watched her talk in awe. Her beauty was overpowering, but there was also something else." He stopped.

"What was it?" Ethan prompted.

Jay sighed, vividly remembering that moment. "She sneezed."

Ethan and Shawn exchanged a look.

"Is this supposed to be a germ fetish I'm not aware of?" asked Shawn, reaching for the hand sanitizer in his pocket.

Jay denied with his head. "She was having some allergy flare-up that day. She kept sniffling, and sneezing into a Kleenex, and apologizing. And every time she did, it was like a train of memories ran me over. There was only one person in the world I'd ever met who scrunched her nose like that when sneezing." He hesitated before concluding. "My Grace."

A long silence fell in the room. The therapist's stone face became more unreadable than ever, while apprehension and disappointment flashed on Shawn's and Ethan's faces. Jay braced himself for the explosion.

"No, no, no! Not again!" Shawn exclaimed.

And there it is.

With a loud sigh, Shawn rose from his chair and spread his arms wide. "Jay! We've been through this before! Not every blond woman in the world named Grace is your childhood girlfriend. And that's not even her name, so why would you think Allison is her?"

Jay stood up to meet Shawn's teal eyes. "Grace's middle name was Allison! And she might've changed her last name since, but... Shawn, I think this time I found her!"

Shawn placed his hands on his temples. "This obsession that your childhood girlfriend is the only woman who could ever make you happy is really getting old. You need to get out in the world and have a meaningful, positive relationship."

"I've had plenty of meaningful relationships."

"I mean lasting longer than a week."

"Of course, I've had relationships longer than that. For a whole year, I was with"—he snapped his fingers twice—"what's-her-face."

Ethan signaled him to slow down. "Wait! Then, the day Allison almost ran you over with her car... Did you stage that?"

Jay shook his head with enthusiasm. "I owe that encounter to Shawn and Fe!" He paced around the room. "Shawn, remember when I stopped at the beachfront hotel to congratulate you on your wedding day?"

"And then refused to stay for the ceremony? Yes." Shawn scowled.

"That was the day I ran into her! I was looking through your suite's window with your binoculars, and I noticed Allison's car passing by on the highway, and a little later she made a U-turn and headed back. So I rushed to see if I could stop her with an excuse. I never imagined things would go that well!"

Shawn stared. "She almost ran you over and you call that well?"

"Wait!" Ethan's brow lines showed he was making an effort to keep up. "How did you know that was her car?"

Jay made a dismissive wave. "Easy. The gunmetal gray Mercedes with the bumper sticker that reads, 'Men suck' and the license plate number 'N0-80YZ.'" To his friends' inquiring look, he confessed. "And I know that because sometimes I've gone to park near where she works at five o'clock to watch her leave."

Ethan and Shawn shared a worried look, and the therapist reached for a pill in a desk drawer and placed it under his tongue.

"You're stalking her for real?" Shawn exploded first. "Jay, haven't you learned anything from the trouble you've gotten into in the past? Have you forgotten you almost got arrested for stalking that other blond woman you thought was Grace?"

Jay gave his friend an apologetic half-smile. "That was Allison."

Shawn whipped his head on Jay's direction. "The woman you chased all over the city in a taxi, trying to take her picture? The one you followed to her building late at night, trying to talk to her, and almost got caught by security?"

He assented again. "Both times. Allison."

Color drained from Shawn's face and he sank back on the chair.

After a long silence, Ethan rested a hand on his chest. "This is beautiful. So romantic."

Shawn sent Ethan a murderous glare. "No! This is sick!"

Shaking his head, Ethan rose to place his hand on Jay's shoulder. "Don't listen to him, Jay. I know what it is to long for a woman who hardly knows you exist. You're my hero for taking this step. You should go for her."

"No. He should get himself back on therapy—and probably also on medication!" Shawn argued.

Ethan got his face closer to Shawn's. "Life is too short to be cautious."

Shawn got even closer to Ethan. "And if we stopped being cautious, it would be even shorter."

"Guys, enough!" Finally reacting, the therapist raised a hand. "You should let me take it from here."

Muttering an agreement, Shawn stumbled out of the office.

Ethan unfolded his walker and slowly followed after, mumbling under his breath, "Lucky bastard. If I tried that move, I'd get run over for real—by a steamroller *and* a dump truck." He used his elbow to close the door on his way out.

Dr. Hazenberg reached for an inhaler in a drawer and gave himself two puffs. Taking a deep breath he asked, "Jay, if you're so sure this woman is your childhood girlfriend, how come you haven't just inquired directly? You could simply ask, 'Hey, isn't your real name Grace? What elementary school did you go to?'"

Jay tensed up. "I... I tried. She refuses to talk about her childhood. And years ago I sent her a Facebook message saying I was a friend from Port Popsicle, Wisconsin, and she ignored me."

The therapist leaned forward. "Or, which I consider more likely, you're afraid of pressing the issue because a part of you knows she's not her. You'd rather hold on to an illusion than face reality."

Jay didn't answer. The man had a point. Every time in the past he thought he'd found Grace and the woman wasn't it, the disappointment crushed him.

Dr. Hazenberg adjusted his wire-rimmed glasses. "You need to learn that adult relationships aren't stormy, adrenaline-driven romances. Nor are they just admiring someone from the distance, unable to reach them, like the imaginary father you had in your early years."

Jay frowned. "I can't believe I'm paying you a fortune to tell me what Shawn tells me for free."

"Well, if you don't like that topic, let's pick up where we left off when you walked out last time." The therapist opened a folder and pointed at a line. "Could this obsession with finding your childhood girlfriend be an attempt to return to the past and undo the moment your father showed up in your life?"

With an impatient huff, Jay looked up to the ceiling. No wonder he'd stopped coming to see this Freud-wannabe. "No, thank you. Let's stay on the topic of Allison."

Dr. Hazenberg closed the folder. "Have you considered giving this woman a chance for herself, not for the possibility of her being that girl from your past?"

"What do you mean?"

"She may've started out as the unreachable woman in that conference room. But now you've met her in person and even had intimacy with her. She's now real, and the fact that you're still interested in her is promising. Maybe we can find a silver lining in this."

The therapist seemed inspired. "This could be another instance in your life when you're about to replace an addiction for a healthier one. Years ago, your addictions used to be food and alcohol, and you replaced them with an addiction to exercise and an obsession for healthy eating. That's great. You've channeled all that energy into something that's good for you. You can attempt the same with this woman."

Puzzled, Jay surveyed the doctor. "I still don't get it."

"My point is: Instead of stalking her, I encourage you to pursue her—in an open, healthy way."

Jay hadn't expected this from his stuffy therapist.

The doctor resumed his explanation. "You'll be exercising social skills you never developed. She'll probably reject you again or disillusion you. But, hey, that's life. Can you think about something nice you could do for her to woo her and impress her?"

Jay considered it, reviewing his last conversations with Allison in his mind. "I may have an idea for a present she can't refuse."

* * *

On the balcony of Emery's apartment, Hope face-palmed herself. "I want to slap you. Allison! How could you do this? You don't turn down a man who looks like *that*!"

Allison cursed the moment the conversation sprang out of control. Tonight, Fe was practicing Emery's hair and makeup before the wedding in two days—yes, Fe was better than a professional beautician. But Hope had the sniffer for gossip that an airport dog had for drugs and had immediately noticed Allison's changed mood. After taking them apart, she'd practically beaten the confessions out of her and Joy.

Staring at Jay's pictures from a Google Images search on her phone, Hope shuddered. "Don't get me wrong, I'm happily married, but…" She fake-sobbed and her voice turned high-pitched. "Have you seen the picture where he has his shirt off?"

Truthfully, it had taken all of Allison's self restraint not to pick up the phone and call Jay for the past three days. "Hope, I've seen Jay with *everything* off. I get your point. But I'm proud of myself for imposing my brain above my hormones. Stepping away from him was a matter of principle as a psychotherapist."

"I give up. You're a lost cause." Hope left the balcony, returning to the scantly decorated living room, and dropped herself onto the Ikea sofa with a groan.

Allison and Joy followed Hope back inside. There was still no sign of Emery and Fe; they were probably still in the bedroom working on makeup.

Allison sat next to her friend. "Hope, you have no idea how often a client cries her eyes out in my office because of some heartbreak. I have to politely nod and be all-supportive." Allison used her fist to punch her own palm repeatedly. "But deep inside all I want to do is shake her and yell, '*Come on*! You *really* didn't see that coming?'" She dropped her hands. "It didn't occur to you that if your boyfriend cheated on every single girlfriend he had before you, he'd cheat on you too?"

Her phone rang with another call from Tiffany. *Speaking of which.* She sent the call to voicemail. "Or that if your latest man only texted you for drunken booty calls at two in the morning… *maybe* he wasn't interested in a real, deep relationship?" She stopped, realizing she was losing her cool, and cleared her throat. "Well, I'm proud of my accomplishment. I did exactly what I preach to my clients and they never listen. I looked ahead, saw the future, and saved myself the headache." She turned to Joy. "Don't you agree?"

Joy took a few seconds before answering. "Let me see if I got this right." She narrowed her eyes and held her chin, mimicking Allison's therapist face. "This big 'accomplishment' you're so proud of is that you finally met a man you really liked and was good in bed. He deeply impressed you with his work. He went out of his way to be nice to you and stay in touch—and yet you pushed him away, hurting his feelings and crushing his male self-esteem." She paused. "So, that is your *accomplishment*? Did I get it all?"

Allison blinked rapidly. *Darn it!* Joy really knew how to twist her logic.

Joy reached for her hand and held it. "You know, Allison, I've always suspected you had a bad heartbreak in early life you don't talk about. That's my only way to explain your mistrust of men."

Allison had another flashback of the large oak tree and the tire swing hanging from it. She shook it away and slanted Joy a glance. "Joy, you know my story. You know about my abusive stepfather and my mess of a mother, jumping from useless man to useless man in her life. Do you really have to wonder where my lack of respect for men comes from?"

Joy shook her head. "I'm not convinced. If your stepfather was the root of your attachment issues, how come they didn't get better after you reclaimed your power and sent him to jail?"

"Get out of here!" Hope clapped. "You put your stepfather in jail?"

Allison made a dismissive flick with her hand, but Joy spoke enthusiastically. "Allison is my hero. The minute she turned eighteen she denounced him for his drug dealing activities. The police had never taken the domestic abuse charges against him seriously, but she found a different way to make him pay."

To Hope's surprised look, Allison explained. "That's how I ended up changing my name. His brothers threatened to make me pay for that, but he wasn't a 'big enough fish' for the police to consider me eligible for witness protection services. So I went to the farthest-away college that accepted me—University of Florida—and changed my name legally from Grace Allison Maxwell to Allison Connors, taking my middle name and my grandmother's maiden name. And still if anybody asks where I was born, I tell them I'm from Canada."

Fe exited Emery's bedroom at that time. Her unusual lack of a smile warned everybody that something wasn't right.

"Emery's not coming out to show us her hair and makeup?" asked Joy.

"Let me guess," Hope said. "She's upset because her black eye isn't going away in time for the rehearsal dinner."

Fe shook her head. "The rehearsal dinner has been canceled." Sudden silence filled the room. She licked her lips and looked away. "Because the wedding has been canceled."

The three friends gawked at Fe. With a grimace, she added, "Someone texted Emery pictures of Ken in a... compromising position with the stripper from his bachelor party."

Chapter 11

LYING ON THE RECLINER IN ALLISON'S OFFICE, TIFFANY Wetzel-Donovan-Carlson-Blanche whimpered. "That man is a monster!"

If Allison had a dollar for every time she'd heard those words, she'd be a millionaire.

With her blond hair and blue eyes, Tiffany could've passed for Allison's younger, richer sister. Maybe that was why she affected her so much; sometimes Allison felt like she was looking at herself in a parallel lifetime.

She realized she'd let her mind wander for too long. "I'm sorry. Remind me; which ex are we talking about today?"

"No, no. I'm talking about my brother Jacob."

Allison went back in her mind. "You mean the one who has split personality disorder, who you hate for stealing the spotlight at your Sweet Sixteen party?"

"No. That's my brother Zeke. Jacob is the one with the rage issues. The one I hate for being Dad's favorite."

Keeping her face impassive, Allison nodded. Even after five years as Tiffany's counselor, she still had trouble keeping up with Tiffany's dysfunctional siblings—and that was *after* having met them in a couple of family therapy sessions. "What's Jacob doing now?"

"His lawyer called me! He wants to take Gracie away from me!"

The mention of Gracie immediately refreshed Allison's memory. "How could he? You're her mother; an uncle has zero legal weight."

"He has a copy of my ex-husband's will where he appointed him as her legal guardian before he died. He's now threatening me with asking for Gracie's custody! He argues he can convince the judge I'm not psychologically stable to take care of her. Can you believe his nerve?"

Allison tried to frown—her Botoxed forehead wouldn't respond. "I've counseled you for years. You've shown some judgment issues and made some mistakes, but from that to saying you're unstable there's a long distance." *Well, some distance.*

"It's all an excuse. He doesn't care about being her legal guardian." Tiffany huffed. "All he wants is to enforce being the trustee. All he cares about is the money Tim's family left Gracie."

Allison's thoughts returned to Gracie, Tiffany's eight-year-old daughter. What a coincidence that the little girl had the same name Allison had before her name change. Tiffany might not be the most nurturing mother in the world, but the worst thing that could happen to that little girl would be being separated from her and sent to live with a sketchy uncle.

"Don't worry, Tiffany. I'll help you in any way I can. Accusing a woman of being a bad mother just to hurt her is below the belt, bullying behavior." She paused, noticing something. "Speaking of which. Isn't Thursday your nanny's day off when you bring Gracie with you? Where is she today?"

Tiffany's face went blank. "Yes. Where is Gracie?"

The office door slammed open and Tiffany's daughter appeared at the threshold, carrying a one-year-old baby on her hip and a diaper bag on her opposite shoulder. Her blond hair appeared soaked in sweat.

"Where the hell were you?" asked Tiffany. "And why are you so sweaty?"

Piercing her mother with her sky-blue eyes, little Gracie limped toward her. "You forgot to feed us lunch. I had to walk to the building across the street, to buy us crackers from their vending machine.

Why am I sweaty? Because the sun's hot and your newest stepson is super heavy!" With a groan, she sat the baby on the recliner.

Surprise flashed on Tiffany's face. "I could've sworn I fed you Pop-Tarts five minutes ago."

"That was breakfast—hours ago." Gracie glared at her mother.

Tiffany covered her mouth with a hand. Her body trembled before she burst into tears, hugging her daughter. "I'm so sorry. There's so much going on right now." Between sobs, she whispered, "Jacob is right; I'm a bad mother."

Allison's first thought was to remind Tiffany she wasn't supposed to leave an eight-year-old supervising a baby. But she first had to tend to her therapist's duty to offer her client unconditional support and no judgment. "Don't say that, Tiffany." She rose from her chair to pat the woman's shoulder. "Anybody can make a mistake once." She turned to Gracie with inquiring eyes. *Only once, right?*

Gracie avoided Allison's gaze. With a loud sigh, she stroked her mother's back. "It's no big deal, Mom. Stop crying. Did you forget to take your antidepressants again?"

Allison felt a twinge of pain in her soul. This girl reminded her so much of herself at that age it was bordering on dangerous counter-transference. It wasn't only about physical appearance, but in the way she'd had to mature so fast in order to handle her volatile mother.

Tiffany's phone rang, and she glanced at it with a sniffle. "Sorry, I have to take this. It's my manicurist." She released the hug and picked up. "Hi, Bihn. What? What do you mean you have to reschedule?" She walked out of the office, pressing the phone to her ear. Allison noticed her tears had vanished suspiciously fast.

With another loud sigh, Gracie dug in the diaper bag, extracted a bottle of formula and stuck it in the baby's mouth.

"You must be thirsty after that long walk," Allison commented, her eyes glued on Gracie. *Gosh, she's grown so much!* "Would you like some water?"

"That would be great," she agreed.

Allison moved to the nearby cooler and served the girl a paper cup of cold water. She accepted with thanks and drank eagerly. Then, she turned back to the baby to make sure he was holding the bottle upright.

Allison had trouble shaking the rumble of memories of herself at that age, taking care of her younger sister while their mother was passed out drunk. She'd bragged to her friends she knew nothing about kids precisely because she wanted to forget those scenes of childhood.

She opened a drawer in her desk, removed a box and smiled at the girl. "It's no lunch, but would you like a chocolate-chip cookie?"

Gracie eyed her with a serious expression. "Sugar is not good for you. It gives you a high, but then it makes you crash and feel hungrier later."

"Oh! Sorry." Allison put the box away.

Gracie held the bottle to the baby's mouth with the commitment of a soldier.

"He's cute," Allison commented.

"I know," Gracie mumbled. "I'm trying not to get too attached to him. Mr. Jordan is only keeping him for the month until his mom is out of rehab."

"That's probably wise," Allison assented. She wondered what kind of childhood that little girl would have between a former child star mother and stepfather, both stuck in the "glory days" and unable to face the world of being grown-ups. She made herself a note to investigate what was really going on in Gracie's household.

Gracie patted the baby's head. "My nanny Miranda calls him 'my stepsibling of the month.' You know, because of those other stepbrothers I had when Mom was married to Mr. George, and the kids I met when she dated that other guy before she married Jordan." Her smile withered. "But it's okay. My uncle says that when I turn eighteen, I can find them all on social media, and host big 'ex-step-family reunions' to complain together about how our parents screwed us up."

Allison wished she were a little warmer and could give the girl a hug.

Gracie glanced around the office. "Speaking of Mom's divorce. Do you still have those puppets you and I played with back then? I had so much fun when we did that."

Allison was surprised the girl still remembered that time, three years ago. The Wetzels had been one of the last families Allison took on as a family therapist before she changed her practice to focus on single women. When Tiffany divorced her second husband, Allison felt obligated to run a few sessions with the little girl, to make sure she was doing okay. Working with a five-year-old was tricky, so she had limited herself to letting the girl use puppets to express herself. "No, I gave those away. And yes, I had a lot of fun, too," she said, sincerely.

Gracie's face lit up. "Do you think if Mom divorces Mr. Jordan, we'll get to do it again? I never get to go on playdates."

Allison felt sorry for the girl, but there was no hope of that for now. Tiffany was getting along better with her husband and putting the divorce on hold. No surprise; whenever she was getting her drama fix from somewhere else, she didn't need to find it in him.

Tiffany returned to the office. "Sorry. Manicure emergency. My nail salon is closing early today and I have to rush." She stormed out the door, leaving the kids behind.

With a resigned shake of her head, Gracie carried the baby. "Well, I have to go. Thanks for the water, Dr. Allison."

"Do you need help?" Allison asked as the girl hung the diaper bag on her shoulder.

"Thanks, I got it." She limped away, following her mother and closing the door behind her.

I know that pride of not needing anybody.

Allison dropped herself on her chair, covering her face with her hands. She'd tried very hard not to remember her childhood. But that little girl was a constant threat to her self-imposed amnesia.

Her secretary knocked on the door, interrupting her musings. "I'm sorry, Dr. Connors, there's a phone call you may want to take right now."

Allison mumbled through her hands. "Who is it?"

"Ms. Carrie O'Brian."

Allison's hand flew from her face. "Her producer is finally calling me back?"

"Not the producer." The young receptionist was giddy with excitement. "It's Ms. O'Brian herself on the phone."

Confused, Allison mumbled a thank you and took the call on hold. "Hello?"

"Dr. Connors?"

Allison swallowed hard. She'd been sure there was a mistake, but this was Carrie's voice. "Ms. O'Brian! What an honor! How can I help you?"

There was a brief silence on the other end of the line. "I... I need to ask you a favor... and it's difficult to explain."

Allison's pulse raced. "Yes?"

"I'd like to invite you to an event my show will be covering. It starts in two weeks. I'm sorry about the short notice."

Someone must've canceled on Carrie last minute and she needs an emergency replacement. The personal touch of calling must be to soften the blow of not being the first choice. *Who cares? Hell yes!* She felt like climbing on her desk and jumping up and down, but kept her voice calm. "I'd be honored!"

Carrie sounded relieved. "Great. My assistant Trey will contact you later today to sign some NDAs."

"Nondisclosure agreements?" That sounded juicy.

"Yes," Carrie explained. "It's... not the typical show recording."

Allison was intrigued. "What do you mean?"

"You'll be on a series of roundtable discussions with three other guests. The topic is women's self-esteem and body image. I'd tell you more but the idea is... still evolving."

"May I ask who the other guests are?"

Carrie hesitated. "Well, we… we're still finalizing that. But we hope to also have Karen Knight—"

Excellent news! This would be her chance to stand up next to Karen and differentiate herself from her.

"—And Wayne Nash."

Allison's grin fell. *What does Wayne have to do with women's self-esteem, except that he can erase anyone's self-esteem in a second?*

"Who's the fourth—?"

"Oh, well, look at the time!" Carrie rushed to say. "Trey will be in touch. Have a nice day."

Allison frowned in her mind to the sound of the clicking phone. Why would Carrie be reluctant to talk about the fourth panelist?

Slowly, an idea dawned on her. Karen Knight. Wayne Nash. Carrie O'Brian. When was the last time she mentioned all three names in the same day?

Her heart dropped. *No. It can't be.*

She had a burning suspicion that the fourth panelist was Jay.

Chapter 12

I T TOOK ALLISON SEVERAL PHONE CALLS AND USING HER STERN voice on a few people, but she soon confirmed that the fourth panelist member was the famous Triple J. Carrie had manufactured the whole event just to please him, as the price to pay for an interview with him.

Allison remembered where Jay mentioned he'd set up his office. Not wanting to give him the benefit of a warning—or the pleasure of a phone call—she called the Riverside building's front desk and verified he was on the premises.

She sped the entire twenty minutes to his office, livid with rage. She'd made it a point in her life to show she didn't need any man coming to her rescue. Even less if she'd once slept with that man and it could be interpreted as if she was working her way up through sexual favors.

She parked in front of the building and went straight to his office. She slammed the door open, startling him at his desk.

His face lit up when he saw her. "Allison! What a pleasant sur—"

"How dare you do this?" she cut him off. "Are you trying to bribe me into bed with you? Do you really think I'm going to sell myself for a TV appearance?"

He didn't answer immediately. Blinking rapidly, he stared at her blankly. "Uh… *You're welcome?*"

She clenched her fists, fuming inside. "Don't try to pretend you did this selflessly, just to do me a favor. You're trying to bribe me. You just want to sleep with me!"

Reclining back in his wheeled office chair, he linked his fingers and narrowed his eyes with a serious expression. "I think this might be a case of what therapists like yourself call projection. Now the question is: Allison, could it be that *you* are the one who wants to sleep with *me*?"

She was taken aback. "So, you don't want to sleep with me?"

Jay laughed. "But of course, I do! Why do you think I went through so much trouble just to see you again?"

She felt like screaming, but kept her voice extra calm. "So you admit that you put all of this together just to get me in bed?"

He raised one hand. "No. I said *to see you again*. But you can't blame me for wishing that something might eventually happen as a result of that."

She processed his answer; he had a way of confusing her with words. "Did you or did you not have Carrie call me as a bait, to get my attention?"

Indicating the office chair in front of his, he agreed. "Carrie *is* bait. It was the best way to convince you to hear me out about a business proposal."

"*Business* proposal?" She crossed her arms and ignored the seat.

He stood and walked around the desk, getting closer. "I've been thinking about what you told me the other day; how I've been blocking my own success, because it scares me."

She was surprised and flattered. "That's great. But what does that have to do with me now?"

"You told me that I couldn't afford to alienate half the population. So the first step I'm taking toward greater success is a trial run to see if my Warriors Boot Camp can be expanded to accept women. Do you see where I'm going?"

"I still don't." She eyed him with caution.

He slowly walked closer and stood in front of her, only inches away. She still hadn't gotten used to how tall he was, forcing her to lift her chin to hold his gaze.

"Since you were the person who planted that idea in my mind," he explained, "I'm expecting you to be the volunteer who will prove to the world that women are capable of completing this training."

She was caught so off guard she had to take a step back to regain her balance. "Are you asking me to participate in your all-male boot camp?"

He twinkled. "It starts in two weeks. Sorry for the short notice, but the idea just came to me."

Shaking her head, she backed away. "You have the wrong person. I have no training in martial arts, or extreme sports, or any of those things your seminars or that boot camp are about. I'm pretty much a couch potato."

"Don't forget my boot camps are designed for people out of training. You're in better shape than many of the men who'll be attending."

She almost frowned. "And my opportunity to appear in *The Carrie O'Brian Show* is conditioned on whether I accept or not?"

"What? No!" He seemed offended. "I would never tease you with something that big and then take it away. The roundtable with Carrie is merely a token of gratitude for hearing me out. But it would make more sense if you do take part in the boot camp—as Ms. Knight and Wayne Dash will be doing." Noticing her inquiring expression, he added, "They're invited as a way to divert attention from you. All Carrie knows is that I plan to bring an evil feminist to my boot camp for publicity reasons. She thinks I'm bringing both you and Karen so at least one of you finishes the training. Wayne is supposed to be a 'male control subject.'" He winked.

Pacing around the office, he continued, "The roundtable discussions will be based on your impressions from participating in the training. And Carrie will be choosing the best parts and filming some segments of the boot camp in a documentary style, to release it as a special edition of her show."

She was tempted. That would be an amazing opportunity for promotion.

Gathering herself, she shook her head. "I know what you're doing. You're making a display of your influence, delivering Carrie and my two nemeses into my hands. Your belief that I need to be helped is condescending."

He studied her with a puzzled expression. "Let me see if I get this right. So, when a man is mean to you, he's a bastard and proof that we men are evil creatures. But then when a man tries to be nice to you... he's being *condescending*?"

She couldn't come up with a reply.

He continued, "Just imagine what participating in my boot camp would do to your fan base. You'd become a true feminist pioneer. And the possibilities for promotion are endless for both of us. I can direct people from my website to yours, and you can do the same, boosting your search optimization. You can blog about your experience and request people's email address before giving them access to the full posts—that will grow your email list. We can even stage a whole war of the genders for publicity purposes. You can use your well-known wit to come up with clever ways to ridicule me on Twitter, I can pretend I'm challenged by that and reply back to you."

She gawked at him. Maybe she'd misjudged the man; he was a business genius. "So, it is true, then? You're doing this for promotion, not because you want to impress me, or to seduce me?"

With a grave expression, he declared, "But of course, I plan to seduce you. That's why I'm doing this; everything else is an excuse."

Her breath caught at the intensity of his gaze.

A spark fired in Jay's eyes. "Oh, darling, it's adorable how you believe everything I tell you." He slapped his own thigh, roaring with laughter.

She impatiently tapped her foot on the floor, waiting for him to recompose himself after the guffawing attack. *Yup. This man is going to drive me completely crazy.*

He wiped tears from his eyes and continued. "I have no intention of seducing you. For the duration of your stay in my boot camp, you and I are bonded by the personal trainer-client proper behavior agreement."

She sighed in relief. "Is that true?"

His lips curved as he waved a hand. "Nah! I just made that up. I have every intention of seducing you."

She stiffened, then surveyed his face looking for any sign of hilarity. "I'm not falling for it. You're joking again."

His face was dead serious. "Am I?"

She wanted to pull out her own hair. *This man will be the death of me.*

Jay took a step toward her with a soft smile. "Darling, relax. Whether I'm joking or not, I'd never make an advance on you unless I had evidence that you want me to. So, if you have no doubt that you're completely immune to me and you *don't* want me, then you have nothing to worry about. Right?"

The intensity of his gaze was unsettling. She noticed for the first time the way his white shirt stretched tense over his wide chest and shoulders as if about to burst—had his torso bulked up even more since the last time she'd seen him? His dark pants made his waist and hips impossibly narrow in comparison. His cleanly shaved face offered no distraction for his attractive features and his golden-green eyes. The faintest scent of his sweat hit her and a movie-reel of flashbacks from their night together months back avalanched over her.

He pivoted away and packed his laptop and charger inside a laptop bag. "Darling, I have a meeting to go to now. Think about it, and let me or Carrie know your decision by the end of the day."

After positioning the strap of his bag across his back, he squeezed her hand and kissed her on the cheek. The gesture was so casual it didn't occur to her to resist. But he managed to land his lips exactly at the edge of hers, teasing her with a rush of electricity. He let his mouth linger next to hers a little longer than appropriate before releasing her hand. With one last beam, he left her alone in the office.

Chapter 13

"**D**UDE, IF YOU SMILE ANY WIDER, YOUR JAW WILL dislocate." Shawn frowned at Jay.

Sitting in Shawn's family room, Jay suppressed the grin that had overtaken him since his meeting with Allison. He was ecstatic by the success of his plan. If he'd known that pulling a few strings would bring Allison into his office so fast, he would've done it months ago. "Sorry, man," he answered. "I'll try to tone down my cheerfulness by thinking about sad things. Like world hunger, and sick puppies, and… pathetically whipped married men like you."

Balancing her five-year-old stepson—a mini-me of Shawn—on her hip, Fe slapped Jay on the back of his head, almost making him drop his teacup. "Hey! More respect for my husband," she protested.

"My dear love!" Jay put his cup down and opened his arms. "From all the women in the world, if someone had to whip my friend, I'm glad it was fabulous you. Hey, isn't Aidan too old for you to carry him around?" He quickly changed the subject.

Aidan squirmed away from Jay's attempt to touch him and hid his face against Fe's shoulder. She ran her fingers through the boy's auburn hair. "Give me a break, he's not feeling well. And I'm a Latina mom. I'll be cleaning after him and packing him a lunch until he's both forty-five *and* married."

Beaming, Shawn raised a hand. "Her grandma still packs *me* a lunch."

"Hey, Fe," Jay stopped her before she walked away. He forced a casual tone. "I read somewhere that your friend Allison grew up around the Great Lakes area and I was wondering if she's from near my town. Do you happen to know where she grew up?"

"You know, she's very secretive about her past," Fe replied, changing the boy from one hip to the other, surprisingly balanced in her platform high-heels. "But I think she said once she's from Canada."

A wave of disappointment hit Jay. *So she's definitely not Grace.* To his surprise, that didn't eliminate his enthusiasm about her.

Fe turned to Shawn. "Let me see if I have better luck putting Aidan to bed. I'll see you in a bit."

Shawn rose from his seat to reach for one quick kiss. Then, Fe walked away, clicking her heels on the tile floor.

Jay felt tempted to tease Shawn about his own grin, watching Fe walk away, but he decided to give him a break.

Shawn reached for his hand sanitizer and cleaned his hands. "It's making me really nervous to keep your stalker history secret from Fe, Jay. Please tell me. What are your intentions with her friend Allison?"

Jay eyed him warily. "*Intentions?* Uh. My intention is to ask her father for her hand, three cows, and ten acres of land as her dowry. What is this, the eighteenth century?"

"Aren't doctors supposed to be extra smart?" Ethan asked from the kitchen counter, where Fe had forced a plate of Dominican rice-and-beans on him, claiming he needed to gain weight. "Dr. McDevitt, you should know by now that a man's intentions are *always* to screw the woman. Anything that happens around that— from marriage and family to conquering kingdoms—is a byproduct."

"Whoa! Slow down! *Marriage?* No need for cusswords." Jay shuddered.

Shawn tapped Jay's shoulder. "Man, it's not like you have a shortage of women eager to jump in bed with you; why do you have to hit on one of Fe's girlfriends she's passionately protective about?

Where are you going with this?"

"You doctors are so psycho-rigid. You need to open up your mind and think like entrepreneurs." Jay picked up his tea again. "You don't need to know where every business you start will take you; some ideas float, some sink." He took a sip. "I have no clue how things will end with Allison. Nothing is certain in life."

With a groan, Shawn added Splenda to his tea. "One thing is certain. If you screw up and hurt this woman, Fe's gonna kill you. And I'll be in the middle of it all, unable to defend you." He picked up his cup. "Luckily, I have a strong feeling that you stand no chance. For what I know about her, Allison is not easy on men." He sipped from his tea.

"I know!" Jay grimaced. "She's really put up a fight so far. And she doesn't even know yet that she's my sister's therapist."

Shawn put his cup down, coughing uncontrollably.

Ethan forgot his walker and rushed from the kitchen, to the family room, gawking at Jay. "What?"

Jay nodded. "My sister Tiffany is Allison's client. I've been debating whether I should tell her. But I don't think Allison's going to like it."

Shawn's blue-green eyes seemed about to protrude out of their orbits. Still coughing, he gaped at Jay. "Man, I know you're crazy. But are you *fecking* crazy? You can't date your sister's therapist!"

"Why not?" Jay asked, honestly baffled.

"Because that violates professional boundaries!"

Jay scoffed. "Says the man who married his son's speech therapist."

"No, it's not the same." Ethan shook his head. "Even *I* know that, and I'm the one with chemo brain!"

Shawn's grave expression worried Jay. "Psychotherapy and counseling associations have dead-serious rules about that, man. You can get Allison in real trouble. Like disciplinary action and licensing issues. I mean, it's probably not as severe as if she'd slept with one of her clients, but I'm sure it's a close second."

A feeling of impending doom slowly crept into Jay's soul. "Define client."

Shawn drilled him with his eyes. "Jay, is there anything else you haven't told us?"

Jay swallowed, his pulse starting to speed up. "Let's just say, hypothetically, that before Allison became Tiffany's therapist she was something like… our family therapist?"

Color drained from Shawn's face.

"Do you remember the story I told you that I met Allison briefly in a conference room? That was a failed attempt at family therapy my stepmother organized," Jay explained. "My four siblings and I met with Allison and she was supposed to be working on our issues, but then it didn't work out. The rest of us dropped out, and she stayed on as Tiffany's individual therapist."

Looking wobbly, Shawn held on from the table. "How many times did you see her?"

"Just once. But I didn't even talk. She was just talking to my other siblings."

"That doesn't matter! Did you sign a consent for treatment? Did you pay for the session?"

Jay shrugged. "I guess. That was five years ago; I barely remember."

Shawn placed his hand on Jay's shoulder. "I have bad news for you, my friend. Allison Connors is officially, for all legal purposes, your former therapist. She can't date you or she's at risk of losing her counseling license."

Jay's chest tightened in fear. That sounded illogical, and he had to find out if it was true.

Picking up his phone, he searched for his therapist's number.

* * *

Dr. Haagen-Dazs, or whatever his name was, seemed delighted by Jay's sudden request for an appointment.

"Seeing you return so soon after your last visit is encouraging. Have you had any new breakthroughs from our latest—"

"Yeah, yeah. Uh. Listen, Dr. H. Before we dive into the session and I forget. I have a… friend… who has a situation and I'd like to run it by you."

"Yes?"

Jay scratched the back of his head. "Uh… My friend… Ethan, yes, Ethan." He cleared his throat and looked back at the doctor. "He likes this woman who happens to be a psychologist and has been… kind of dating her. And it turns out she's the therapist of a relative. Would that be a problem?"

Dr. Hazenberg's thick gray eyebrows knitted together. "How close of a relative?"

A sister. He swallowed. "Pretty close."

The man's headshake didn't promise anything good. "That's a no-no. That therapist should immediately terminate any contact with your friend and notify her client, so they can decide if the client-therapist relationship is compromised."

His stomach knotted. "Are you serious?"

"The American Counseling Association Code of Ethic section A.5.b explicitly prohibits sexual or romantic relationships with the family members of clients. This woman could have her counseling license revoked for something like that."

"Even if she didn't know it?" *This is ridiculous.*

Dr. Hazenberg hesitated. "Well, if she had no idea, there's room for argument. She would need to face a disciplinary committee and prove that she had no wrong intention. I guess if the relationship never went very far her chances are better."

So, having slept together doesn't help, right?

The therapist considered it before adding, "I guess if she can claim complete ignorance of the situation under oath, and stops seeing your friend immediately after finding out, she should be okay. I mean. It's not as bad as if she'd slept with a former client—now, *that* I don't wish on my worst enemy."

A cold drop of sweat slid down Jay's forehead. "Oh… Sure. Because that's even worse, right?"

Dr. Hazenberg bobbed his head. "Lay people may think there's a time limit. But every self-respecting therapist knows that we must never, *never*—it doesn't matter how much time has gone by—get sexually involved with a former client."

Shit. I screwed up big this time.

He'd better stay away from Allison. That would be difficult considering they were about to spend two weeks together in a resort, at the boot camp.

And for her own protection, so she could claim ignorance, he'd better not tell her the reason why he had to stay away.

Chapter 14

THE OPENING CEREMONY FOR THE WARRIORS BOOT CAMP took place at a local theater and doubled as one of Jay's ticketed inspirational lectures. Friends and relatives were encouraged to attend. Trying to get Emery out of her recent slump, Allison had invited her when she'd visited Emery's office to get the medical clearance required for participation. Off from her work as a business consultant for a hotel chain, Hope had invited herself.

"At another time in my life I would've wondered if my soul mate was somewhere in that crowd—but not anymore," Emery said with a sigh. "I'll probably die alone."

Doubtful, Allison eyed her from head to toe. Emery sported wrinkled scrubs, wore no makeup and contained her frizzy, reddish hair in a simple braid—yet with her exotic Swedish-Korean-Jamaican racial mix, she couldn't help turning men's heads wherever she went. That was Dr. Emery Love's curse. Accomplished, and beautiful in such a stunning way, the average nice guy assumed she was way out of his league—so only overconfident megalomaniacs like Ken Carter dared to approach her.

Emery's lips quivered and her green monolid eyes glistened. "Do you guys think I should freeze my eggs?"

"So, Allison, you'll be in a resort for two weeks?" Hope blurted out.

Allison appreciated Hope's efforts to steer away from the topic of Emery's canceled wedding. She almost didn't mind catching Emery up about Jay, as long as it distracted her. "A double-decker bus will be picking us up from here later to take us there. The main principle of the boot camp is that it takes thirty days to re-program the brain to create new habits," Allison explained. "This time of physical training and 'diet detoxification' isolated from the world is the jumpstart. Then the following two weeks we continue the work at home while receiving online and phone support."

High-energy music that seemed vaguely similar to the *Superman* theme played through speakers. Projected onto the closed curtains in front of the stage, a clock displayed a countdown of the minutes and seconds before the seminar started. Spandex-clad trainers circulated among the boot camp attendees, picking up folders.

Emery eyed the fit young woman, wearing athletic shorts and a sports bra, as she walked away after picking up Allison's folder. "What's in that file?"

"We all had to fill a long questionnaire about food intolerances, favorite meals and activities, and about our childhood favorite games," Allison replied. "They'll use the information to customize our plans."

In the same fashion she did when she was coming up with a diagnosis, Emery pursed her lips and scrunched her nose. Allison could almost see the wheels turning in her mind. Emery's brain was dangerous, combining the intelligence of her physician father with all the dramatic potential she'd inherited from her mother, the diva supermodel.

"Something doesn't make sense here," Emery whispered, pointing at the female trainer. "If that woman is an example of the hot babes Jay works with, why would he go through so much trouble just to get Allison?"

Allison shot Emery a dirty look. "Thanks for reminding me I'm a flabby old lady."

Emery held up her hands. "Come on, gorgeous, let's look at this with scientific detachment." She rested her elbow on the chair armrest and her chin on her hand. "The Triple J the media talks about and Fe describes would never chase a woman. Why would he be so obsessed with *you*? Did you inherit a billion dollars recently, or something? Do you happen to have out-of-this-world skills in bed?"

Hope snickered. "Uh… well, *you* tell her, Allison."

Matter-of-factly, Allison announced, "More than one man has called me a cold fish."

Emery spread her fingers. "So you have to admit this behavior doesn't make sense. Why would he go through all this to get you, or anybody, in bed?" Widening her eyes, she gasped and held Allison's hand. "Maybe that night he fell in love with you and now can't forget you!"

Leave it to Emery to leap from scientific analysis to cheap soap-opera plot in one second.

"I don't know and I don't care why he'd want me," Allison answered in a whisper. "I'm only attending the boot camp because it is a tremendous promotional opportunity. But if he thinks I'm going to even socialize with him, he's wrong. Jay Johnson's *Titanic* just met its iceberg."

Hope perked up. "*Titanic*? Is that a nickname you have for his junk, or something?"

The countdown clock reached zero. The lights dimmed, the music changed, and the audience went silent. Slowly, the curtains opened, revealing a stage decorated in a way Allison could only guess was a fantasy video-game world including magical woods, hanging bridges, and the backdrop image of a castle against a starry sky. A loudspeaker announced, "Ladies and gentlemen, welcome the founder of Legendary Heroes. Triple J."

The attendees' applause and cheering were deafening, but nothing seemed to happen on the stage. Allison wondered what the fuss was about when she heard a rhythmic sound coming from the back of the theater; the roar of the audience peaked. Within a few seconds Jay arrived on the stage.

He was riding a horse.

What the heck?

She was barely recovering from the impression when a member of the staff helped Jay dismount and she caught a first glimpse of his clothes—or lack thereof. He was dressed in some form of modern gladiator outfit, yet no one in the audience seemed surprised.

"Yup, he's completely crazy," Emery affirmed.

Fanning herself, Hope commented, "But you have to admit he's hot!"

Ditto. And DITTO.

Allison's mouth went dry, staring at Jay waving at the cheering crowd. From the waist up, he was naked except for a dark red cape and a brown leather strap—the strap of a quiver carrying a bow and arrows—lying oblique against his shaven chest. His wide shoulders, strong arms and muscular torso on display would've been too much, but glittery body paint made them less graphic. An elaborate wide belt reminiscent of wrestling belts cinched his narrow waist and doubled as a holster for a sword. From the waist down, he wore a short maroon tunic skirt and knee-high brown leather gladiator sandals. He should've come across like a psychotic patient; instead, he looked like a sexual fantasy.

Jay stood front and center on the stage and lifted one hand, making the whole crowd fall silent. She became sharply aware of the hypnotic energy he radiated from the stage. The audience watched him in a state of euphoria. Victim of the same hypnosis, she completely forgot about the unusual outfit and his breathtaking body.

So *that* was what people were after! They were there to drink from that energy. She couldn't blame them.

Wearing a microphone headset on his ear, he finally spoke. "Do you remember how it felt to be a five-year-old?" He paused, as if letting them process his words. Allison had trouble accessing any early childhood memories; she knew it was a defense mechanism to forget about harder times.

Jay continued, "Wasn't it wonderful? Every birthday was a reason for huge celebration, instead of a dreadful announcement of aging. Money was a magical token you exchanged in the store for candy— nobody knew or cared where it came from. There was no concept of work, no concept of taxes."

Some snorts and giggles sounded in the audience. Allison smiled.

"Heck, wasn't it great being five?" he continued, pacing around the stage. "When you could run at top speed without fatigue or fear of injury. Before the birth of limits when you still hadn't learned that some things are supposed to be impossible. Before the birth of shame when you and your best friend thought nothing of taking your clothes off and jumping into your favorite swimming hole in your underwear."

A flash of a memory blindsided Allison. It was the memory of her at age six, swimming in Lake Michigan, in Port Popsicle, Wisconsin, with her little friends Ginger and Cowlick. A bittersweet feeling rose in her chest.

Jay continued, beaming. "Remember when the world was a never ending string of new amazing discoveries. When every little flower, or rock, or bug, or crawling creature was fascinating?"

He lifted his head and she could almost swear his eyes met hers across the theater. "Do you remember when your soul mate was a pet, a doll, or a stuffed animal you loved with passion, and the other love of your life was your little best friend? Sometimes if you were lucky, the two of you could find treasure chests hiding in attics or basements—full of old clothes from long-gone grandparents—and play dress-up. From a space traveler to a mermaid, you could magi- cally become anybody you wanted to be."

Incredibly vivid images of herself as a little girl, wearing a long dress and oversized high heels, dancing, entered her mind.

Then she saw the image of the oak tree and the tire swing again. And suddenly, she couldn't take it anymore.

Discreetly, she wiped an annoying, unexpected moistness from her eyes. Excusing herself, she left her chair and walked toward the exit. Confused, Emery and Hope followed her.

As she arrived at the door, Jay's words reached her. "It was so wonderful to be a five-year-old. And starting with these two weeks, and for the rest of your life, I challenge you to become one again."

* * *

Allison didn't get far in her attempt to escape. Less than an hour later, one of Jay's crewmembers came to get her at the theater's coffee shop, claiming Jay needed to talk to her before the bus arrived. As she approached, she could hear the audience roaring in applause at the end of his speech. Music announced the end of the opening ceremony.

A dozen people stood in line at the stage to shake hands with Jay or to express their admiration. Jay greeted every one of them as if he'd known them all his life.

As he posed for selfies, his eyes found her and he signaled her to come over. She braced herself. It was now a matter of pride, and she was determined to resist his attempts to charm her.

The last person in line seemed to be an elderly man, with an oxygen tank and cane. Jay embraced him for a while, and after he released him, Allison realized he was a frail young man.

Jay beamed at him. "Ethan! You decided to come!" He kissed the top of his friend's bald head.

With a smile, the young man pushed him away and ran his hand over his bare scalp. "Stop it!" he joked. "You're ruining my hairstyle."

"I can't help it! Your head looks like a baby's; I want to kiss it every time I see it!"

The man's glee vanished and he sighed. "My facial hair is growing again, but nothing on my scalp. What if my hair never grows back?"

"It will; you'll see." Jay patted his back.

The man's eyes flicked to Allison, standing now near Jay. "New girlfriend?"

Allison felt the tingle of a blush on her face. *Darn it.* She didn't recognize this blushing woman.

"Ethan, this is Allison." Jay seemed reluctant.

Ethan lowered his voice to a whisper. "I see. She *is* your girlfriend, but she doesn't know it yet." He winked.

Ethan shook her hand and she met a pair of deep blue eyes in a puffy face that once must've been attractive. He jabbed a thumb over his shoulder to indicate Jay, without looking at him. "Don't let this guy's crazy act fool you; he's worth his weight in gold and diamonds. And I'm not saying that just because he let me into his super-expensive boot camp for free; I wouldn't have survived my chemo without him."

Allison was moved. She still processed the man's words as he slowly walked away dragging his oxygen tank, supported by his cane.

As they strolled out of the stage through a side door, Jay said, "I hope Ethan didn't offend you joking about you being my girlfriend. It's an inside joke between us. See, Ethan has a crush on one of his doctors, and he keeps saying that she's the future mother of his children—except she doesn't know it yet."

"I see. How do you know each other?"

"We connected a few years ago when I was considering buying a place here. Ethan works in real estate and home remodeling—or he used to, before his health issues."

Allison hesitated before asking, "What happened to him?"

"His lymphatic cancer required such a tough treatment he was in the hospital all the time with complications. He lost most of his muscle mass from lying in bed so long."

She was afraid of asking the question. "Is he cured?"

The long pause before Jay answered worried her. "He says he's not allowed to use that word yet. He is… 'in remission.'"

Swallowing hard, she nodded.

"If the cancer ever comes back his best option would be a bone marrow transplant," Jay continued. "But he's so weak right now the treatment would kill him. So my goal is to have him back in shape as soon as possible."

Allison was touched. Silence fell for a moment until she finally said, "Every time I think I'm wrapping my mind around you, you throw a curve ball and I have to start from zero."

He shot her a curious glance. "Why do you say that?"

"You're the self-proclaimed pleasure-seeking hedonist, yet you're practicing altruism, saving the life of a cancer patient."

Jay chuckled. "Are you kidding me? Altruism is the ultimate pleasure-seeking behavior. It gives the highest high with least amount of hangover." His cheerfulness disappeared. "But I also really care for Ethan and value the lesson he brought to my life. If I ever want to complain about growing old, his story reminds me of the alternative—dying young."

Darn it. This man was turning out to be so much more likable than she expected. It was much easier to play the game when he was only a sex symbol.

"So, what did you want to talk to me about?" she asked.

A flash of something she'd never seen in him before crossed his eyes. Was it sadness? "I needed to apologize for the way I pushed you to join this program. I agree that we shouldn't see each other again afterward."

If he had slapped her across the face, she couldn't have been more surprised. "What?"

He avoided her gaze. "You were clear that you didn't want to re-connect with me and I shouldn't have pressed the issue. I want to reassure you that I won't harass you in any way during the boot camp. And that you won't hear from me after that."

Allison's brain froze for a moment, unable to comprehend. "You're kidding again, right? The moment I fall for it, you'll crack up."

His expression was dead serious. "No. I mean it."

She scrutinized his face for any sign that he was bluffing. A faint ripple of disappointment pulsated in her, but she pushed it away. "I know what you're doing and it's not going to work. This is reverse psychology; you're doing this to entice me."

There was no joy in his voice or his eyes. "Sure. Let's say that's it."

Without another word, he walked away, leaving Allison standing in the hallway, still baffled.

Chapter 15

A S THE ONLY WOMEN AMONG THE BOOT CAMP ATTENDEES, Allison knew she and Karen would get tons of attention. But, to her annoyance, men seemed disproportionally interested in *her*. It might've had something to do with Karen's sweatpants and baggy sweaters.

The minute Allison entered a room, half of the men turned into sweaty-palmed teenagers tripping over their own shoelaces. The other half turned into testosterone-overdosed Playboy-wannabes, throwing glances in her direction while puffing their chests and flexing in an effort to show off. Allison was convinced that the worst part of the experience would be having to deal with so many idiotic men.

But she was wrong. The worst part was—everything.

The first three days of the boot camp were designed to "thin the herd." Traditionally, twenty percent of attendees quit by the third day, unable to keep up. Allison now understood the need for medical clearance ahead of time and wondered how Ethan had sneaked in: the program wasn't suitable for anyone in less than perfect health.

Loud music playing through speakers awakened them at an insanely early hour the first day.

"Wake up, everybody! The fun is about to begin!" yelled the staff members, banging on doors while cheering and hooting.

As the disoriented participants crawled out of their rooms, the staff presented them with an "organic, health-boosting, antioxidant smoothie"—which she suspected was heavily caffeinated. After separating them into three groups by fitness levels, the first activity of the day was a run along the dark beach.

Allison got assigned at first to "Group B." She almost protested, until she realized that group A, led by Jay himself, consisted of half-a-dozen fitness freaks who were in the boot camp not to get fit but insanely ripped—mostly professional athletes and gay body-builders. They took off running and soon disappeared from her sight.

She had so much trouble catching up with the other joggers in group B she soon demoted herself to powerwalking with group C—the older participants and a few people with injuries. When she couldn't keep up with even them she ended up founding "Group D," strolling with Ethan and his oxygen tank, and a five-hundred-pound attendee named Kurt.

After the so-called run, Shania, the attractive female trainer she'd seen at the opening, guided them through basic yoga stretches at sunrise. Only then were they allowed to shower and meet for breakfast.

Breakfast doubled as a cooking and nutrition lecture. Since she had checked "no" in the boxes for vegan, vegetarian, gluten-free, dairy free, low carb and food allergies, she ended up assigned to Jay's group in a session on how to create their own version of egg-white omelets.

"To lose weight and keep it off, the goal is to change your eating habits not for a 'dieting period,' but *for life*," Jay explained, while stubbornly avoiding looking at her.

"That's not possible," Ethan argued, raising his hand. "You can't give up junk food forever and live on broccoli and celery for the rest of your life."

Smiling, Jay replied, "You don't give up junk food forever. You give it up for the next twenty-four hours. And then the next day you do it again. And then again. That's the way I've been dealing with my own junk food addiction. It has been five years one month and three days since my last donut."

The group laughed. Jay strolled around the kitchen and added, "But you're wrong; I'm not asking you to survive on broccoli and celery. On the contrary; I want you to find healthy, tasty dishes you absolutely love to eat and wouldn't mind repeating over and over—otherwise, you'll never stick to good eating." He served each a sample of the omelet he'd made and she had to admit it was surprisingly tasty.

He made no effort to address her all through the class. To make things worse, she was convinced that Shania kept finding excuses to interrupt with messages, touching him and shooting him flirty looks. Whatever reverse psychology he was using on her, it was annoying.

And it was working.

The rest of the morning, the group joined conferences on stress relief and Jay's favorite topic: how to incorporate pleasure in life through all the senses, so food didn't become the only source of enjoyment.

"This is not about 'discipline.' I never do anything that I don't want to do, and my biggest goal is enjoyment," he continued from the podium at a later lecture. "But when you're really in tune with your body, you learn to identify what will give you a little pleasure right now, but then will give you a lot of pain tomorrow."

He took a grape from a fruit plate and put one in his mouth. He ate it slowly, with his eyes closed, and then moaned. "Now *this* is cellular joy! You can't get a rush like that from donuts and pastries." He opened his eyes. "For me, junk food isn't worth the few seconds of great taste before the sugar crash. I get more pleasure out of liking what I see in the mirror than I get from eating greasy or sugary foods."

Darn it. He's good.

She was back in his group on the second nutrition and cooking lecture of the day, over lunch. He taught them to replicate their favorite meals in healthier versions that were as equally flavorful and texture rich as the originals. Allison had to give him credit for her enjoying green beans for the first time in her life.

"Starting now, nobody is allowed to talk during meals," he said as they finished cooking. "Savoring food slowly and with no distractions is a critical weapon against overeating."

As they ate in complete silence, she found herself fascinated by the pleasure on Jay's face with every bite he took. It brought flashes of memories of that one night when she'd seen him make a similar face for different reasons.

* * *

Jay wanted to slap himself for his now useless idea of bringing Allison into the boot camp. It was enough torture having her so close and being unable to touch her; but her very presence was proving to be a hazard. The minute she stepped into a room, wearing her spandex workout clothes, every straight man in the place lost his focus, risking injury. *Yup. She has a point; we men are hopeless.*

She'd done a decent job keeping up with the guys during the afternoon "playtime session"—the camp's name for exercise. A self-proclaimed tomboy, she played dodge ball and hung from the monkey bars like a champ. He knew she was fueled by the extra caffeine they'd fed them in the "smoothie snacks" and would be flattened by the end of the day. He admitted half the program's effect came from inducing a state of brainwashing in the attendees by causing sleep deprivation.

"I've had it with the attitude of your guinea pigs," Shania complained after the group returned from a mandatory post-dinner powerwalk along the beachside.

"Which one?" Jay asked.

"All three, but especially the two women," she replied. "Karen complains about everything. Dr. Connors doesn't complain; but I'm tired of her I'm-better-than-you attitude. Look at that," she pointed at a group nearby.

The camp staff was splitting the participants into small groups around campfires for a group counseling session. He could see Allison's eye roll from where he stood.

"Well, she does have a PhD in psychology," he justified her. "She probably considers our life-coaching techniques crude."

A FaceTime call from his niece lit up his phone and he excused himself. He walked back to his improvised office while taking the call.

In all the years since he'd split with his family, Jay had only missed Wednesdays with Gracie when he was hosting that boot camp—even when it meant flying weekly from Atlanta.

"Hello, chipmunk! I'm already missing you."

On his phone screen, Gracie's beautiful face was scrunched with worry. "Uncle Jake. You have to rescue me! Mom and Mister Jordan hate me!"

He entered the office and got comfortable in the rolling chair at his desk, facing a wall. "That's nonsense, munchkin; it's impossible to hate you. You're so adorable you're annoying."

Moving the iPad closer, she whispered. "They want to get rid of me."

"Not your mom," he tried to reassure her. "She loves you." *In her style.*

"Yesterday, Mom forgot me and my stepbrother at the store," Gracie said. "I had to borrow a phone to call her to come get us."

Jay became speechless for a moment. "What?"

Tiffany's high-pitched voice sounded in the background. "You, snitch! Stop dissing me! It was *your* fault for not getting in the car fast enough."

"*You* sent me to change the baby's diaper!" Gracie replied in a defiant tone.

"And you were gone for so long, of course, I forgot you were there. Why can't you change diapers faster?"

Her eyes squeezed shut, Gracie shook a fist and yelled, "I'm only eight!"

Feeling the fire of anger build inside him, Jay's fingers tightened around the cell. He wondered if everybody's relationships with their baby siblings were like his. He loved Tiffany; he'd beat up anyone who dared to hurt her—yet on days like today he seriously wanted to feed her to the sharks.

Counting to ten in his mind, he wished there were a way to help Gracie that didn't imply damaging his sister or starting a war with the family he never wanted to face again. "Have patience with her, munchkin. You know your mommy's brain works differently than other people's." That's what he repeated to himself all through his adult life.

Miranda called Gracie for bedtime and she rushed to end the call. At least he felt reassured that, as long as she was with her nanny, the girl was safe.

Could he ever do what Miranda proposed and take over caring for his niece? *But I'm a big kid myself!* What if he broke the little girl's heart, like he'd done for so many women before for being unable to grow up and settle with them?

Jay pondered for a while, torn. Gracie was the only thing in the world he felt attached to. He'd loved her from the first time he saw her baby face at the nursery. That was why he'd suggested naming her Grace—like that other time in his life he'd fallen in love at first sight.

As with any time he wanted to escape worrisome thoughts, his memory returned to his childhood girlfriend. *And now I know Allison is not her.*

He walked back to the beach area, where the group counseling sessions went on. Allison's group, led by Shania, was a mish-mash of anyone who consented to have her and Karen there.

She sat between Ethan and five-hundred-pound Kurt. Alf, a lanky, four-eyed Silicon Valley genius finished the story of being bullied as a kid for being a nerd. Holding the 'talking stick,' Kurt opened up next, talking about the ways the world discriminated against him for being overweight. Allison leaned forward, completely absorbed and taking it all in with no sign of mockery. From where he was he could swear she was teary-eyed.

He smiled. Maybe something good would come from this event and she'd walk out of it having a little more compassion toward men.

Chapter 16

J AY HAD BEEN SO ABSORBED IN RUNNING THE BRUTAL FIRST three days it hadn't been difficult to avoid Allison. He wasn't kidding when he told her that the boot camp was exhausting for him and he couldn't host it more than twice a year. Thank heavens the fourth day had arrived. As a reward for everybody who stuck through the seventy-two hours of hell, the participants' morning run that day was being replaced by a bonding moment at sunrise, followed by a professional massage. And he would've been enjoying that too if his job didn't include putting out every stupid little fire in the program.

He hated having Carrie's crew breathing down his neck, recording every step with the zealous devotion of reality TV directors. He tried to ignore them while having a one-on-one session with Ethan.

"I can't do this!" Ethan complained in a weak voice, shaking. "I'm having withdrawal symptoms."

Jay tapped his back. "The first days are the hardest. I promise that the cravings will get better."

"They won't!" Ethan protested. "My body is telling me it *needs* saturated fat and sugar! I need a burger with french fries! I need a cholesterol-loaded steak! I need cheesecake!"

Ethan's voice was rising. Placing both hands on his shoulders, Jay held eye contact and sent him hypnotic reassurance. "In a few days you'll detox. You need to make sure the weight you gain is from healthy, lean protein, not junk food."

"But I need comfort food! My hair isn't growing and I'm feeling miserable. Plus, I learned Dr. Love broke her engagement, but I can't go face her looking like this!" he lamented. Then, with a forced sigh, he changed to a weak tone of voice. "Plus, you never know if my next meal could be my last one." Fluttering his uneven eyelashes, Ethan pouted his lips slightly and gave him the tilted guilt-trip expression Jay was now very familiar with. "You know... because I had *cancer.*"

With a loud sigh, Jay looked up to the ceiling. "Stop it! Your blackmail is not going to work this time."

"Jay, we have a problem with one of your guinea pigs again." Calvin, his event director, got Jay's attention.

He signaled the camp's official counselor to take over Ethan and walked toward him. "What's going on?"

"Dr. Connors just attacked another participant."

Jay's jaw dropped. "What?"

Mumbling cusswords, Jay followed Calvin out of the improvised office and onto the beach, wondering what could be the problem now. Allison had seemed to be handling the men fine by herself. With her icy-glares, her no-nonsense attitude and sticking to the workout, she'd earned their respect and was now one of the group.

They arrived at the beach where the clouds in the sky were just turning from orange to golden as the sun rose, dyeing the crashing waves.

Shoulders straight, leaning forward as if about to attack, Allison stood in front of Brad, a giant even taller than Jay, craning her neck to glare at him. Brad held his bleeding nose with a Kleenex and appeared terrified.

"What's going on?"

Brad exhaled sharply. "This... wild woman elbowed me in the freaking nose. It may be broken!"

Allison raised her index finger. Her voice was glacial. "Listen to me, Brad Pitt with a pituitary disorder. Hands off."

Brad huffed in exasperation. "I was just following directions from the team leader!"

Before Brad the prima donna launched into an outraged rant, Jay mumbled an excuse, grabbed Allison's arm and walked her away, toward the office. Trey and his cameraman followed them.

The second they arrived at the empty office—Ethan and the counselor were gone—she shook off his arm. Defiance and guilt blended in her expression as she faced him in the middle of the room.

"What is this about, Allison? Are you trying to get me sued?"

Frowning, she crossed her arms and looked away. "He tried to hug me. I don't like to be hugged."

He stared at her. "Allison, this part of the program was designed by nationally recognized psychotherapists. Having the participants hug and offer each other support is—"

"I don't care," she interrupted, sounding like a petulant child. "I don't need any sticky fingers on me."

Losing his patience, he sighed. "Would it make you feel better if we got you a female hugging partner? Karen, or Shania perhaps?"

She growled. "I'm not worried about Brad getting handsy. Come on! I can spot a gay man from a mile away—I was married to one!" She turned away from him. "I just don't like to be touched. That's it."

Jay ran his fingers up through his face, then through his hair. These small, senseless crises were the reason why this event only happened every six months.

"Jay," Trey intervened. "If she doesn't go through this and complete the program, that means she's admitting defeat on behalf of all women."

For a flash, Allison's eyes were shaded by fear as they searched his. Jay realized this wasn't the tantrum of a brat he could argue away. And this wasn't another way for Allison to assert her feminism. She was frightened.

"Trey, crew, give me a few minutes with Dr. Connors," he asked.

Trey and the cameramen found their way out, mumbling something about high-maintenance women.

It didn't matter how much he needed to stay away from her; he had a responsibility as program director. Slowly, Jay took a seat in one of the chairs and indicated Allison to sit in another one.

"Do you want to talk about where your phobia of being hugged comes from?" he asked.

She tensed. "I don't have a phobia of being hugged. I just don't like it."

"Darling, you're not fooling me." He tilted his head. "I was there the night we slept together."

He didn't have to explain. Getting her to accept caresses that night had taken the creativity of MacGyver. He had to let her have all the control. He had even agreed to let her immobilize his hands at times—a placebo effect, since she couldn't make a dent in his strength, but at least it was something that allowed her to relax at the end.

She averted her gaze without answering.

"In your bio you claim to be a survivor of childhood abuse. Is that what this is about?" he asked.

Her eyes turned shiny, but she kept bracing herself in silence, avoiding eye contact.

"That's admirable," he added with a soft voice. "Overcoming that and becoming a counselor for others must be something you're proud of."

She half sighed, half grunted. "I don't deserve to be called an abuse survivor. I'm a big farce."

"Really?" He rolled his chair one step closer to hers. "So you were never physically abused?"

Lips sputtering, she flicked her wrist. "My mother used to spank me and my sister—no big deal. She used to vent her frustration on us whenever my stepfather hit her."

Stunned, he processed her words. "Your stepfather used to hit your mother?"

"He only beat me one time—I mean for real, hard enough to leave bruises."

"He hit you?" In spite of her efforts to minimize the story, he was appalled.

She made a dismissive, impatient wave. "Only once, when I was eight. It was just one big blow between my left cheekbone and my ear. That's how I got the facial palsy; somehow the swelling pinched my facial nerve."

Imagining her hurt at that age, he wished he could travel to the past, find that man and rip his head off. *She's definitely not my Grace.* The Grace he remembered was the happiest, most worry-free girl in the world. "I'm so sorry."

"Don't be," she rushed to say. "I'm glad that happened because that ended up driving my mother to leave him for the first time. And I've made a point all my life to never see myself as a victim. On the contrary. Defining moments like that are where I've gathered my strength from."

For a moment he felt the urge to take the little girl she'd once been in his arms and console her. But he had to stow his feelings away and stay in the role of coach. "That sounds like a lot for a little girl to handle."

She gave a sour chuckle. "I lost the ability to evoke any sadness from these memories a long time ago. And after you volunteer for years in a women's shelter, you gain a new perspective. My story is nothing compared to the average case I saw there."

She was determined to intellectualize, so he decided to go along with her instead of fighting her. "Well, you're a therapist. Tell me, what's your theory about why you don't let anybody hug you?" he asked.

Talking about her field of expertise seemed to be a relief. Tension eased from her body. "Well, whenever I tried to rebel against my stepfather, calling him out on his bullying, my mother would rush to immobilize me by hugging me. I'm going to take a wild guess and assume that's where my knee-jerk reaction comes from."

He got it. "So, in your mind being embraced is linked to being restrained, to losing your freedom."

Rolling her eyes, she huffed. "Come on. I know all that on an intellectual level. And I've done all the debriefing and regression therapy in the world, but there's a long road between knowing something and being able to do something about it."

"Well, I'm more into re-wiring the brain for the future than I am into focusing on the past traumas. What you need are new pleasant and unthreatening associations with touch, to override your previous messages. Maybe then your brain will stop having those automatic reactions."

She lifted her eyes to look at him. "What you're talking about is called neuroplasticity. It's a formal theory in applied behavioral therapy."

With a simper, he shrugged. "See? Maybe life coaches are not such a farce after all."

She considered it. "How would I start?"

There was so much he wanted to answer. He wanted to volunteer to show her that touch could be pleasant and unthreatening. Offer her hours of pleasurable foreplay, sensual touch and afterglow cuddling.

But he couldn't.

Instead, he replied, "You can start by letting your closest friends and loved ones hug you, and then make an effort to savor that love and support they're offering you." Resigned, he stood up from his chair and opened his arms. "Come here."

She shot him a skeptical look. "No, thank you. I pass."

"I swear I won't touch you inappropriately. There has to be some advantage in the fact that I've done much more than hug you before."

With the hesitation of someone dipping her toe in icy water, she took a small step in his direction. Her face resembled a little girl who'd just taken a mouthful of broccoli.

He wrapped his arms around her; she let hers hang limp next to her body.

"Allison, to hug, you have to use your arms."

Grumbling in protest, she clumsily moved her arms up and seemed to debate on where to place them. She finally settled on one around his waist and one around his mid-back.

In her running shoes instead of high heels, her face was at the level of his neck and the top of her head right under his nose, offering him a whiff of rose scent. The softness of her body in his arms brought flashbacks from their night together, and he had to breathe through it, so he wouldn't taint the moment with lusty thoughts. He closed his eyes and imagined a light of compassion radiating from his body and wrapping her. She seemed to sense it, and for a moment he could feel the tension leave her body like a deflating blood pressure cuff—one millimeter of mercury at a time. He felt the beating of her heart against him, racing at first, then slowing down, and he knew she was making progress...

And then she pushed him away and punched him in the chest, knocking the wind out of him.

"Ow!" he protested holding his sore ribcage.

"Sorry," she blurted out. "But... hey! That was progress! That was exactly thirty seconds—I counted."

Rubbing his side, he probed. "But for the time it lasted, it wasn't that bad, was it?"

She squared her shoulders and slanted him a look. "Considering you're a life coach—not a therapist—and considering you're *a man.* This little session wasn't bad at all."

On an impulse, he touched the tip of her nose. "I'll take that as a compliment."

Reluctantly, she half-smiled.

"But now we have to hug again in front of Trey and his cameras," he added. "I'm not risking you getting me into an injury lawsuit with another participant. From now on, I am your campfire hugging buddy."

Before she could protest, he caught her wrist and led her out of the office.

Chapter 17

AFTER THE PAINFUL FIRST THREE DAYS, THE BOOT CAMP GOT only marginally better. Even if the schedule was less hectic, Allison dealt with the sleep deprivation and achiness affecting every muscle in her body from the previous days. No wonder the high desertion rate.

She'd been so busy trying not to die of exhaustion she'd almost forgotten about Karen and Nash and had barely paid attention to the cameramen around them. She was delighted to hear Nash quit on the second day—she'd never let him live down his defeat by two women.

In spite of the soreness in her body, Allison made an effort to dress up and look her best for the first roundtable, scheduled for the end of the fifth day. Carrie O'Brian's assistant, Trey, explained that the plan was an informal hour-long conversation between them and Jay. Later on, Carrie would choose the best snips for the documentary. The underlying message was: "Controversy sells. Be as outrageous as possible, and we'll edit later."

"So, Karen," Carrie started, patting her glossy mahogany bob. "Tell us your impressions of the first few days of the boot camp."

Facing Jay, Karen straightened the collar of her baggy striped shirt. "These days have confirmed my opinion that Mr. Johnson's attitude toward women is condescending and fosters gender segregation. Allison and I have not participated in all the activities the men do."

Mumbles rose in the audience and Allison cringed inside.

She suspected Karen was intentionally causing trouble to generate publicity.

Jay threw Karen an exasperated look. "I'm proud of being a feminist, and your insinuations that I wouldn't treat a woman with respect are offensive. I separate activities for men and for women solely for safety issues."

"You insinuate that women are weaker than men." Karen's face twitched.

Jay sighed in fatigue. "Karen, saying that a man is physically stronger than a woman is not sexism; it's acknowledging biology."

"All those are myths created by society." She sneered at him.

Extremists like Karen give feminism a bad name. "Actually, Karen, what Jay says is true," Allison intervened. "Men's predominant sex hormone is testosterone, the natural anabolic steroid. Even at the same height, weight and training level, a man will have more muscle mass and physical strength than a woman."

"My point exactly!" Jay shot Allison a grateful look and turned back to Karen. "Saying that the average man is physically stronger than the average woman is not a crime—it's a truth of nature. The same way that everyone knows that the average woman is a hundred times stronger than the average man emotionally."

His answer surprised Allison.

Rolling up the sleeves of his charcoal blazer, Jay continued. "The days when brute force was indispensable are gone. Most of the strength people need nowadays is the power to tap on a screen or type on a keyboard. Your emotional strength beats our physical strength any day."

His words sounded sincere, impressing Allison.

"Emotionally strong?" Seated next to Jay, Wayne snorted. "That's bull crap! Women are temperamental and hysterical."

Tilting her head, Carrie scoffed. "Then explain to me why a minor cold leaves my husband incapacitated, while I still manage to drive my kids to school and go to work with the flu."

"And let's not forget," Allison added, flashing Nash a smirk. "I'd love to see *you*, Wayne, with menstrual cramps. Or better yet—in labor."

"That's always the excuse." Wayne rolled his eyes. "'Oh! Poor us! We have to give birth and get periods!' Well, I'm sorry. If *you* drew the short straw, don't make *me* pay for it."

Jay intervened again. "But that's *why* men must be nice and kind to women. Don't you get it? It's not anti-feminist or condescending that we want to help you lift your luggage into the plane's overhead compartment. If a man has integrity—straight or gay—he knows deep inside that he got the better end of the deal. Being a gentleman is about knowing, 'Shit! It could've been *ME* with periods and pregnancy; I'm soooo lucky to have dodged that one! I'd better be nice to this fellow human being who has to put up with all that so I don't have to!'" The audience laughed and Allison had to restrain herself from cracking up too. "And you, gals, instead of complaining about it, should say, 'Thank you. You're right; we deserve a break!'" He turned to Allison. "Like you say, sometimes it's all a matter of widening your focus instead of narrowing it."

It was a direct quote from Allison's first book—the one on goal achievement few people had ever read. She was baffled for a moment. *Didn't I unpublish that book*?

She and Jay locked eyes across the table and everyone around disappeared. He then flicked his eyes away.

"Give me a break!" Karen huffed. "Those so-called chivalrous behaviors have nothing to do with manners. They're all about seducing women. For men, women are nothing but objects of pleasure. Just look at advertisements. Even to sell toothpaste they have to show a model in a bikini."

"Which leads us to the topic of this roundtable," Carrie said, trying to pull the conversation back on track. "We're here to discuss how those unrealistic body image expectations affect women's self-esteem. Triple J, would you say that the fitness industry and seminars like yours worsen that?"

Jay reclined back in his chair. He seemed so comfortable in front of the cameras Allison felt a pang of envy. Looking so gorgeous and having no self-consciousness certainly had to help. "My fitness classes are not about losing weight. They're about health. About finding the point where you feel most comfortable with your body and the most energetic," he said. "Do you really think that most models are healthy? Anorexia, bulimia, surviving on champagne and cigarettes. That's the opposite of what I want to teach."

Resenting losing the center stage, Karen took over. "That's exactly what I explore in my latest book, 'Killing Barbie.' Barbie dolls should be banished from stores because they create unrealistic body expectations and contribute to women's low self-esteem."

A flash from childhood reached Allison. She'd stared at a Barbie doll at the toy store, begging her mother to get it for her for Christmas. She felt like a traitor to feminism for still liking those dolls.

Jay intervened, "Never feel threatened by Barbie. She's just a caricature of a woman, not the real thing. Getting angry at her for having a too-narrow waist is just as senseless as getting angry at a cartoon character for having too-large eyes." He relaxed even more in his chair. "Women's bodies are *not* supposed to look like that. What sane man would want his woman to have boobs that hard and a butt you can't pinch?" He rolled his eyes and the men in the audience clapped.

She couldn't help chuckling. *This guy is completely crazy. But he's not that bad.*

Why did he have to resemble the cover of a steamy romance novel? If he at least had the physique of a normal man, she would've been less embarrassed to admit she'd really enjoyed their brunch and had considered seeing him again. But with him looking like that, her followers would assume she was brainlessly in lust with his smashing body.

Not that they'd be wrong.

"And also trust me, I know about unrealistic body expectations," he added. "It's getting to me too. My body's not the same as it used to be."

Allison scanned him in disbelief. *He must be fishing for compliments.*

"Come on, Triple J." Carrie gave him a once-over. "You could not be in better shape."

He shook his head with a sad smile. "You should've met me in my teens and twenties, before my weight gain. Now there's no way I can compete with the twenty-something-year-old bodybuilders, coming onto the scene with the youthful, bulk bodies. That's why I'm trying not to get too attached to this career; it's coming to an end sooner than later."

This was the first glimpse of vulnerability Allison had seen hiding under his inhuman self-confidence. *Another curveball.*

"But we're digressing." As if trying to lighten the mood, he straightened and looked into the camera. "Ladies, do you really think men want you to look like Barbie—or worse, like a supermodel? Supermodels are just hangers for clothes. And the only reason fashion ever considered them beautiful is because most fashion designers are gay. Have you ever seen a fashion model naked, without the airbrush and the few pounds the camera ads?" He raised a hand. "I have. They look like famine survivors or patients affected by a wasting disease. And don't get me started on trying to get physical with one! Nothing is less sexy than ribs poking you all over."

The audience roared and Allison felt like celebrating. She'd agonized, imagining the goddesses he'd probably dated before and comparing herself to them.

As if reading her mind, he returned his gaze to her. "Men like to touch *soft* bodies—bodies that feel like comfy pillows when we lie on them. And all that obsession you gals have about cellulite, spider veins, and stretch marks only *you* can see… trust me, that's the last thing we notice when we have a naked woman in front of us." He seemed to caress her with his eyes. "You're perfectly airbrushed, in soft focus, and you've never looked better. All we see is your beauty."

She held her breath, hypnotized by the intensity of his gaze. Everything around them disappeared for a moment, and she knew he was remembering their night together.

Chapter 18

THE BOOT CAMP RULES INCLUDED THAT ALL PARTICIPANTS had to surrender their cell phones at the beginning of the event. Allison had cheated, giving away her old phone and keeping the real one. Now late at night, she hid in the hallway bathroom—the only private place where she had signal—to return a phone call from her lawyer and friend, Mercy Kind.

Mercy's Southern accent always reminded Allison of *Steel Magnolias*. "Conan Wetzel, Tiffany Blanche's father, requested my services as mediator regarding his granddaughter, Gracie Donovan."

"To mediate between his children?" Having been absorbed in the program, Allison was caught off guard. "Is Tiffany's brother insisting on claiming guardianship of the girl?"

"Yes, there's a lot of drama going on in that case," Mercy added. "Apparently he's estranged from the family and this is their first attempt to talk in years."

Allison retraced her memory trying to remember that man. "That's Jacob Wetzel, isn't it?"

"I haven't met him yet. And I think he goes by a different last name now. Anyway, Mr. Conan Wetzel has also requested that we bring you back as family therapist to try to open a dialogue with his son," Mercy explained. "And to help explore the girl's wishes in this situation. It would take months for Gracie to bond with a child therapist, but she's already known you for years, hasn't she?"

When Allison decided to move away from family therapy and

focus on single women, years ago, she'd never officially changed her contract with Tiffany. Technically, she was still working for the Wetzel family. And she'd been worrying about Gracie ever since the episode at her office weeks back.

"I'm not sure about the rest of the family, but I definitely can manage the girl," she said after some consideration.

"That's a start. I'll make an appointment at your office."

After quick goodbyes, Allison disconnected the call and walked out.

It was a cool night to stroll in her pink satin pajamas, but she saw no point in the modesty of a robe when she'd been walking around in spandex capris and a sports bra all week. But she was thankful for the warmth of her fluffy kitten sandals—a personalized gift from the event organizers—as she walked the pool area toward her room.

"Allison?"

Jay's voice took her by surprise and she halted in her tracks. *Shoot.* She discreetly hid her phone inside her pajama pants pocket before turning around and facing him at the poolside outdoor sectional. Barefoot, he wore mismatched pajamas with Star Wars bottoms and a Captain America T-shirt that looked pretty sexy stretched over his chest. *Darn it. That man would look good wearing a potato sack.*

"What are you doing out of your room so late?" he asked.

Hiding her restlessness at being caught, she shifted her weight from one foot to another. "You're not the only one who gets insomnia sometimes."

On the table next to him she noticed a two-liter bottle of diet ginger ale and saw her opportunity to detract attention from her escapade. With a theatrical gasp, she joked. "Oh no! The health guru is abandoning water and berry smoothies and surrendering to the dark path of diet soda!"

With a groan, he mumbled, "Cut me some slack; I had a hard day."

He seemed to resent the invasion and, for a moment she considered leaving. Then, he reluctantly got up, walked a few steps and reached behind the tiki bar where he retrieved a glass to serve her a drink.

What are you doing? she asked herself as she accepted the ginger ale and took a seat. *Don't fall for his reverse psychology.*

He tilted his head and brought his ear to his glass. "Do you hear that?"

She hesitated. *Here's the crazy behavior again.*

He seemed to be having so much fun she finally gave in and imitated him. The bubbles bursting in the drink made a sound she'd never noticed before. "Wow! It's loud!" she commented, amused.

"Doesn't it sound like crickets?" he asked.

He had a point. "Yes, a little."

"How would you describe that sound?"

She considered his question, feeling vaguely aware of how crazy they must've appeared listening into their glasses. Maybe insanity was contagious.

She finally came up with an answer. "I'd say it sounds like the way bubble bath feels against my skin."

"Not bad!" He beamed. "You're making progress in fine-tuning your senses."

He took a long sip with his eyes closed. His face showed more delight than she'd seen anyone show when tasting the finest wine. Maybe being crazy wasn't that bad if it made you enjoy life that much more.

After a short while sipping in silence, he commented, "I hadn't had a chance to thank you for taking my side in the argument against Karen. That was cool."

She bowed her head in response. "I found it pretty cool that you defended Barbie."

His face lit up. "Did you ever get yourself that doll we talked about?"

"No, I chickened out." She considered it, thinking back on their talk at the roundtable. "But I think I'll use my fifteen minutes of Internet to order it tomorrow."

He smiled in approval and silence fell again.

She then said, "I also found it pretty cool that you referenced my line about widening your focus. That wasn't my most popular book."

"I've read them all."

The answer was not what she expected.

He added, "My favorite quote of yours is that marriage is the ultimate happy ending—"

"It ends your happy!" she blurted at the same time as him, then they cracked up together.

"Finally, someone gets that joke!" She clicked her glass with his in a toast and took a sip. "I was dying, trying not to laugh at the end of the roundtable when you made all those jokes against marriage."

His eyes sparkled and his chest shook in a suppressed laugh. "I have a whole collection of them, maybe I'll tell you someday."

She set her glass on the table. "I have to admit, your contempt for marriage nearly matches mine. May I ask where it comes from? Bad divorce?"

With a sour grimace, he shook a hand. "No way. I didn't have to make that mistake. My father cured me from any desire to attempt it."

"He had a bad divorce?" she inquired, interested.

He shot her a mistrusting look. "You're not trying to psychoanalyze me, are you?"

She raised a finger. "Just redeeming my right on our questions game. I answered a bunch of questions for you yesterday morning— very personal ones. It's my turn to ask now."

He half chuckled, half grumbled. But didn't protest.

"So," she charged again. "Your father had a bad divorce."

He avoided her eyes, sipping on his drink. "That was my welcome present shortly after I moved in with him. Turns out my first stepmother wasn't as cool about my father's bastard as she thought she was at first."

For a moment she could see him as an eight-year-old, carrying the guilt of thinking himself responsible for his father's divorce. When he didn't add anything else, she said, "You mentioned you have a conflicted relationship with—"

"Change of subject." He forced a smile that made it clear the conversation was over. "Now it's your turn. Why do *you* hate marriage so much? Because of the gay ex-husband?"

She considered giving him a generic response; but something, maybe the sleep deprivation-brainwash, brought out the truth. "Oh, I always knew he was gay. That was part of the plan. He needed a 'beard' and I wanted the social status of being married, to look more 'respectable' in the eyes of my clients."

"So it was all a business transaction?"

"It was also a failed experiment." Reclining in her seat, she sighed. "As a therapist, I'd seen so many relationships fail that I thought I had it all figured out. I thought that by marrying someone I was *not* infatuated with, I'd save myself the disappointment when the 'magic' unavoidably wore off. And my theory was that couples fight because they had expectations—that the key was entering the marriage ready to take care of myself and not expecting anything from my partner. And then we'd grow old together peacefully as sexless roommates, like most long-term couples I knew were anyway."

Raising his eyebrows, he nodded. "Interesting theory."

She lost herself for a moment, observing the lights reflected on the pool. "I had the perfect scenario. Ryan was a good friend, also a therapist—a great source of intelligent conversation. He was the only man I knew who wasn't a slob and always smelled nice."

"And, of course, he was gay," he remarked. "Then what happened?"

With a weak shrug, she raised her palms. "We just got sick of each other, the same way real couples do. After a while, we argued just as much. He decided he needed 'more' and pursued a relationship with his now-husband. I'm still trying to figure out what went wrong."

"That's easy." He huffed. "Your marriage experiment failed for the same reason most people can't stick to healthy eating."

She eyed him with skepticism. "And that is…?"

"If you're not crazy about something, you won't stick to it."

She assimilated his words slowly.

"All the clients I ever worked with who were able to lose the weight and keep it off for life had one thing in common," he continued. "They found food they loved to eat, and an exercise program that brought them joy. And they were passionate about their new lifestyle. You can't stick to something you're half-hearted about."

"You're saying the opposite of my theory," she said tentatively. "I say the key to avoiding disappointment is *not* to care."

He raised his glass. "And I'm telling you that the key to not giving up when things get rough is to really, *really* care. Only when you have your whole heart invested in something, are your chances of quitting it much less."

She was impressed by his answer, yet she still felt compelled to refute it. "If what you say were true, then couples who are uncontrollably attracted to each other would have a better chance. But that hasn't worked out for many of the women I've counseled."

"Because that was *physical* attraction," he said, setting his glass down on the table. "That wears off with time. You need to be crazy about the other person in more enduring ways." He paused, and his eyes caressed her. "Like… I never plan to get married and I seriously doubt I'll ever stick to one woman for life. But if I ever did, that person would have to be someone who has earned my respect. For example, by sticking with what she believes, even when the whole world criticizes her for it."

There it was again. His hypnotic stare. When that golden-olive gaze was grabbing her like that, she felt weakened.

"I agree," she said. "I never plan to tie myself to a man either. But if I ever did, it would have to be someone who has earned my respect too. For example, because he does exactly what he wants and refuses to mold to the world."

Assenting, he slid toward her on the outdoor sectional, while holding her gaze. His hand casually brushed her arm. "It would need to be a woman who blows me away with her strength and intelligence, yet also lights up my day with her dry sense of humor."

Automatically, she slid closer to him too and, less discreetly, touched his knee. "A man who blows me away with his kindness and his surprising, deep wisdom I would've never expected to find in someone so hot."

He moved the hair off her face with his fingers. It was happening. And somehow she had no desire to stop it. Painfully unrushed, his head inched forward, lips reaching for hers. She found herself stretching toward him, eyes closing against her will, as her lips parted, eliminating the last distance between them.

Cellular joy. His words from the day one seminar returned to her mind as his soft lips brushed hers. Every particle of her body hummed. The world vanished. She longed for the next instant when his mouth would fully take hers.

And then she felt his hands on her shoulders, pushing her away.

Her eyes snapped open, and she saw him look away as he cleared his throat. "I'm sorry." He sprang from the seat and staggered backward. "It's late. You should go to sleep."

He then pivoted on his heels and strode off as if running from her.

What the hell just happened?

Her body trembled in frustration, yearning for his touch, as she watched him disappear into the dark without once looking back at her.

Chapter 19

ENDING THE KISS WITH ALLISON TORE JAY UP. THAT BRIEF moment their lips touched had been greater than any junk food sugar rush he'd ever had. The fantasy of kissing her senseless, then carrying her to his room still caused a dangerous uproar in his workout shorts.

But he had to stay away. And the worst part was that to protect her from the situation he'd dragged her into, he couldn't tell her why.

He'd avoided her the following day, sending a different trainer to run her group's cooking class. He'd often felt her eyes on him during the daily lectures, but he fiercely ignored her. It helped keep him busy when, the morning after the roundtable, in a publicity-seeking move, Karen had quit the program to protest 'Jay's misogyny.' Trey and his film crew had a blast with the scandal.

But he could no longer escape Allison. Today the participants would start martial arts and fighting training—the part of the boot camp that concerned him the most about accepting women. With Karen quitting, and Shania off today, he no longer had a female contender to match Allison with.

He had hoped for Carrie's film crew around to ease the tension between them. But of all days, Karen had chosen today to hold a protest along with a group of feminists, right outside the resort's property fence. All cameramen had gone to cover the protest, and with all trainers busy with other participants, he was left alone with Allison.

He walked into the improvised training room—a conference

126

room where the floors and walls had been covered by gym mats. Near a corner of the room, a large punching bag hung from the ceiling.

Allison sipped the last of her morning smoothie through a straw, her free hand already sporting a boxing glove. When she saw him arrive, she set the empty cup down on the nearest stool, then straightened to face him.

He made an effort to keep his eyes on her face and off the appealing curve of her breasts under the sports bra. "It seems like you lost your assigned contender," he commented. "I'm going to be sparring with you today."

"You're kidding me, aren't you?" she deadpanned.

"Since I'm trained on how to do this, I'm less likely to injure you."

As he helped her with the second glove, she eyed him coldly from head to toe. "Because you have such a lower chance of hurting me than Ethan, the guy on oxygen, or Alf, the ninety-pound techie," she stated.

"Yes. Believe it or not, it's not about the physical force of the opponent; it's about controlled motions so you don't get hurt for real." He held the large punching bag. "Now, let's start with a warmup, practicing some boxing moves, and then we'll put on the protective gear and—"

Before he completed the sentence, she punched the bag he held. The forceful blow threw him off-balance and almost knocked him over. He recovered quickly and held the bag firmly.

He watched in surprise as she hit the bag again and again. Her excellent rhythm indicated this wasn't her first time with boxing gloves.

"This is great, but—whoa! Allison, slow down. This is just supposed to be a warm—"

She alternated punching the bag with kicking it. She was so intense he could've sworn she was angry at the bag.

"You're good!" he commented.

"I've taken some self-defense classes." Her breathing was

becoming labored, but she didn't stop.

"Allison, I think this is enough warm up. We should put on the gear and—"

A kick nearly hit him in the stomach and he caught her foot midair, forcing her to balance on one leg. "Allison, are you okay?"

"I'm wonderful." She freed her foot, took off her gloves, and sent a karate chop in his direction that he narrowly avoided.

"Are you sure? You seem to be quite… aggressive today."

"We're supposed to be fighting, aren't we?" She pushed him, using both hands and he took a step back to regain his balance.

"No. We're supposed to be fake-fighting. It's just for fun."

She attacked him with a single leg take-down, making him fall back to the cushioned floor. "Oh, trust me. I'm having lots of fun."

That's it. He grabbed her ankle, making her fall, too. Before she could react, he had her pinned to the ground, arms to her sides.

"Allison, are you angry with me?"

She scoffed. "Why would I be angry?" She flexed her knees and kicked him in the chest with both feet, propelling him away.

He landed on his back, and before he recovered, she straddled him with her legs while holding his arms outstretched. He swallowed, feeling turned on. In a second, he had reversed the positions and was immobilizing her, but she wiggled herself free. She was taking full advantage of the fact that he couldn't risk hurting her and had to measure his strength.

He tried to get up from the floor, but she pulled his ankles and knocked him over again, then elbowed him in the stomach.

Why is she so angry? I apologized for almost kissing her.

They'd been wrestling for a while, rolling and writhing on the training mat, when a light bulb went on in his brain.

"Wait a minute," he said lying on his side, as he entangled her legs with his, not letting her move. "How can you tolerate this amount of physical contact and not tolerate a hug?"

She squirmed free and rolled him to his back, spreading his arms and sitting astride him again. She seemed fatigued. "I don't know. Maybe because here I'm in control?"

He broke the hold and reversed their positions, pinning her to the ground. "But there has to be something more than just control. Not every hug makes you snap. You didn't push me away when we kissed the first time at the beach, and I'm pretty sure I was hugging you at the time."

Taking advantage of his distraction, she shoved his chest with her feet again and climbed back on top of him. "Would you stop it with your life-coach-y stuff?" she asked, breathing heavily. "You can't just magically fix me."

He hooked her leg with his to throw her off balance, and she fell on top of him, chest to chest. Her hips slid to meet his and a rush of excitement went through his body.

Her panting halted and her body tensed. He felt the throb of arousal in his lower body and knew she could feel it against her, but she made no effort to move.

Wait. Is that why she's so angry? Because I didn't kiss her?

He brushed his lips with hers briefly and retreated immediately, observing her. She didn't move. He closed his eyes and nipped at her lips, slowly and softly, stopping, then coming back for more, then more. He sensed that if he forced the kiss she'd push him away. So he limited his touch each time to a light tease of the lips.

She cussed. "For goodness' sake, will you stop fooling around?" She pulled his face eagerly, deepening the kiss herself.

Still tasting of berry smoothie, her tongue invaded his mouth, and every bit of logic and self-restraint disappeared from his mind. He kissed her with ardor, deeper and deeper, inhaling her fragrance as they rolled to their side on the mat. She was frantic, but for him, this wasn't the desperate kiss that had launched their first night together. He sensed a new tenderness and wonder he hadn't felt before.

As he feasted on her smoldering mouth, one of his hands moved through her silken hair, as the other tentatively moved to clasp her thigh. Her fingers roamed his back, pressing his chest against her breasts. The distance between their bodies disappeared, and his hands slid out of his control to cup her buttocks, pressing her even closer. She arched against him and every molecule of his body screamed in hunger for her.

Her fingers reached for the waistband of his shorts and he cussed. He wanted so much for her to keep going, but he couldn't allow it.

"Stop." He held her wrist.

"Are you trying to drive me crazy?" Groaning in frustration, she freed her hand and scrambled away from him on her hands and knees, then rose to her feet.

Panting, he sat up on the mat. "This is a mistake."

"Of course it is!" She braced herself and changed her weight from one foot to the other, avoiding his eyes. "I have no intention of ever hooking up with you again." With a grunt, she paced around the room. "I have a responsibility to my readers and clients. I would never fall for such a low trick as reverse psychology."

Jay wanted to slam his head on the floor mat again and again. He covered his face and mumbled with a weak voice, "Yes. That's exactly what this is, reverse psychology."

She didn't seem to notice his despair. Her subtle trembling and fluttering lashes announced she was close to crying. "I mean, I don't even understand why you'd be interested in me! I'm a flabby granny compared to women like Shania."

Who is as gay as someone can be.

"You're obviously not after my warm and cozy personality," she continued, pacing. "And I know I'm lousy in bed."

A storm of conflicting feelings rose in Jay. The desire for her. The fear of hurting her. The frustration about the absurd situation he'd shoved himself into. In the midst of it all, the only thing he managed to do was laugh.

"What are you talking about?" he asked between chuckles. "You are *not* lousy in bed!"

Stopping short, she whipped her head around to face him. "Excuse me?"

"You're amazing!"

She studied his face as if trying to gauge his sincerity. "Are you sure you're not confusing me with someone else? I mean, it has been months."

He got up from the floor and moved toward her. "No. I'm talking about *you*. The woman who challenged my creativity because she wouldn't let me hug her. The woman who's slow to warm up but then when she does... watch out."

"Yes, that sounds like me." A small, proud smile lit up her face. Her eyes darted away, then met his again, both eager and cautious. "Sooooo... you didn't think I was too bad? I mean, at least not too difficult?"

"You were great. You just need to loosen up a bit." Narrowing his eyes, he tilted his head from side to side. "And it wouldn't kill you to make a little more noise to guide the man. It was hard to guess what you liked and what you didn't like."

"Come on!" With a huff, she waved him off. "Like you didn't know I liked *everything* you did."

He couldn't help grinning. "You did?"

"Stop faking surprise." Allison averted her gaze, cheeks reddening. "You know you're a woman's fantasy come true. And I've been told more than once that I'm cold like a fish and comatose from the waist down. It doesn't even make sense that you were ever after me."

He chortled again and took a few steps to place his hand on her shoulder. "Darling, if a man ever said you're cold and comatose, it only means he didn't invest the time and effort to turn on your heat and wake you up with soft kisses."

She scrutinized his face as if searching for a sign of sincerity. "Then why? Why are you pushing me away now?"

With a sigh, he sat cross-legged on the padded mat and patted the space next to him, inviting her to sit. After she did, he held her hand.

"Allow me to set the record straight." He paused, sustaining her gaze. "The night we spent together was one of the most amazing memories of my life." He looked away, feeling unexpectedly shy. "And I confess. Yes. It's true that I originally put all this together—Carrie's call, the roundtable, your invitation to the boot camp—just to see you again. And yes, my hope was to convince you to sleep with me."

"I knew it!" She slapped a hand on the mat. "Then what happened? Did you change your mind?"

Hesitant, he glanced at her. "Darling, I learned something recently that made me realize it's better if I stay away from you. I wish I could tell you more, but the less you know, the better off you are."

She stared at him. "That covers anything from, 'You stink' to, 'I'm involved with the mafia.'"

He couldn't help cracking up. "None of that. It's something that makes me think *I* could hurt you."

"Okay, and that covers anything from, 'I have a pet you're allergic to' to, 'The long-lost wife I thought was dead just came back'—"

"Stop!" He covered her mouth with his hand, feeling weak. He wanted to laugh. And cry. And kiss her again. "It'll come out sooner or later." He removed his hand. "For now, I just ask that you accept my apology for having dragged you into this program and that we finish it the best we can."

He extended his hand in offering. Her eyes darted back and forth from it to his face and he could sense her struggle. Slowly, the unease left her face and her usual mask of indifference took over.

"Oh, well. I can think of worse things to do for the next week than getting national attention and hanging out with Carrie O'Brian." She accepted his hand and shook it.

Chapter 20

A LL EYES WERE ON JAY AND ALLISON DURING THE RECORDING of Carrie's roundtable on the tenth day of the program.

"You insist on saying men constantly objectify women, but I disagree." Jay's gaze focused on Allison with such intensity she got goose bumps. "It's not that we objectify the female body. Rather, we *worship* the female body. We're addicted to it."

The softness of his words contrasted with the fire in his eyes. His gaze seemed to disrobe her and caress her at once, yet the respect filling them made her feel adored instead of exposed. She was afraid everyone else at the table could see the flying sparks.

Since their wrestling/kissing session three days earlier, Allison had poured all her energy into her performance in the boot camp. She'd made sure to never avoid Jay, to show how little she cared about his rejection. He'd made an extra effort to be attentive and helpful to her as if flaunting how okay he was. They were in fierce competition for the title of the most civilized and friendly person in the world.

And the only opportunity to vent their frustration was Carrie's roundtable debate.

"And you can't say objectification is a problem affecting only women," he continued. "I'm the subject of objectification regularly. Just Google my name and the first image that pops up is a picture of me, half-naked, with my chest hair shaven and glitter rubbed all over me."

They'd been locked in an argument for a while and their chairs had slid closer and closer until they were practically in each other's face.

"As the regular recipient of it, I'm allowed to say this about objectification," he said. "It's only as dirty as the mind of the beholder. As long as you agreed to it voluntarily and don't take yourself too seriously, it's fun to see pictures of yourself afterward all glammed up and nicely airbrushed—everybody should try it."

Allison moved closer, her face inches away from him, his minty breath reaching her. She felt like kissing him and hitting him at the same time. "Mr. Johnson, it's not the same. First of all, you're in the fitness business. Glitter aside, by showing your body you show exactly what you advertise. What I resent is using a woman's body to sell unrelated merchandise—for example, a car. Second of all, you said it, you agreed to those pictures voluntarily. But somewhere out there, a poor young aspiring model or actress believes she'll only make it in the world if she takes her clothes off. Do you see the difference in the power dynamics here?"

Raising his eyebrows, he eased back in his seat. "I do see your point."

"In addition to that, we also have to remember the constant battle of women against unrealistic body expectations," she added. "Women are being bombarded with images of size zero models, and sixteen-year-olds wearing a ton of makeup to make them look older. Everywhere, the message we receive is that the ideal body is a toothpick with big breasts." When the audience cheered and hooted, she went on. "Come on! There's no natural way to have extra-large breasts and not have at least a little roll somewhere else! Even the fittest woman will have some fat around her abdomen and her hips. That's what estrogen does!"

"And thank God for it." Jay rose from his chair and clapped, making other people join.

He extended his hand. "Dr. Allison Connors, I concede defeat."

The skin touch during his brief handshake made her long for

his hands on her body. But, too soon, he'd let go to resume clapping along with the audience. "We have a winner."

Allison beamed, taking in the satisfaction of the roaring of applause.

* * *

"You should've been there yesterday, girls! It was the best moment of my life!"

Hiding in the hallway bathroom to get cell signal the next night, Allison FaceTimed her girlfriends, sharing her enthusiasm about the last roundtable. Joy was absent from the call, on a date with the Neanderthal Agent Fields. But not even the mention of his name could spoil Allison's mood tonight.

"We saw you!" Fe replied. "Jay posted the snip on his video blog. You were on fire!"

"Oh, not only that," Hope added. "He posted another one choosing the best moments of your verbal duels with Wayne and Karen. Under the video he added a link to your website. I bet your site visits are skyrocketing."

Allison was out of words. She'd hoped he'd keep his promise to help promote her, but she never imagined he'd do it so quickly. Grinning, she held the phone and paced around. "Now *this* is worth the pain the boot camp has been. If I can keep this going for the last few days, I'll be a celebrity by the time Carrie's show releases."

"But what's up with the sexual tension boiling between you and Jay in that last roundtable?" Hope asked. "I assume the Titanic hasn't sunk yet?"

Allison dismissed her with a wave. "I guess the conversation got heated up for a moment there. But to call it sexual tension—"

"Sweetie," Hope interrupted with a raised hand. "I needed a cigarette after that—and I quit smoking years ago."

Emery's face entered the screen. "I've never smoked in my life.

And I needed one too." She shuddered.

"Drop it, girls," Allison warned. "I told you, Jay and I had a reasonable conversation and agreed to keep a distance from each other."

Allison stumbled over something and only then realized that, in her distraction, she'd moved out of her hiding place into the hallway.

She raised her eyes and met Ethan's face, gawking at her.

"You have a cell phone!" he exclaimed. "How did you get to keep yours?"

Shoot. "Uh, gotta go, girls." She disconnected the call and faced Ethan.

Ethan had turned into a bouncy, fidgeting kid. "I can't believe you have a phone! You have Internet for more than the miserable fifteen minutes a day they allow us here!"

Allison rushed to shush him. "If someone hears you, they'll kick me out of the boot camp." She begged with her eyes. "Ethan, you wouldn't tell on me, would you?"

"Of course not!" he snickered. "Because you can order real food!" He clapped once and pumped a fist.

She stared at him, confused.

"I'm so sick of those damn healthy smoothies and egg-white omelets!" he explained. "We have to order something sinful. MSG-loaded Chinese. Fried chicken. Cheese-smothered Mexican food. All of it!"

Allison wanted to protest, but the rumbling of her stomach denounced her temptation. *Darn it.* She really liked Ethan and his "life's short, enjoy it" ideas.

* * *

In the temporary office, Jay talked to Gracie on FaceTime. He didn't like keeping her up so long past her bedtime, but lately, they could only talk like this after Tiffany was asleep.

"Pleeeeease, Uncle!" she begged. Her spiked hair and the

upside-down background suggested she hung head down from the back of the couch. "Hell is breaking loose here. There's a lot of cussing. And Mom threw a lamp at Mr. Jordan yesterday."

Jay prayed that Gracie's innocence protected her from learning about the drugs behind those behaviors. It was amazing how his sister and brother-in-law could look so cleaned up and picture-perfect in public; it must've come with the acting ability.

He sighed in despair. "Chipmunk, I told you what the lawyer said. The only way to get you to stay with me is if we fight your mom in court. We don't want that."

"Why not?" she asked. "Mom's fighting with someone all the time, anyway."

He ran a hand through his hair. "But this would be worse. You would need to say ugly things about your mom and Jordan. I'd need to tell the judges she's acting crazy—"

"But she *is* acting crazy. And Miranda says she's willing to help us prove it." She lowered her voice. "We've been shooting videos of them with my iPad every time they break something in the house. I've been uploading them to YouTube as private videos like you taught me."

He was impressed. "Munchkin. Do you understand that means you'd barely ever see her again?"

"I barely see her now. I'd rather be with you. Don't we have the best time ever? Wouldn't it be great if we could be together all the time, forever and ever?"

All the time, forever and ever. The words sent a surge of panic through Jay's chest and he felt like going for a run—to Alaska. He'd never been able to stick with someone for long. He was the man who'd rarely had a romance that lasted longer than a week.

His own words during his recent chat with Allison returned to his mind. "*Only when you have your whole heart invested in something are your chances of quitting it much less.*" He regarded his niece's face on the screen, feeling the warmth of soft love in his heart. Yes, if there was something in his life he was crazy about and really cared for, it was her.

He made a decision. "Okay, chipmunk. I'm going to court to fight for you."

"Yay, Uncle! You're the best!" Gracie spun around to sit straight on the couch and clapped, and that made the fear worth it. This might be a doomed battle, but he wasn't going down without a fight.

"And in the meantime," he added. "If you ever feel scared that 'hell is breaking loose' and you're not safe there, you have Miranda text me a code word—let's say, 'Mayday,' and I'll come pick you up. Now it's bedtime, munchkin."

After they said goodbye and disconnected the call, he noticed the express mail package addressed to Allison sitting on his desk. By the return address he guessed it was the doll he'd encouraged her to order. His thoughts flew to her.

Now that he knew he'd be fighting Tiffany in court soon, it was best to come clean about who he was. With only four more days left in the jumpstart program, they'd both proven they could be appropriate and civilized. He picked up the box and headed her way.

It had rained on and off all night, and a cool breeze blew. As Jay made his way to the guest tower in the dark, he avoided the puddles on the ground, remembering a time when he and Grace had earned a reprimand for stomping in some, getting covered in mud. Maybe now that he'd decided to end his fixation with Allison, he could return to his obsession with finding Grace.

When he entered the courtyard where Allison's room was, the complete silence and deserted hallways announced it was much later than he thought. He glanced at the time on his phone realizing it was past eleven and she was probably asleep. As he turned around to leave, a familiar smell hit him.

Oh yes. For a recovering junk-food-aholic like him, that scent was unmistakable.

With the precision of a hound, he sniffed at the air and followed the muddy footprints right to the source of the delicious smell. He grabbed his master keypass and opened the door.

And he caught them *in fraganti*.

Allison and Ethan were together in her room—stuffing their faces with pizza.

"What is this?" he roared from the door.

Startled, she dropped her pizza slice onto the bed beside her.

From the nearby chair, Ethan pointed at her and talked with his mouth still full. "She ordered it online. She has a cell phone."

With a gasp, Allison gawked at Ethan. "*You* made me order it!"

Ethan wiped his mouth with a napkin. "Oh, come on! Like I had the strength to twist your arm. I can't even fight a kitten!"

Jay felt frustrated; they were supposed to be detoxifying from unhealthy food. But half of him also wanted to laugh at Allison's greasy fingers and Ethan's tomato-sauce-smudged face.

Still, he had to play the part of program director. "Sneaking in outside food is a direct violation of our rules."

Flinching, she rose from the bed. "Jay, I swear, he blackmailed me! He gave me puppy dog eyes and said—" She pitched her voice low. "'How can you refuse me a pizza? I had *cancer*.'"

A spark of satisfaction flashed in Ethan's eyes and his lips twitched, fighting a smirk.

"I'm very familiar with those puppy dog eyes and that blackmail," Jay remarked, shooting Ethan a withering look. "He uses them to get away with not doing the dishes." He snapped his fingers and pointed at the door. "Back to your room. You and I will talk about this later."

Ethan headed for the door. Before exiting, he sent Allison a half-naughty, half-apologetic smile. "By the way. The 'I-had-cancer' excuse also works when it's my turn to clean the bathroom."

"Worst roommate ever! Out!" Jay stamped a foot on the floor.

Ethan snatched one last slice of pizza from the box and ran out.

Way to run! He must be getting better.

He turned to Allison, giving her his sternest look. "Ethan broke one rule. You broke two, by keeping your phone with you."

"I'm really sorry." She placed her phone on the table, mortified. "Please don't kick me out. I'm only four days away from making history. The media attention I'll get if I complete this training is unprecedented."

He was torn between his desire to reassure her and his duty to lecture her. He went with both. "I'm going to treat you like I'd treat any man in my program and tell it to you like it is." Taking a seat on the chair Ethan had vacated, he gestured her to sit back on the bed.

She trembled, as the perfect student not used to being reprimanded by the teacher. Piercing her with his eyes, he said, "This is not the last time you'll slip and fall, so stop beating yourself up." He raised a hand. "It has been two days since my last donut."

She jerked in surprise.

"We're kids learning to walk and we'll fall and get back up constantly," he continued with a smile. "When you give in to temptation and break your diet, you don't use that as an excuse to throw it all away. The next day, you pick yourself up and start all over."

For a moment, her body relaxed, and she appeared relieved, then a second later she slumped her shoulders and clasped her hands together as if overcome by guilt. "I don't want you to give me any special treatment. But I don't want to get kicked out of the program, either. If you'd caught any of the men doing this, would you impose some form of penalty on them? Make me pay for the slip-up by cutting my calories tomorrow. Or make me exercise extra to burn off the pizza."

She seemed to *need* punishment to soothe her conscience; he considered it. The next three days were mostly one-on-one training, helping the participants design a custom-made exercise program they could enjoy sticking to. "I guess I can instruct your trainer to work you extra-hard, to compensate for this infraction."

She bobbed her head effusively. "Yes! I'll do it! I'll pay for this."

"And I would move you from this suite to a regular room in the main hotel tower, where we can watch you better. No more special privileges."

"Anything! Just please don't kick me out now."

He extended his hand to pick up her phone and only then realized he was still carrying the package under his other arm. Remembering the reason for his visit he lifted the box. "I came to give you this. And also, I needed to talk to you about—"

"My doll came already?" The unusual excitement in her voice startled him.

She snatched the box from his hands and rushed to tear apart the cardboard package, revealing a box containing a blond Barbie doll in a silver gown.

Allison jumped in excitement. He'd never seen her that happy and expressive—ever. Her face flushed, her uneven grin so wide it defied the Botox. Her eyes crinkled and her right cheek dimpled.

"My doll! My doll!" She squealed hugging the box while doing a silly happy dance.

Jay felt like he'd been slapped. *Oh my God, she is Grace.*

It had to be her. He remembered that silly dance vividly, along with that expression of delight and the sound of that squeal.

He forgot all about the confession he was there to offer. "What are you waiting for? Get her out of the box!" he encouraged her. His own voice sounded different to him. It was also tinted with the enthusiasm of a kid.

Clutching the box, Allison beamed. "I can't open it, Jay! This is a limited edition collectible doll. If I leave it in the box, in ten years it might be worth ten times what it's worth now."

"And ten years from now you might've died in a plane crash." He *tsked*. "Come on! What good are toys for if you don't play with them?"

Her trembling fingers moved to the flap on top of the box, then she stopped. "What if I regret it?"

"Trust me." He shook his head. "I have a huge collection of

action figures that aren't worth half the price I paid, because I refuse to leave them in the box. It's absolutely worth it!"

She sank onto the bed, him beside her. She took a deep breath and slid her finger under the round piece of tape holding the top flap together, breaking it. She then opened the box and slid the doll out, still tied to the cardboard backing.

She took a whiff at the doll's hair. "Ah! New doll smell."

She produced scissors from her purse, cut the tiny plastic cords tying the doll to the cardboard backing, and then stopped. "This is the irreversible part. Once you free their hair, it starts getting frizzy, they're no longer in mint condition, and the resale value goes down dramatically." Still, she cut the last plastic bands on the head, separating the doll from the backing.

Allison placed the doll on the nightstand with its back against the wall and sat on the bed, staring at it in awe. The shine in her eyes transformed her into a little girl. Another flashback rushed through Jay's mind.

Yes, she has to be Grace.

Trying to reel his thoughts back in, he examined the doll and commented, "She looks exactly like you."

"Are you crazy?" she tittered. "She's blond like me, that's it! But she's *a Barbie*! Never in a million years will I have that waistline!"

He snorted. "What are you talking about? Your body is a million times better than the body of a Barbie."

"Oh, stop it!" She rolled her eyes, but it was obvious she was pleased.

Slowly, her face darkened. "I know you men would rather screw a plastic doll than a real woman—so you don't have to deal with her feelings and opinions."

Aaaand… she's back. His glee vanished.

"Darling, haven't you ever, in your whole life, been treated well by a member of my gender?" he asked. "Isn't there anyone who can be the saving grace for mankind—one exception to the rule that we're all evil?"

The deepest shadow fell over her expression. She denied with her head.

Please be Grace. Please remember me. He insisted, "Not even in your childhood? A little playground friend? Someone who ever stood up against the bullies for you?"

She half-shrugged. "My childhood memories are sparse and hazy. I'm aware that's a defense mechanism to forget the painful experiences of my early life."

He nodded in silence, recalling the story of her abusive stepfather.

She picked up the doll and caressed its hair. "Years ago I remembered just enough to get therapy and now I'm fine. But in order to keep the bad memories under control, the good ones are gone too."

He frowned at her. "That must suck. So you don't have any happy memories from childhood?"

"Minimal."

He fought the temptation to extend the hand and touch her face. "We'd better get started making childhood memories now, then."

The little snort and wheeze in her laughter brought another surge of memories of Grace. "That's nonsense!" she said. "I can't make childhood memories; I'm not a child anymore."

"Who cares?" he argued, beaming. "You know the saying: you can decide to have a happy childhood at any age. And do you know what?" Having an idea, he stood up from the bed and took her elbow, making her rise too. "We are starting right now! When was the last time you stomped in puddles?"

Chapter 21

"LISTEN. ISN'T THAT THE MOST RELAXING SOUND EVER?"

Three days after the pizza incident, Allison and Jay lay on the beach with their eyes closed. Following his lead, she focused on the hypnotic sound of the crashing waves while the afternoon sun warmed her skin and the sand beneath her.

"Now shift your attention to your sense of smell," he continued, guiding her. "Can you smell the ocean?"

She inhaled deeply. "I smell nothing."

"Your sense of smell must've tired out. But I came prepared. Keep your eyes closed."

His hand let go of hers. Seconds later, he said, "Now, what do you smell?"

"It's lime peel. I love it." She delighted in the scent of zest.

After a few moments, he moved the lime away. "Now try again. Can you smell the ocean now?"

He was right. Now that her nose had re-booted, the strong scent of the ocean became noticeable again. "Yes! I can!" She beamed, proud of her accomplishment.

Thank God Carrie's film crew was gone already. The last three days had been a boot camp of returning to childhood.

When Jay invited her to stomp in puddles in their pajamas, Allison had agreed reluctantly, considering it part of her punishment for the pizza. The morning after, Jay had rearranged the one-on-one training sessions so he could be in charge of hers. While the other participants designed their custom workouts, he'd driven her to a beachside park where they climbed trees, played hopscotch and jumped rope. She'd followed his directions with serious discipline, yet by the end of the session was actually enjoying it. She'd never guffawed harder in her life than when they chased each other playing tag.

That night, as the rest of the attendees slept, they'd laid on their backs on the roof of the hotel, looking at the night sky and remembering names of constellations.

"The world will make you believe it's normal to become cynical and sour with age," he'd told her, his eyes searching the stars. "But I've spent the last few years of my life refuting that. Returning to that state of grace before the fall—the joy we had in childhood before the world wounded us—is my greatest goal."

She envied him so much for even having that dream.

The following day they'd played dress-up. She couldn't believe he'd ordered a load of costumes just for her, to add to the male superhero outfits they usually kept for the participants. She'd reluctantly tried on wigs and dressed up like a modern Amazon warrior per his request. But she most enjoyed dressing up like a medieval lady and a vampire princess. It helped to tame her giddiness that any costume Jay chose, from an ancient warrior to a modern superhero, made him look like temptation on a stick.

In the late afternoon, he'd made rainbows in her new room by hanging a prism in the beam of light filtering through the curtains of her west-facing window. Her mouth fell open in delight, wondering how he'd guessed she was fascinated with rainbows when she was little.

And that night, he'd delivered a different treat that he'd ordered from who-knows-where: a butterfly farm.

"What I really wanted to get you were fireflies," he apologized. "Apparently they're hard to ship."

As they'd released the butterflies and watched them flutter

around her room, she was transfixed; forgotten happy childhood moments flickered in her mind.

"We should probably head back," she said now from her resting place on the beach. "I have no idea where we are."

He tapped her hand reassuringly. "We're about five miles south of the hotel."

"*Five* miles?" Gasping, she sat up. "How did that happen?"

Amusement playing on his face, he stopped smelling the lime and sat up too. "Don't you remember walking here?"

She vaguely recalled the walk—sometimes running, sometimes skipping and spinning—while chatting, collecting seashells, and occasionally chasing birds.

"I can't walk five more miles today! Especially not barefoot! We need to call a cab."

He jumped off the ground. Crossing his arms, he clicked his tongue and shook his head. "Do I need to carry you?"

"Don't you dare!" She shot him a warning glare. "The romance-novel image of a man carrying a woman is demeaning and perpetuates the myth of the weak gender."

"Well, I guess that means you have to prove you're the strong gender and walk with me."

He pulled her up to her feet and took off, dragging her by the hand despite her protests.

After they'd been walking a while, her eyes caught a glimpse of gray roots in his temples. *Does he dye his hair?* "Jay, how old are you? You have to be younger than me to have the stamina you have."

He seemed to suppress a smile. "You and I are exactly the same age. We even share our birthday."

She narrowed her eyes. "Which is…?"

There was a short silence before he answered. "The day your car almost ran me over. That's the day we both were born."

"Nice save!" Giggling, she reached in the pocket of her white capris to retrieve a hair band. "You're just trying to make me reveal my birthday. But seriously, don't you *ever* get tired?"

"Of course I do. That's the whole point. The more tired I am, the better chance I have to sleep at the end of the day."

As she gathered her flyaway hair into a ponytail, she studied him. "If your insomnia is so bad, why don't you just get your doctor to prescribe a sleeping aid?"

"I got worried that I was relying too much on sleeping pills at one point." His cheerfulness diminished. "I quit them when I stopped the antidepressants."

She remembered the story of his depression, during his time as CEO. "Was that the time you were trying to make things work with your father?"

With his eyes focused on the path ahead, he nodded. After piercing the lime with his thumbnail he brought it near his nose to take a whiff of its scent. "I tried hard to mold myself into him, to give him what none of his spoiled, legitimate trust-fund babies could give him. But I couldn't keep it up."

A comfortable silence fell.

"You and he didn't end up on the best terms, right?" she asked after a while. "Are you ever going to tell me the story about what happened?"

Groaning, he returned the lime to the pocket on his khaki cargo shorts. "Please stop trying to psychoanalyze me!"

"Is this a double standard?" she joked. "You can pull all your life coach moves on me and make me revisit my childhood, but I'm not allowed to ask you a question?"

He chuckled and shot her a side-glance. After a few more moments walking in silence, he seemed to give up. "When I announced I was quitting my father's company, he didn't take it well. He threw it in my face how I'd quit the MBA classes he'd made me sign up for years back and reminded me of the twenty thousand five hundred thirty-eight dollars he'd paid for that semester. So I did what any self-respecting man would do; I went to the bank and withdrew twenty thousand five hundred thirty-eight dollars plus interest from my savings to pay him back."

She bowed her head. "That sounds like the right thing to do."

"—Then I changed it into coins, rented a dump truck and dumped it all on his favorite car."

Allison cringed. She wasn't sure if she should crack up or be sincerely worried. "That's *almost* funny."

"Except that I didn't foresee how much damage a ton of coins could do to a 1962 classic Camaro." He grimaced. "Have you ever seen a car after being caught in a bad hail storm? Well, my father *didn't* find it funny. Our fight after that, the last one before I left for Atlanta, got... kind of ugly."

"Have you talked to him since then?"

"My lawyer talked to his a lot after he sued me."

She gaped at him, hoping she'd misunderstood. "He sued you?"

"He dropped it eventually. But I did have to go to anger management classes and court-mandated therapy."

And I thought I'd heard every possible toxic family story through Tiffany and the Wetzels.

"And you said your father's still alive, isn't he?" she asked.

He gave a sour chuckle. "Every couple of months I get a panicky voicemail from my second stepmother saying he's dying. Luckily I stopped paying attention after the fifth time."

She raised her eyebrows—darn it, her Botox needed retouching. "Is he sick?"

"He's getting old—he was on the old side when I was born. He's had a couple of heart stents." He picked up a shell and kept walking. "Every so often he gets chest pain, ends up in the hospital and everyone thinks he's finished. But then he gets up from bed and goes golfing the next day." He made a dismissive hand flick. "I've saved myself a dozen trips 'to say goodbye' in the past five years."

She studied the small scar over his right eyebrow, and his attractive features, shaded by a rare case of dejection. "You know," she said.

"Normally I tell my clients that no one should rush forgiveness too soon, before processing the hurt, and risk it being superficial and fake. I tell them, 'You're only ready when you're ready.'"

He considered it for a moment, then tilted his head. "Not bad."

"But," she added. "I would tell *you* that forgiving someone is like weight-lifting. You need to start practicing it a little every day—develop that muscle—or you'll never be ready."

He eyed her from head to toe. "Sometimes you're annoyingly clever."

She raised her hands as if surrendering. "You're the one teaching me to become a child again. You keep talking about returning to that state before the world's cynicism and disappointment reached us. Well, I'm telling you, the way to return to that state of grace—of innocence—is by atonement and forgiveness."

"Did that work for you?" He shot her a cautious look. "Did you ever forgive your stepfather?"

"Oh yes. I forgave him—right after I put him in jail."

To his curious look, she shrugged. "Long story. Sometimes the only way to forgive is to practice a little tough love first." She picked up a mother-of-pearl shell and kept walking. "Can you remember *one* nice moment with your father?"

He thought about it for a while. "One time when I was about ten, he came back from work in a particularly good mood; I don't know why. He sat on the floor with me and we played with my action figures." His soft smile gave away that he was restraining himself not to show how much he'd enjoyed that.

"There you go." She nodded, pleased. "Maybe that's the image you have to hold on to."

Feeling they'd gotten too intimate and it was time to change the subject, she dropped herself back onto the sand. "Sorry, Jay. I can't walk five more miles today. Let's Uber."

With a sigh, he looked heavenward. "Okay, I'll carry you."

She groaned. "I told you, I do not buy into the myth of—"

"Darling," he interrupted her, placing two fingers on her lips. "I never said I'd carry you romance-novel style. I was offering you a piggy-back ride."

It had been so long since Allison heard that phrase she had trouble remembering its meaning for a moment. "A *piggy-back ride*?"

He kneeled down on the sand and offered his back. "Come on. Get up." He wrapped her arms around his neck and scooped under her knees.

"You're not serious, are—?"

Before she finished the sentence, he stood up with her on his back and marched away. She yelped and clung to his T-shirt, giggling nervously.

"What are you doing? You're going to hurt your knees and your back!"

He *tsked*. "You're a feather compared to some of the weights I lift at the gym."

She grinned. That man really knew what to say to charm a lady. "Okay, then go faster!" she requested.

He ran, carrying her on his back. She squealed and laughed harder than she'd ever laughed in her life.

The warm Florida wind blowing across her face. The sound of the ocean and seagulls in the air. His strong body under hers. If *this* was being crazy, she never wanted to be sane again.

Chapter 22

THE LAST DAY OF THE PROGRAM WAS BITTERSWEET. JAY focused on inspirational seminars, wrapping up the main points learned and preparing the participants to return to their normal lives. The following morning they'd have the closing ceremony. Allison couldn't believe it had been only two weeks since she arrived there; she felt ages removed from being the woman who'd started the training.

After-dinner activities were relaxed to allow the attendees to socialize one last time and exchange contact information. Sitting on a stool at the tiki bar by the pool, Ethan poked Allison's arm. "I never imagined I'd say this, but I'll miss you." In spite of his casual tone, Ethan's eyes seemed misty. She guessed everyone was going through the blues of knowing tomorrow they'd say goodbye.

"Do you forgive me for throwing you under the bus over the pizza?" He sent her a shy glance from under his uneven eyelashes.

Darn it. There might be some hypnosis and cult-like brainwashing going on in the boot camp, but she'd really bonded with these goofy guys. They challenged her previous belief that all men were hopeless idiots.

Standing in front of his barstool, she crossed her arms and tapped a foot, joking. "If I say no, will you blackmail me with the 'I had cancer' line?"

"That was my next move." He winked. "Should I?"

Chuckling, she shook her head. "No need. Of course, I forgive you." She patted his head and was surprised when fine, nearly invisible hair tickled her fingers.

"Ethan!" she touched his scalp with her fingertips. "Your hair is growing back!"

"Wait! Is it?" he grabbed a tray from the bar and used it as a mirror to look at his head and gasped. "You're right! Finally!" He dropped the tray to clap, jumping and cheering. She rejoiced in his improved energy.

"I was afraid it would never grow back! I'm so relieved!" Ethan wrapped Allison in a hug.

Without thinking, she wrapped her arms around him and patted his back.

As she released him, she became aware that the rumble of murmurs around her had died away. She could feel Jay's gaze on her, along with the eyes of half the men in the room.

"Oh my goodness!" Brad spoke first. "Allison just hugged someone! How did that happen?"

He was right. She hadn't pushed Ethan away.

Puzzled, she replied, "I… I don't know."

"Can I try now?" Brad asked.

Paralyzed in place, Allison watched the giant man approach, stomping in her direction as if in slow motion. She imagined the earth shaking with each solid step. Then he wrapped her in a bear hug and she envisioned red lights and fire truck sirens.

Blackness swirled around her for a few seconds. The next thing she knew, Brad was bent over on the floor, groaning in pain and holding his crotch. The aching in her knee hinted at the point of contact.

Oops.

* * *

Allison dreamed of riding her bike at top speed while crying. She must've been seven or eight. Tassels hung from the handles of the pink bike and her doll Daisy sat in the front basket. Free from the usual ponytails, Allison's blond hair flew in the air.

The bike arrived at the blue house with the large oak and the tire swing in the front yard, but again, no one was home. Cowlick and Ginger had disappeared.

A loud sound yanked her from the dream and upright in bed.

The sound was a repetitive knocking, but it didn't seem to come from the door, but instead from somewhere inside the room. Her heart thudded. *Darn it!* Here was one argument in favor of having a strong man sleeping next to her in bed. There was no handyman service she could hire to investigate middle-of-the-night noises. Should she call the front desk? Or 911?

With ice running through her veins she followed the sound to where it came from, the balcony door. That couldn't be right; her new room was on the fifth floor. Trembling, she pulled the curtains.

A man stood on the tiny balcony behind the French doors. She screamed from the top of her lungs just before realizing the man was Jay. She clutched at her fluttering heart.

His voice was muffled by the door glass. "Can you talk now?"

"Are you trying to kill me with a heart attack?" Her pulse still racing, Allison jerked open the balcony door. "How did you get there?"

He pointed upward. "I hung down from my balcony. My room is right above yours."

She gaped at him. She'd almost forgotten the guy was completely insane. "I rephrase my original question. Are you trying to kill *yourself?*"

"I know what we've been missing!" Jay interrupted with enthusiasm. "Brad and I are taller than you—like your mother was—and Ethan isn't! When your mother hugged you, she must've placed her arms around your neck and shoulders. If I hug you under that area, around your waist like I did when we kissed, it won't trigger a flashback."

Allison sighed. "Jay, no offense, but that's too over-simplistic—"

Ignoring her argument, he picked her up by the waist and sat her on top of the dresser. Before she could protest, he wrapped his arms around her waist.

Allison braced herself for the usual symptoms—the chest tightening, the feeling of the walls closing in, the seconds of blackness. She expected to break out in a cold sweat any moment and feel the beginnings of a panic attack.

It didn't happen.

Bewildered, she let herself relax a little more, and fully experience the sensation of his strong arms around her waist. Instead of attacked and threatened, she felt... fine.

"Jay, it's working! I'm not panicking!"

"Do you feel ready to try something else?"

She agreed. He slid his arms up just a few inches and stopped. He kept raising them and stopping at times, always staying under her arms, until he was hugging her torso. She was still doing okay.

More than okay. It was delicious. She positioned her arms around his strong shoulders and got lost in the delightful feeling. She widened her knees, letting him come closer, and held him tighter, her breasts pressing against his chest.

She ran her hands over his vast back, enjoying its firmness, when he mumbled a cussword.

"Everything okay?" she asked.

"Um, there's been a side effect."

He didn't have to explain. Allison could feel hardness pressing against her lower abdomen. Her breath caught.

"I'm sorry," he said, without moving. "I know. Men are dogs. I swear I had no intention of tainting this healing moment with lusty thoughts, but I can't help it. Now all I can think about is how much I want to kiss you."

Warmth spread through her and her flesh tingled. Her heart pounding, she whispered, "What are you waiting for?"

His mouth captured hers and she felt her body melt. She kissed him with desperation, devouring his lips, not minding the burn of his stubble on her sensitive skin.

Allison must've blacked out again. Next thing she knew she was no longer sitting on the dresser but lying in bed—her lips fused with Jay's, their tongues entangled, hands roaming all over each other's bodies.

* * *

"We can't... we need to stop." Jay didn't sound convincing even to himself as he kept kissing her neck and undoing her pajama top buttons.

Allison stopped nibbling at his chest to groan in frustration. "Do you realize the bargain you're getting here? The only reason I'm acting this irresponsibly is because of the brainwashing you've subjected me to."

She rolled him over in bed and pulled his pajama top over his head, then trailed down his neck with kisses. He felt the rush of blood to his lower body, making him woozy.

"We need to cool down and talk," he said, but his fingers kept running through her hair and guiding her kisses down his chest and toward his lower abdomen.

Groaning, she stopped tugging at his waistband and glowered at him. "The minute we leave this resort and return to real life, I'm getting a hold on myself and this offer is gone." When he tried to sit up, she pushed him back on the bed, straddled his lap and went back to kissing his neck.

Please stop tempting me. "We can't do this." In spite of his words, his fingers continued sliding under her top.

Gathering all his mental strength, he got up from the bed abruptly, making her roll and fall on the carpeted floor.

"Why are you torturing me like this?" Growling and groaning, she used the bed to help herself rise from the floor and stood in front of him, looking unsteady. "You won! Are you happy now? Your reverse psychology worked."

A chain of cusswords ran through Jay's mind. He ran his hands up his face, then raked them through his hair, leaving them there as he eased down to sit on the bedside. His voice was weak. "It's not reverse psychology."

"Here I am, humiliating myself, just like you wanted," she added. "Do you want me to fall on my knees and beg you to sleep with me? Is that it?"

A few weeks ago those words would've been a dream come true. *This has to be karma. I must be paying for every woman whose heart I unknowingly broke in my life.* "We can't sleep together."

"For goodness' sake, enough with your secret!" She placed her hands on his shoulders, glaring at him. "Answer me a question. This big secret you have, is it that you have another woman?"

Gracie's image entered his mind. "Not... really."

"Do you have another man?"

He whipped his head toward her. "What? No!"

"Do you have a contagious illness?"

He stared at her blankly. "Uh... no."

She threw her hands in the air. "Then I don't give a damn what your freaking secret is! And if *I* don't care, why would you?" She wrapped her arms around his neck. "Let's be together tonight, and then tomorrow it will be like nothing ever happened. You don't even have to call me again. There! That's the best offer a man will ever get in his life. Why can't you just take it?"

Jay had never faced stronger temptation. In the midst of the absurdity, her question made sense. The damage had been done the first night they were together. Did it make any difference if they'd slept together once or a hundred times?

And why couldn't he take her offer if they'd never see each other again after that?

The answer felt like the rumbling of thunder as it entered his awareness, and it sounded even stranger to his ears when it left his lips. "Because I care too much for you."

Color drained from her face. Slowly, she let go of him and stepped away.

He wasn't surprised by her shock; he had shocked himself. He now understood why he'd kept postponing confessing who he was; he was afraid of losing her a second sooner than he had to.

He lifted a hand. "Don't worry. I have no delusion of you being remotely in the same place. But you ask me why I can't take your offer, and this is why." Feeling numb as new epiphanies hit him, he studied her face as if seeing her for the first time. "Because if we slept together and then never saw each other again, I couldn't take it. Because I'm starting to fall in love with you."

She took a step back as if a gust of wind had hit her. "I… um… this is a…"

"Allison, I am—" Jay's phone ringing from the pocket of his pajama pants interrupted him and relief filled her face.

Determined to get through with his confession, he intended to shut off the phone when he realized it was Miranda calling. He also had a missed text reading only "Mayday." He picked up the upcoming call. "Hello?"

"Jay." Miranda's voice was strangely somber. Someone had just died or would be dying soon.

"What's going on?" Jay asked, dread sinking into the pit of his stomach.

"We need you to come right away. Hell finally broke loose."

Chapter 23

A LLISON WAS DISAPPOINTED, THOUGH NOT SURPRISED, when the closing ceremony was run by Calvin and Shania and not Jay. Citing a family emergency, Jay had dropped everything and driven somewhere. She assumed his infamous father must be on his deathbed.

The closing ceremony was effusive, as Allison was honored as the first woman to finish the Warriors Boot Camp. She felt vaguely guilty accepting the honor when she suspected that her one-on-one training with Jay had been much more pleasant than for the other participants.

It did surprise Allison when she showed up for the last roundtable with Carrie that evening and found out it was canceled. Jay had called the studio letting them know that by the time he returned and wrapped up with his crew, he'd barely finish on time to give Carrie the promised one-on-one interview.

"Jay and you have great chemistry on camera. I'll have a hard time deciding which scenes to air," Carrie commented after thanking Allison for her participation. "I wouldn't mind repeating the experience some time in the future."

Allison wasn't sure if that meant she'd be willing to have her on her show without Jay, but she took it as a good sign. "Absolutely! Any time."

Allison didn't feel like facing her lonely condo that night, considering the hotel room was paid until the next day for the roundtable.

She had dinner alone in a fusion restaurant near the studio she'd found on Trip Advisor. She wasn't impressed.

She was about to call an Uber to take her back to the resort when she decided to return to Carrie's studio and sit with the audience, listening to Jay's interview.

Carrie seemed hypnotized by Jay's charm just as his seminar attendees always were. But something was different about his usual magnetic energy. He looked tired, and she could sense the strain in his smile.

He had answered her questions about his trajectory and the basis of his work when the conversation shifted to responding to Karen's criticism.

"Karen Knight is officially filing a complaint requesting that we remove your 'sexist comments' from the show, which she claims are loaded with offensive insinuations. She maintains that the only reason you're famous is because of society's need for sex symbols. What would you respond to Karen?"

Jay sighed, his expression fatigued. "Karen, darling, I have to assume you're not very happy in the sex department right now. In my experience, sex is only a big deal when you're not having enough of it."

The audience laughed.

"Trust me," he continued. "Once you get past that little problem, it stops taking over every spare corner of your mind, and becomes a pleasant background music you can sometimes even forget is playing."

Amused, Carrie asked, "Well, Karen has called you 'the epitome of chauvinist promiscuity.' She claims that giving you attention perpetuates the myth of the man's physical superiority and that it's the duty of any feminist to boycott men like you."

Shoot. What would Karen say if she learned I've failed in that duty so miserably?

Jay's expression changed. For a moment, he seemed to let go of the nuclear energy he radiated on the stage. He seemed tired and vulnerable. "I have no reply for Karen, but a message for all women in the world."

He faced the cameras. "My female fellow human beings, relating to men is not a competition, it's *a game*. And it's supposed to be a friendly one we play for fun. Who cares if I win this hand, if you'll win the next one?"

Carrie clapped, encouraging the audience to join.

"I get tired of being seen as a sex symbol," he continued. "Do you think men don't crave routines and predictability sometimes? Do you think I'd be 'jumping from bed to bed' if I had another choice?" He looked past the cameras and made eye contact with Allison. "Don't you think I'd gladly leave behind a little of the 'surprise factor' in exchange for someone who knows me enough to have learned what I do and don't like in bed? Or someone I also enjoy conversing with? Someone I *care* for, and who cares for me?"

Allison felt a hand squeezing her heart. She wished so much she wasn't dead inside, so she could've answered yesterday with the truth. She did care for him—so much that she scared herself.

* * *

Allison lay in bed feeling tired, but unable to fall asleep. She was still trying to digest the events of the past day.

She wished Joy were there! She could use help putting some things into words so she could better understand herself.

She finally reached for her phone and composed a text to Jay. *"You must be exhausted and I understand if you need to rest. But if you still feel like chatting, I'm available now."*

She hit send, wondering if he'd even answer. A few moments later, the reply popped up.

"I'm scared of hearing what you have to say."

Just that I care about you too. Her fingers refused to type that

160

thought. She struggled for a long time and, instead, she typed, *"That I do want to see you again after we leave here."*

She hit send and for the longest time nothing happened.

Three dots appeared on her screen signaling he was typing a reply. The dots disappeared as if he were re-thinking his words. She held her breath with anticipation.

And then she heard a thud on the balcony, followed by the familiar sound of knocking on the French doors.

Her heart jumped, and she rushed to open the door. He stood there looking exhausted, his shirt untucked and half unbuttoned.

She opened her mouth to greet him, but had no chance to speak. He kissed her desperately, like a starving man finally finding sustenance. Her mind clouded and she kissed him too, ravenous. Her fingers gravitated to his muscular arms as his hands, now expert on her needs, wrapped around her, pulling her body against the hardness of his.

He walked her backward to the bed and by the time they made it there, his shirt and her pajama pants were gone.

And when her brain evaporated at his touch, and she could think of nothing but ending the torture of the minuscule space between them, he tormented her by separating his lips from hers. "I apologize for my sketchy manners. Hello," he said, breathless. "Was your text literal? Did you really mean you wanted to *chat*?"

Panting, she shook her head.

He closed his eyes for an instant and sighed. "Thank God."

Then he released the last button and proceeded to kiss every inch of her skin.

That night, Allison encountered a new universe. If their first night together had been rediscovering her libido, tonight was about something deeper. Every time they touched, her body sang, wanting to melt into his and become one with him. She longed to consume his solid, masculine body; soak up his amazing beauty; steal his DNA. She yearned to inhale his joy for life, to embrace his kindness, to absorb his soul.

Every caress was a vow of admiration. Every kiss was a fantasy of taking him in. Every slide of her hips aligning to receive him was a silent surrender.

I'm starting to fall in love with you.

His words should've pushed her to run away, but didn't. Just for a short time, she gave a corner of her brain permission to admit they echoed her own thoughts.

Chapter 24

BEING AN ETERNAL CHILD IS WONDERFUL.

Over the past week, Allison had to restrain herself from humming songs and dancing as she walked. Her senses were heightened, and the smallest things—from the scent of her shower gel to the taste of her breakfast omelet—filled her with delight. Even strangers around her noticed her good mood and gravitated to her energy. She was the most blissful she'd been in her life.

It was horrible.

This grin stuck on her face threatened her hard-earned reputation as a harsh, cold woman. And if she ever thought she was getting a hold on it, a new text message from Jay, joking against marriage, would make her crack up in the middle of a serious session and set her back again.

This perennially sunny mood handicapped her chances of meeting her deadline for her next book. She needed anger as her muse. How could she write about the history of men oppressing women when she so enjoyed being pressed under the weight of this particular man in bed? How did she complain about being under a man if she *loved* being under Jay. And over him. And beside him. And—

She desperately needed to reconnect with her contempt for men by dwelling on the most despicable ones she could think off. Jack The Ripper. Ted Bundy. Wayne Nash. Agent Richard Fields.

Still in an annoyingly good mood, she arrived at the office for her meeting with the Wetzels a week after the boot camp. During her time there, Tiffany had been admitted with a "nervous breakdown"—she suspected that was the family's code for a drug overdose.

"Dr. Connors!"

Conan Wetzel's eyes lit up when he greeted Allison. Tall, broad-shouldered, and with a full head of silver hair, he looked surprisingly youthful and handsome in his gold-buttoned navy sports jacket and khaki pants. The cane he used for walking support could've passed for a fashionable accessory. Next to him, the much younger-appearing Regina Wetzel shone in a yellow designer sundress and diamond earrings. Other than her blond hair, Regina didn't resemble Tiffany much. It probably had something to do with her cosmetic procedures giving her the generic feline face of a rich woman of indeterminate age.

As they made small talk and discussed updates on Tiffany's health, Allison observed them with compassion. Nobody would've imagined that such an elegant and poised couple had been in Allison's office more than once, shaken and rattled by the unpredictable drama in their daughter's life. Allison had often seen them exhausted, like the parents of a newborn baby that won't stop crying all night.

Except their baby was a twenty-eight-year-old woman.

"Your speech at the fundraiser last month was inspirational, as ever," Mr. Wetzel said. "The women's shelter is fortunate to have such a compassionate therapist as you among its volunteer staff."

Allison smiled. "That's nothing compared to your generous sponsorship."

She wasn't kidding. The Wetzel family's eyebrow-raising donations had single-handedly sustained the shelter during last year's hurricane. She'd never understood why such a wealthy man as Conan Wetzel had chosen to retire to the non-glamorous town of Fort Sunshine.

Regina Wetzel crossed a long leg and leaned forward, getting to the point. "Allison, first allow me to thank you. Our family will never be able to repay what you've done for our baby Tiff in the past five years. She told us about your offer to testify in court and help refute her brother's false accusations about her mental stability. That means a lot to us."

Allison froze. *What?* She didn't remember making such an offer. Tiffany must've assumed she had when she offered to do "anything she could."

"You may not know that ever since our baby Tiff's... nervous breakdown—" Regina cleared her throat. "—our granddaughter Gracie has been in the custody of her uncle. There was a... domestic disturbance between Tiff and our son-in-law."

"Oh no!" Allison pressed her hand to her chest. "Did he hurt Tiffany?"

Regina's gaze wandered around the office, avoiding hers. "Uh, not exactly. *She* hit *him*." She cleared her throat again. "—with a desktop computer. Anyway, the neighbors called the police, then Jacob showed up unannounced, waving his questionable legal guardianship papers, and somehow got a social worker to release the girl to him."

Allison tried to assimilate everything.

"Tiffany will be coming out of the psych hospital soon," Conan commented. "But in the meantime, we believe Gracie would be in better hands with us."

Regina intervened. "But fighting the legal guardianship documents in court would take too long. Our best hope to recover our granddaughter is if you help us clear up any doubts about Tiffany's mental—"

"Or if you help us open a family dialogue with Jacob," Conan Wetzel interrupted.

"I see." Allison rested her chin on her hand. "Have you tried talking to him—"

Regina's widening eyes and subtle headshake warned Allison to stop talking and she got the hint.

Conan's eyes seemed filled with regret. "I hoped you'd resume your original role as our family therapist and help mediate between

Jacob and us. Communication with him has always been difficult and… we need help."

His despair was so profound, Allison felt bad saying the next words. "Mr. Wetzel, I no longer work as a family therapist."

Regina appealed, "We understand your time is much more valuable now than before. And we know you can't collect compensation for the time you testify in court if that becomes necessary, but we really appreciate your commitment to our family and plan to reward you for it. After all this is settled, we'll make sure to put you in touch with people who can really launch your career as an author and professional speaker."

Allison was speechless. Conan Wetzel had been a top executive at Tribune Broadcasting in Chicago before he started his own marketing and communications company. Regina was a retired television actress with friends everywhere. No celebrity boot camp appearance or Carrie O'Brian show would get close to what their connections could do for her.

"Regina! You ruined the surprise. We were supposed to tell her *after* this was over," Conan reprimanded his wife.

Allison finally reacted. "Mrs. Wetzel, that's very generous but unnecessary. All I want is what's best for Gracie."

Regina reached across the desk to pat her hand. "But isn't it wonderful that you can do the right thing, and then, later on, receive a well-deserved reward for it?"

Allison tried to gather her racing thoughts. She was sure that accepting such a large "thank you" gift from the parents of a client had to violate some rule of ethics.

Didn't it?

Conan and Regina Wetzel shook her hand goodbye, but just as they walked to the door, Regina asked her husband to go ahead of her and stayed behind. He strolled away, supported by his cane.

Once alone in the office, Regina said, "Please forget everything he said about reconciling with Jacob. Our best hope is to have Tiffany's competence restored and have her change those guardianship documents immediately." The woman's blue eyes shone with suppressed tears. "Conan is in denial; my stepson will never agree to cooperate."

Allison gave a single nod.

Regina continued, "The last time Jacob and Conan were in the same room alone, things didn't go well. Their fight turned physical. And Jacob… Jake pushed his father, causing him to fall on the marble floor and injure his hip. Conan ended up in the hospital."

Allison was appalled. "God, that's terrible."

Regina lifted her palms in a powerless gesture. "Conan adores Jake, but we've got to admit that he needs help. We've urged him to seek counseling many times, but he doesn't stick to it."

"Has he ever had other violent moments like that?" Allison was now terrified about poor Gracie staying with that man.

"He's been involved in some brawls before—alcohol related. You see, he used to drink a lot in college. He claims that he has it under control now, but you know how those things are."

"Tiffany is under the impression that he's only interested in having Gracie so he can control her trust fund. Have you considered paying him off, coming to some form of financial agreement with him?"

Regina shrugged. "It would be like feeding a black hole. Jake has no job security, he's… 'self-employed,'" she used air quotes, "in some unpredictable online business. I try to keep Conan isolated from anything related to Jake, so we don't know much about his daily whereabouts, but per my understanding, he's always on the brink of bankruptcy. I'm afraid that if we paid him off now, it would be a matter of time until he's back asking for more money."

As Regina exited the office, Allison searched her memory, trying to recall Jacob Wetzel's image from the one time they'd shaken hands in that failed attempt at family therapy. The guy must've been non-memorable, since she couldn't picture him at all.

She made a note to call Mercy, her lawyer and friend, and ask to meet with Gracie to see how she was doing. *Maybe if I can save*

Gracie from this unstable uncle I can finally finish what I started in this career.

* * *

Being a grown-up is not that bad!

"You can do it! Run! We're almost there! I can see the bus!"

A pink backpack on his back and little Gracie by his hand, Jay jogged on the way to the school bus pickup spot. In spite of her significantly shorter legs, she did a good job keeping up.

With the morning wind blowing against his face, he felt ecstatic. If every time he ran he felt like an eight-year-old, today he had his favorite eight-year-old girl in the world by his hand; not only that, he also had the hope of seeing his favorite grown-up girl by the end of the week. Just thinking about Allison made him want to do cartwheels.

Over the past two weeks, Jay had made breakfast and filled lunchboxes, brushed knotted hair, wiped runny noses and taken Gracie to and from the closest school bus stop—quite a distance away until next year, when he could move her to his school district. He didn't know much yet about being a parent, but he did know about being a kid. What he lacked in nail polish application skills, he compensated for with dress-up games. He might not be the best at baking cookies and pies, but he did know how to teach his girl to bake healthy muffins and steam the perfect green beans.

They arrived at the stop where a line of kids boarded the bus. He barely noticed the women accompanying the kids, coughing, giggling, and whispering while perusing his muscular arms, exposed by the sleeveless gym shirt.

Panting, Gracie accepted the backpack from him. "If Ethan's house is not on the bus route, why can't you just drive me to school like normal adults do?"

"Apparently my two-seater Jeep is not suitable for the job.

Someone made a ridiculous law that eight-year-old girls are not allowed in the front seat." As he helped her put on the backpack, he rolled his eyes. "Neurotic precautions. I was planning to stick some handles on the roof of the car and have you ride there."

She shot him a reprimanding glare. "Be serious, Uncle Jake." She finished adjusting the length on her backpack straps and added, "Now, don't you forget that it's Wednesday."

"I know." He looked heavenward. "It's early dismissal and Miranda's new day off. I have nothing booked but you." He touched her nose. "I would never miss our Wednesdays of fun."

Her lips twitched with a smile and she pulled his hand to make him lean down for a hug and a kiss before running to board the bus.

Ignoring the ogling of the women at the stop, Jay jogged back to Ethan's house, anticipating tomorrow with delight. Miranda's workday now started at 5:00 pm, and extended overnight and most weekend days, allowing him to tend to his out-of-home work—private personal training sessions and evening lectures—and to allow him to visit Allison.

He was so thankful for Thursdays and weekends with Allison, when he collected the reward for his hard workweek. Between beach walks, lovemaking marathons and afterglow conversation, the days were a string of bliss. He spent the week planning ahead for the surprises he wanted to bring to her. This week, as they decorated Gracie's room with Christmas lights in May, he'd gotten a set for his hotel room, to surprise Allison.

He found Ethan in the kitchen and could hardly restrain himself from grinning as he waved hello.

"How can you be in such a good mood if you never sleep?" asked Ethan, extending him a cup of black coffee.

Jay accepted the mug. "I slept *four* whole hours last night; that's a personal record! I have so much energy the gym machines stand no chance with me today." He took a sip of coffee and dropped onto one of the barstools at the white granite breakfast bar.

"No wonder you're sleeping better. Adding childcare and the legal mess around your niece on top of your workday must be exhausting."

Jay took a long sip, his eyes lost on the boxes on the living room floor he still had to find a place for after giving the extra room to Gracie and Miranda. "Or maybe my subconscious can now let go and relax better, because I've found what I've been searching for all my life."

"Are you still talking about your childhood girlfriend obsession? I thought you'd decided Allison wasn't her." As Ethan served himself more coffee, Jay became aware of the thickening fuzz of baby hair dusting his head.

Jay walked to the sealed box he'd rescued from his grandmother's attic, still holding memories from that first girlfriend. "Honestly, I no longer feel the need to confirm that Allison is Grace," Jay admitted. "I'm happy *now*."

Ethan raised his growing eyebrows. "As much as I'm rooting for you and believe life's too short not to pursue happiness—how can you be happy in a relationship that's doomed to blow up any minute?"

With a grunt, Jay returned to his stool. "Can you just let me enjoy this and not make a big deal?"

"Of course this is a big deal!" Ethan tilted his head and gave Jay a once-over. "I've always celebrated your refusal to grow up, take life seriously and behave responsibly. But it stops being funny the moment you can hurt someone else. This woman could have her professional license challenged, for getting involved with a former patient."

"I only went to her office once!" Jay groaned. "I didn't even open my mouth, And Shawn is wrong; I didn't sign that consent. *Jacob Wetzel* did; I'm not that man anymore."

"Your last name may have changed, but your social security number is the same. Don't try to dodge this."

Jay twisted in his seat and jiggled a foot. "I have a plan. Allison wants to quit her job as a therapist and transition to full-time author and professional speaker. If I can help speed up that process, then she won't need a counseling license anymore—she can decide to give it up voluntarily. I mean, assuming she still wants me after learning everything."

Ethan pierced him with his deep blue eyes. "Jay, what if she's accused of a serious ethical infraction? Her credibility will be permanently damaged."

Jay swallowed hard. Relying on his great luck, he'd taken huge risks in his life and always won. But this was the first time the stakes were so high and involved someone else. "Dr. H. said it's not Allison's fault if she doesn't know it. I just need to have a solid plan before telling her. And also make sure she's so hooked on me that she's willing to fight for our future." He ran his fingers through his hair with a sigh. "Anyway. I'd better get ready for the gym."

"Wait, my chemo brain makes me slow, not stupid." Ethan raised a hand with a shocked expression. "Fight for *your future*? Jay, did you just suggest you see yourself in a relationship with Allison for the long-term? I mean like… marriage?"

Jay stopped the coffee mug halfway to his lips. He considered it. "Of course not! Are you crazy?" He put the cup down. "Allison and I despise marriage."

Ethan snickered. "You hesitated."

"What?" Jay stared at him, confused.

"When I asked you if you were considering marriage or a long-term relationship you didn't deny it immediately."

He stopped to retrace his own words.

"There it is again, the hesitation," Ethan pointed out.

Jay ran a trembling hand through his hair. "You're making no sense." He pushed Ethan's shoulder and returned his attention to his coffee, ignoring the pounding of his heart.

Chapter 25

*B*EING A GROWN-UP SUCKS.

Jay was now officially the man with freaking health insurance—he needed a policy to which he could eventually add Gracie. He was also the new owner of a car with a second row of seats—a Honda Crossover SUV. And he was officially searching for a place of his own where he could accommodate Gracie and Miranda without having to invade so much of Ethan's space.

But now the worst possible part about being a grown-up had arrived: meetings with lawyers.

The big items had taken so much of his time that he'd failed to care for the small details and was now paying for it. This morning, Thursday, his stepmother had shown up at Gracie's school long before dismissal time, waving some paperwork, and had taken his girl with her.

He now sat in a mediation meeting with his and Tiffany's lawyer at a neutral location. He felt like chewing someone's head off but was trying to stick to what his counsel advised and instead act confident in his legal rights.

Pulling out some of the anger-management strategies he'd learned over the years, Jay summoned his child-like brain to imagine people in the room as cartoon characters. His own lawyer, Lewis Wall, had white hair and a matching thick, bushy mustache. Jay fantasized about using Easter egg coloring to dye them some pastel color while he slept. Next to him, wide-shouldered Ken Carter, Tiffany's lawyer, had no facial hair but wore a blond pompadour that Jay enlarged in his imagination to envision him as a suit-clad Johnny Bravo.

After handshakes and pleasantries, the mediator Mercy Kind—a young red-haired lawyer sporting the haircut of a teenage surfer and the suit of a ninety-year-old man—invited them to take a seat in a small, all-brown conference room.

Jay opened the conversation. "Regina had no right to take Gracie to her house and she knows it. *I* am her legal guardian. Before his death, my former brother-in-law Tim Donovan appointed me in his will in the event that neither he nor Tiffany could take care of her." He laid a copy of the documents on the table.

Ken Carter rubbed his prominent, dimpled jaw. "Mr. Johnson, I'm sorry to inform you that yesterday my client signed standby guardianship documents assigning her parents as temporary guardians of her daughter." He laid another document on the table.

Tensing up, Jay looked at his lawyer, who took over. "And since she's not competent to make decisions, my argument will be that such documents have no legal weight. We're reclaiming my client's guardianship rights. Then, we're ready to file for termination of parental rights, proving that Tiffany Wetzel-Blanche is not mentally fit to be a reliable mother."

Ken turned to Jay. "If I were you, I'd let the grandparents keep her and just work out some visitation rights."

"If I let Conan and Regina take Gracie, I'll never see her again." He glared at Carter.

"If we go to court, the judges will likely rule that the grandparents are better candidates for guardianship. You're already questionable for the task, given your history." Ken opened a folder and lifted one eyebrow. "So, I see you were sentenced to court-mandated therapy for attacking your father?"

Jay cursed the moment he'd let his hot temper get the best of him. "I gave him *one* push."

"One push that made him fall and mess up his hip."

"His hip was messed up long before that. And he pushed me first. He was harassing *me*."

"Because you vandalized his car."

Jay groaned. "It was a stupid prank."

"Well, imagine how that's going to look in the eyes of—"

"We're not here to dissect my client's history," Jay's lawyer interrupted. "But I assure you that if we had to compare his record against Mrs. Wetzel-Blanche's he'd look like a saint."

Raising a hand, the mediation lawyer intervened in her heavy Southern accent. "Let's not lose sight of what this meeting is about. We're here to explore mediation." She opened her own set of folders. "Mr. Conan Wetzel wants to open a dialogue between his two children and avoid court."

"Oh, please!" Jay groaned. "He's bulldozing his way to what he wants as usual. He took Gracie away without my permission!"

Ignoring his words, the lawyer continued, "He's willing to pay for the totality of my mediator fees, and he's requesting the intervention of the Wetzel's former family therapist, Dr. Allison Connors—"

Jay's stomach dropped to the floor. A cold sweat misting his forehead, he felt the urge to ride his bike at full speed until he made it to Patagonia.

"No!" He interrupted. "I will not take part in that."

"Why not?" Attorney Kind asked. "Why engage in a legal battle that may take years and risk the court making an arbitrary decision regarding the girl's guardianship?"

His pulse racing, Jay searched his mind for an answer. He couldn't confess that he was opposed to Allison specifically as a family counselor. "Because that would be pointless. The damage done to my relationship with this family is beyond repair." He cleared his throat. "And let's cut through the bullshit here. Tiffany doesn't really care if I have guardianship. All she wants is to make sure she controls the Donovan family's trust money. I'm willing to forgo that part and any child support from her. That's my offer. Now get me an answer and let's move on." He rose from the table to signal the meeting was over.

As he walked to the parking lot, Carter caught up with him. "Mr. Johnson. Mr. Johnson!"

Jay turned around and found him extending his hand.

"I just needed to tell you that I'm a big fan." Ken beamed. "Your abs workout has become my daily religious ritual." Proudly, he punched his own flat abdomen with his free fist, as he shook Jay's hand.

"Well, thank you."

Ken walked with him on the way to his car. "I have the feeling this attempt at mediation will lead nowhere and we'll be on opposite sides of the battle, ready to rip out each other's throat—but I hope you understand it won't be personal."

Jay bowed his head. "I understand."

Ken stopped walking and placed a hand on Jay's shoulder, making him stop too. "And a fair warning. Just like I know you'll be doing everything in your power to assassinate my client's character, I will be leaving no stone unturned to do the same for you. Leave it to us to find every dirty secret you ever hid and bring it to light in front of the judge."

Jay shot him a cold glare. "That's not what I want. Yes, Tiffany has enough skeletons in her closet that I know we'll find plenty of material to show to a judge. But I really hope we can fix things through mediation, without hurting her."

Carter crowed and patted Jay's shoulder. "You have scruples; that's *cute*. Lucky for my client, I don't."

The attorney's cell rang and he took the call without excusing himself. "Hey, Emery, did you get my flowers?" The smile fell off his face. "W-wait. B-babe, wait. You want me to stick them where?" Without saying goodbye, he walked away.

Jay strolled to his car dwelling on his thoughts. *Why did you have to be our so-called family therapist, Allison? If I had one shred of common sense left, I'd stay away from you.*

* * *

Allison was used to the routine now and wasn't surprised when Jay's constant flow of emails and text messages got interrupted on Wednesday. She did find it intriguing when she didn't hear from him by Thursday afternoon, but she dismissed it, making herself a note to text him by the end of the day.

She tried not to let the Wetzel case ruin her recently great mood as she met her girlfriends for dinner. It seemed like an eternity since she'd returned from the boot camp, but amazingly, it had been just over two weeks. She'd been surprised to find out not much had changed back home. They'd never figured out who had sent Emery the anonymous text with the pictures of Ken with the stripper, and the friends were still tiptoeing around her as if she were a psychiatric patient recovering from a violent psychotic breakdown. It was a se-cret relief that "The MDiva"—a nickname of Emery's that suited her quite well—was on call that night and couldn't join them for dinner at their favorite Thai restaurant.

"What's up with you lately, Allison?" Fe asked as she dipped a bite of sushi roll in eel sauce. "Right now Emery needs someone to support her through the 'all men in the world suck' phase. But right when we need you to be your usual man-hating self, you suddenly decided to like men?"

"Who says I like men?"

"No, she likes one particular man," Hope chimed in with a smirk. "The Titanic broke the iceberg—and then sank in it."

Fe frowned. "It makes me nervous that you're dating one of my husband's best friends."

"Oh, we're not dating!" Allison spun her steamed vegetables, let-ting them cool down. "We're just… hooking up from time to time. Like I said in chapter seven of my third book: A powerful woman knows how to treat herself to candy now and then."

"Didn't you just go through candy detox?" asked Joy, distracted, trying to maneuver chopsticks to grab her noodles—and failing miserably at the task, dropping them on her dress.

"It's a metaphor," Allison explained, handing Joy a napkin. "*Candy* may be sending yourself flowers, instead of waiting for a man to send them; or buying yourself a new pair of stunning shoes." She rested the fork down and added, "Or treating yourself to a hot man with no expectations of a future." She returned her attention to her food. "I have no delusion that this man will ever grow up, take off his gym clothes, put on a… *tuxedo*, or whatever, and kneel in front of me, giving me a 'happily ever after.' So don't worry about me being disappointed when it all ends."

"I *am* worried," Fe insisted. "Shawn has been acting weird every time I mention you and Jay. He gave me a long speech asking me to forgive him because he can't betray his friend's trust by talking to me about 'anything he might know.'"

Allison felt like someone had slapped her, and the image of the tire hanging from the oak tree flashed in her mind. *I knew I should never lower my guard with a man.* "What do you think Shawn's talking about?"

"He won't budge. I wonder if in medical school they beat the crap out of them to teach them secrecy. But if I had to guess, I'd go for Jay having another woman."

Allison felt a wave of hot nausea. "I asked him; he said no."

"But don't cheaters always deny it?" Fe's expression was more puzzled than cynical. "I mean, my three Latin-lover-wannabe brothers can't keep their pants on to save their lives. And they can beat a lie detector when they're bullshitting their women." She made a low-pitched voice. "'Oh no, I'm not seeing someone else right at this moment'—Meaning they slept with someone else at 'another moment' an hour ago."

Allison recalled Jay's answer the day she'd asked if he had another woman. "*Not… really.*"

Fe had a point. "What do you know about that 'friend' he used to see on Wednesdays?" *Or still sees?* "What else have you heard him talking to Shawn about?"

"I overheard once that Jay had some old girlfriend he's been obsessed with. He even followed her all around the city in a taxi once."

"Like stalking her?" Hope dropped her chopsticks and leaned forward.

Fe nodded. "And according to Shawn, Jay forgets about her for a little while to pursue other women, but then returns to his obsession with her."

Allison remembered Jay's words. "*It's something that makes me think I could hurt you.*" She felt quite sure that Jay wouldn't lie about sleeping with someone else, but was it possible he had a platonic relationship with another woman, bordering on emotional infidelity? Was Allison just a placeholder, a distraction, until the woman he really wanted decided to accept him?

That would explain his hesitation. No, there's no other woman— at the moment. But there's the shadow of one. *And the impending threat that he will choose her over me any minute.*

It hurt. Having his body should've been enough. But now she had this unreasonable need to also have the totality of his heart and mind.

And now I'm turning into a freaking romantic.

"You know what, girls? This is irrelevant. I'm seriously just giving myself permission to indulge in a fling," she said, more for herself than her friends. "This man and I have nothing in common, and I feel nothing for him but physical attraction." She was the most surprised to realize it was a blatant lie.

She quickly thought of an argument to save face with herself. "I'm telling you, if I learned today that I'd never see him again, I'd be perfectly fine."

Her phone vibrated announcing a text. She threw a quick glance at it and her heart dropped. All the blood drained from her face and she felt faint.

The partial text displayed read, *"This is a friend of Jay's. I'm using his phone to notify all his contacts that he just died."*

Allison's body trembled uncontrollably. With quivering hands, she unlocked her phone.

It was another joke from Jay. He'd taken a picture of a sign at the Orlando convention center announcing. "Wedding Vendors Forum: The Largest Annual Fair of Bridal Services."

The caption under the picture read, *"Jay ran into this and had a massive stroke. He died instantly. He will be missed."*

She pressed a hand to her chest, feeling life return to her body. *Jay and his weird sense of humor.*

She typed back. *"Oh well, I guess it was fast and painless. Let's hope his ghost doesn't come back to haunt us."*

The answer came nearly instantly. *"Care to go out with a ghost tonight?"*

Wanting to make him beg a little, she typed. *"I'm not sure. I've heard when you try to touch a ghost your hand goes through him. I prefer dates I can touch."*

The answer took longer than before. Next to her, Hope cleared her throat. Without deviating her eyes from her phone screen she lifted a finger, asking for a minute.

The answer arrived in the form of a picture. Jay had taken a selfie in the bathroom mirror, wearing only his briefs. The caption underneath read, *"Does this look good enough to touch?"*

Allison choked on her own breath and coughed. "I'm sorry, girls. There has been an unexpected emergency. I'm going to bail on our dinner."

Without waiting for a response, she dropped some bills at the table, left her dinner behind, and ran out of the restaurant to her car.

Chapter 26

ALLISON LAY ON THE HOTEL BED, TWISTED IN THE BLANKETS and interwoven with Jay's limbs. Her brain and her body floated in bliss.

The evening had been a dreamy string of sensuality and amusement. Whether Jay was daring her to swim in the ocean or suck on a lime wedge with a straight face—a guaranteed way to split their sides, staring at each other's grimaces—she'd never met someone who got such joy out of the smallest things.

She still couldn't understand how he could make her feel like a five-year-old one moment, then like a lustful woman a minute later.

After kissing her head, he turned her around to rub her shoulders and commented, "I needed this night so much. Only you can make me feel this good after the horrible day I had."

"What happened?"

"It's not worth ruining this moment talking about it."

If he really felt down today, he knew how to hide it. She moaned, enjoying the caress of those large hands—had she ever said she didn't like touch?

And did she ever call men "hairy, smelly creatures, slaves of their testosterone?" she asked herself as she started to doze off. *Thank God* for testosterone, which gave this wonderful male specimen those strong muscles and his raging libido.

Who was this woman, betraying feminism, submitting to a man as his toy?

The thought made her jerk awake. "I better get going."

She wiggled, trying to leave the bed, but Jay's arms held her in place. "Why are you always in such a hurry to leave?"

She forced a chuckle. "Well, real life goes on."

Feeling a sudden urge to run away, she slid out of his arms and sat on the edge of the bed to get dressed.

"Will you come back tomorrow and stay the weekend?" he asked. "Some… project got canceled and I'm going to have plenty of free time."

One of her self-imposed rules was not to see him more than two days in a row. Tense, she buttoned her wrinkled-beyond-repair shirt. "I can't. I… have plans."

He was silent for a moment as she picked up her light blue jacket and put it back on. "Oh. Too bad, this may be my last weekend here for a while."

"How come?" Surprised, she turned around to face him.

Running a hand through his disheveled dark hair, he half-shrugged. "The following weekend I'm speaking in Atlanta. And from there I'm supposed to travel to LA to meet Matt."

"You mean your friend the Hollywood actor?"

"He got me an invitation for some movie premiere and af-ter-party in LA to get me networking with Hollywood people. There's a red carpet and everything." With an annoyed eye roll, he groaned.

Interested, she leaned forward in bed, propped on her elbow to face him. "That sounds like a great opportunity!"

"Nope. It sounds like torture. Why would I want to rub elbows with a bunch of megalomaniac actors and anorexic actresses? Plus, listen to this! I'd have to wear *a black tie*." He fake-gagged. "Talk about funerals! As if a regular tie wasn't horrendous enough!"

She giggled and his face lit up. He ran his thumb alongside her face. "You have such a beautiful laugh. I was bending over backward the first day we met, trying to get it out of you. It was all worth it." He gave her a small kiss on the lips.

Damn it. She had to admit she'd miss him terribly if his deal with Matthew Hester went through and he moved to LA.

But it didn't matter. She'd kick herself later, but she couldn't let him pass up the chance of a lifetime. "Jay, you have to listen to your friend's proposal."

"No, I don't." His face fell and he dropped himself back onto the pillow. "Matt doesn't understand that in this project he's just risking money; I'm risking my lifestyle and my peace of mind."

She touched his strong arm. "At least go to the party. Maybe you'll like the Hollywood people more than you think."

Frowning, he considered it for a moment, then blurted out, "Would you come with me?"

The unexpected invitation stunned her speechless.

Looking away, he continued with a forced casual tone. "Matt is offering to cover the travel and hotel expenses for five days. I'm sure I can get him to pay for your plane ticket too."

It took her a while to digest the tempting offer. The prospect of spending five days with him twenty-four seven was scary beyond her initial doubts about his sanity.

She soon found a logical answer hard to refute. "I'm honored, but I can't. I'm making a name teaching women to be happy without a man. I can't risk being photographed in public holding hands with a semi-celebrity like you."

His face went blank. "Oh. Okay." He pondered for a moment. "I guess that answers it for me. I'm not going."

She felt both disappointed and strangely relieved. It was a pity that he'd pass on that opportunity—yet she wasn't ready to see him move to the West Coast.

As he slid away from her, she noticed his tension. His good mood had evaporated and his voice was dry. "Didn't you say you had to leave?"

He sat on the edge of the bed and reached for his clothes to get dressed. Allison eyed him, faintly raising one eyebrow. "Excuse me, did I miss something? Are you angry with *me* now?"

He didn't answer, busy retrieving his pants from the floor.

"Something obviously bothered you," she insisted in a calm voice. "You'd better tell me, instead of sulking like a three-year-old. I don't take the silent treatment from anybody."

He whipped his head toward her. "You want me to talk? Fine, I'll talk. First, you refused to spend the weekend, then you rejected my offer to come to LA with me." He zipped up his pants.

She slowly rose from the bed and crossed her arms. "Are you making this into a male ego thing?"

"This isn't about *my* ego." He snatched his shirt from the floor.

"And what *is* this about, according to you?" she asked dryly.

As he shoved his arms into his white button-down shirt, his voice rose. "You'd rather die than accept you want to spend time with me. Everything you do is about proving you don't need anybody— making a point that *you* are in control."

She felt as if his words slapped her.

But he had a point.

"Are you pulling a life coach move on me? Because I don't need this crap." Furious, she grabbed her purse and stilettos from the floor and headed for the door barefoot. She wanted out of there as soon as possible.

Before she made it to the door, he intercepted her. "I'm sorry. I didn't mean to raise my voice; I had a hard day. Please don't go."

She felt the sting of tears she couldn't comprehend. "I don't play these type of games."

"I'm sorry," he repeated, taking her in his arms. His voice sounded weaker than usual.

This caring about someone sucks. She felt the unreasonable urge to push him and run away, crying. She felt there was nothing he could say that would make her want to stay.

"Please have patience with me. You were good at diagnosing me with anger problems and unresolved father issues the first time we met," he muttered. "In case you missed this part, I have abandonment issues too."

His words stabbed her, and if he hadn't been holding her, she'd have taken a step back.

He continued, stroking her spine. "And I'm still sensitive when I think someone is ashamed of me—like my father was back then."

She could only imagine how difficult it must've been for him to know his father hid him from the world the first eight years of his life. Raising her arms to embrace him, she murmured, "I'm sorry too. I do want to spend the weekend with you. If I said no, it's because I'm scared."

Slowly, he walked her back to bed, sat her on his lap and cradled her in his arms. She couldn't explain why, but Jay cradling her made her want to cry even more.

"What are you scared of?" he asked.

Scared of how much I'm enjoying these visits. Scared of getting used to this. Scared of what will happen when your career skyrockets and mine stays behind and I never see you again.

"Of everything."

She reached for her silver-gowned Barbie, sitting on the nightstand next to his Hulk action figure. "Do you remember the day I got this doll? It made me think about the way I approach life: my career change, getting close to people, taking risks." She got up off his lap and sat on the chair near the bed. Holding the Barbie in one hand, she used the other hand to touch its hair. "While unboxing her, I realized *I was her*. I've been trying to keep myself in 'mint condition,' like a collectible item. I'm afraid that if I get out of my box, I'll get dirty, and scuffed, like the dolls that are played with. And so, I've been living my life inside it, watching the world through the plastic window but not engaging with it."

He reached for her hand and caressed it with his thumb. "But you can take yourself out of the box any moment you want. You just have to decide it."

She gave a mirthless chuckle. "It's not that easy. Fear is paralyzing."

"Take my word for it, fear is *self-limiting.*" He tightened his grip on her hand. "It's worse right before taking the step. And the longer you postpone it, the worse it is."

She rolled her eyes. "Says the man who's done everything twice—bungee jumping, skydiving, shark cage diving—and is not afraid of anything."

"Oh, I *am* scared of something," he refuted. "I have a recurring nightmare that leaves me terrified." He scanned the room as if making sure they were alone and whispered, "I dream that I wake up with a wedding ring on my finger."

She appreciated his attempt to lighten the mood. "I have that recurring nightmare too," she teased. "And when I wake up, I scratch myself until I bleed and then throw up."

He tugged on her hand and guided her to sit on the bed, next to him. "But you know what? Once you take the risk—once you jump out of the plane, or rappel down the rocky wall—it's exhilarating. You realize you've been worrying over nothing. And nothing in the world compares to that thrill."

"Really?" She slanted him a look. "So, if you are so fearless, how come you're still refusing to go to LA?"

His hand, running through her hair, halted. "That has nothing to do with fear."

"Oh yes, it does," she contradicted. "You're afraid of success getting out of control. You'll be so famous people will recognize you on the streets. You'll have to wear a jacket and a tie more often. You are scared of having to grow up."

"Stop it!" He shifted, clearly uncomfortable, then rose from the bed and dropped on the carpeted floor to do sit-ups.

"Didn't you say at that roundtable that you know your career has an expiration date?" She slid over to get closer to him. "What are you going to do when you can't make a living out of showing your muscles anymore?"

"I'll figure it out," he said without stopping his exercise. "If I want to be poor, free, and happy instead of rich, enslaved, and stressed out, it's my choice!"

She placed a hand on his chest to make him stop the sit-ups. "But don't you realize that having job security and money is part of being stress-free? Don't you have any dreams and goals that cost money? Anybody in your life you'd like to be able to help financially?"

He remained silent for a few moments. Then, he sat up on the carpet and answered. "Yes."

"See? Go, and at least listen with an open mind to what your friend has to say."

He closed his eyes and whipped his head. "Damn it! You're good!"

With a gasp, she clasped her hands together. "Wait, did I just convince you? Are you doing it?"

With his eyes still closed, he nodded.

Not even the Botox could conceal Allison's excitement as she clapped and cheered.

"Not so fast!" He opened his eyes and lifted a hand. "There's a catch!"

She gave a half-smile. "There's always a catch."

"Well, this is *my* catch," he replied. "You say that I have to go to LA to overcome my fears. I'll only do it if you do something you're scared of, in exchange."

She eyed him with caution, hoping he wasn't talking again about blindfolding her in bed to enhance her other senses. "What did you have in mind?"

He shrugged. "Skydiving? Hand gliding? Grade-four whitewater rafting? The point is that if I do something that I find terrifying, you do something you find terrifying."

She was touched. This could be a life changer for him. "Yes! I'm willing to take a risk, as long as you take it with me. That's my catch.

If I'm going to jump out of a plane, you're jumping too."

He beamed as he extended his hand. "Deal!" They shook hands, then he said, "And I already know what your risk will be."

She stiffened her spine in preparation. "Okay, I'm ready. What is it?"

He made her wait for the answer much too long.

"You're coming with me to the red carpet event."

Her jaw dropped. *Shoot.* She should've seen that coming.

Chapter 27

I T HAD BEEN A WEEK SINCE GRACIE LEFT AND THE HOUSE FELT too quiet without her. It was a relief for Jay that Conan and Regina hadn't tried to stop her from communicating with him. They'd FaceTimed every day, and besides complaining about the loss of their Wednesdays together, she seemed happy with the novelty of staying in a house with a pool. That morning, before she left for school, she'd shared excitedly how Miranda was dropping her off at some new friend's house for a playdate that afternoon.

Sitting in front of his laptop, Ethan growled. "I can't even type on the damn keyboard since I got this neuropathy. How am I going to find a freaking job if I can't use my tools anymore because my hands are numb?"

Jay wished he could help his friend. In debt from all his medical bills and unable to return to his previous job in home remodeling, Ethan faced an uncertain financial future. Allison had a point when she said that it might be worth losing some freedom on behalf of a cause that required money. Helping Ethan was one such cause. Affording the astronomical legal fees he knew were coming from fighting for Gracie was another.

Luckily, Ethan didn't let anything upset him for long. He turned to Jay, commenting in a casual tone, "Hey, what are you after, bringing Allison to LA and to a televised event? Someone's going to recognize you and tell Allison that Jay Johnson and Jacob Wetzel are one and the same." He closed the laptop, his trace of re-growing eyebrows knit together. "Don't risk someone else telling her. If you want a minimal chance that she won't kill you, you have to tell her yourself."

Jay shifted on his kitchen stool. "But if I want to have the most minimal chance of her staying with me, I need something to offer her in exchange for her career as a therapist."

Ethan eyed him, interested. "What do you mean?"

"This trip is as much about her career as it is about mine," Jay explained. "Matt and I sent Allison's last book and videos from the roundtable to a few of his Hollywood friends who will be at that red-carpet event. When they witness Allison's beauty and dry sense of humor, I know they'll see that she has the potential to become the next celebrity doctor for the heart. If she no longer needs to practice as a therapist, she wouldn't need her license. She can decide to surrender it voluntarily, discreetly."

"Wow!" Ethan rested his jaw on his knuckles. "You seem to have a clear plan, for a change."

Jay tapped his fingers on the granite counter. "I need to fix this soon. The special from Carrie's show releases the week after. If someone tells my family they saw us there, the truth will come out. So I'm planning to come clean to Allison during the trip. Then, I'm willing to confess publicly that she didn't know who I was and I tricked her."

"Shoot. There's too much that can go wrong with that plan."

Tell me about it. Another time of his life, Jay would've fully trusted in his good luck. This was the first time he wondered where the border between "daring" and "reckless" lay.

"When are you planning to tell her?" Ethan asked.

"On the flight home from this trip."

Snickering, Ethan slapped his own knee. "You're smart. When she's stuck with you in a plane for hours and can't run away. And when she's feeling indebted for what you did for her career."

And also after I had a few days with her, enjoying her to the max. In case the plan doesn't work, and she does end up dumping me. "I plan to savor this trip like you always tell me to do. As if I only had a few days to live."

As Jay walked to the living room to start moving the boxes back to Gracie's old room, his phone rang. He grimaced when he saw it was Ken Carter, but still picked up. "Hello?"

Amused chuckles sounded on the line. "I know what you're doing, son of a bitch. You're dating Allison Connors!"

Shit. How did he *find out?* Before he could react, Ken laughed. "You have my respect! Now *that* is playing low. You found the only person who could testify that your sister is not crazy and you're going to force her to recuse herself from the case because of personal involvement with the opposite party." He snickered. "And I almost bought your story that you had scruples. Way to go, evil genius!" His voice changed to a business-like tone. "Now seriously, you give me no choice but to play dirty. Brace yourself for what's coming next."

Jay's phone rang on the other line with a call from Shawn. "I don't have time for this, Carter. I have to go." He disconnected the call and took Shawn's. His brain was still boiling from the bomb Ken had just dropped on him.

"Hello?"

Shawn's worried voice sounded on the other side of the call. "Hey, man. I'm not sure if this is good or bad, but you better know it. Did you hear our girls have a playdate today?"

"You mean Gracie and Gabriela?" Jay walked away from the boxes and to the back porch, seeking better cell signal. Still organizing his thoughts, he leaned over the railing and took in the lake view. "Gracie mentioned she was meeting a couple of girls today after school and was quite excited. Did Fe organize it?"

"No. That's the problem. *Allison* did for some reason."

Jay froze, and his fingers clasped the phone. "What?"

"I know. When Fe mentioned it, I almost fell on my face. I was hoping that meant you finally came clear and we're no longer hiding Gracie is your niece?"

A chill went through Jay. Gracie always carried her iPad with her. She was constantly showing people pictures of him. "Uh... not yet. Is Allison there too?"

"I don't know for sure. I'm at work."

Jay's pulse sped up faster than in any of his most strenuous workouts. "Sorry, man. I have to go." He disconnected the call and took off, running.

Ignoring Ethan's questions, he sprinted across the house and front yard and rushed to his car, while searching for Fe's number in his phone. He needed to stop Gracie from talking about him or showing her friends his photos. And he needed to find a way to create a distraction until he got Miranda to pick her up—if Miranda wasn't available, he might need to go get her himself.

After a few rings, Fe answered as he was pulling out of the driveway. He skipped the greetings. "Fe! Are you home?"

"Hi, Jay! I'm just coming home from work and parking in the garage, why?"

"I heard Allison is there with my niece."

"Oh! Is that the same Gracie? I thought the name was just a—"

"Why is Allison there?" he interrupted.

Fe's slow speech showed her surprise about his abrupt questions. "I don't know. It's something related to Allison's work." She tittered. "Now, that's funny! Allison used to criticize me for getting personal with my speech therapy clients, and here she is—"

"Sorry, Fe!" he interrupted again. "I don't have time to explain it. It's an emergency! I need you to hide Gracie's iPad."

* * *

Allison hadn't forgotten Gracie's comment about longing to go on play dates, so she was satisfied with the play date/therapy session she'd designed. With the help of Hope's stepdaughter Liz and Fe's daughter Gabriela, she'd warmed up Gracie to playing with dolls. Through doll role-playing, Allison hoped to get a sense of the girl's family situation. Eventually, she'd have her use dolls to represent her mother, stepfather, and uncle.

The girl was so immersed in the game she had stopped fretting about her missing iPad. Allison observed in silence, noting how much drama seemed to be going on in the world of Gracie's doll.

"Look at what you did to me! You spilled juice on my new dress!" Gracie's doll yelled at Liz's dolls while stumping her little plastic feet on the floor. "I'm calling my lawyer! And my therapist!"

"D-dat's n-not p-polite!" Gabriela's doll remarked from the girl's wheelchair. Earlier, Liz and Gracie had been braiding Gabriela's dark hair, and it was now covered in little braids on all sides.

"Sorry! I'm just clumsy when I'm jittery!" Liz said with her nasal voice of chronic allergies, waving her doll. "It comes with my ADHD."

Poor Gracie. Allison looked at the girl with compassion. She had no idea how narrowly she'd escaped living with a man who was potentially dangerous—violent, unscrupulous and greedy. And yet the girl had spoken wonders about her "Uncle Jake." *That man must be a sociopath, able to charm a little girl like that.*

"Can we have a snack now?" Gracie suggested, putting her doll down. "I have a hankering for green beans."

"Eeew!" Liz and Gabriela said at once.

"Green beans?" asked Allison with a smile. "That's an original craving."

"I didn't use to like them, but my uncle makes the best green beans in the world," Gracie said. "The trick is a little butter, salt and pepper, and steaming them to the perfect point: not too crunchy, not too soft."

Allison went back in her mind trying to remember where she had heard that before.

Fe placed a plate of crackers and cheese for the girls on the coffee table. "Uh, Allison. How about we leave the girls with Grandma for a minute, and you and I... uh, take a little walk?"

Allison noticed the unusual fact that Fe wasn't waving her hands as she talked. "Everything okay, Fe?"

"Excellent question." Fe hooked her arm with Allison's and slowly walked her to the door. "Let's take a stroll to the park and dwell on it." Fe's phone dinged with a text message. She read it and stopped walking. "Uh… change of plans. Let's not go out. Why don't you come to the lanai for a bit? *Abuela!*"

Fe's sweet grandma peeked her head from the kitchen. Fe sputtered some instructions in machine-gun fast Spanish and pulled Allison's arm, walking her through the French doors connecting the family room to the pool area.

Over the edge of the infinity pool, where Fe's two boys Diego and Aidan practiced swimming with an instructor, the magnificent view of the Indian River was a visual treat. Fe invited Allison to sit on a wicker sofa.

"Is something wrong, Fe?" asked Allison.

Fe's grin seemed forced. "My point, exactly."

Allison noticed Fe's jiggling foot. "Fe, what's going on?"

"I don't know. But trust me, I have every intention of finding out." She got up and rubbed Allison's back. "In the meantime, let's just stay on this lanai for a little longer."

Allison opened her mouth to ask why when her phone rang with a FaceTime request from Joy.

Joy's understated beauty entered the screen next to Emery's exotic face. From the background, Allison guessed they were in the hospital's physician's lounge. "Hey, Allison. This may not be a big deal, but I told Emery she should make you aware." She indicated to Emery to take over.

Emery bit her full lower lip. "Is it a problem if my ex-fiancé the slug knows you're dating Jay?"

"Hell, yeah!" Dread gnawed at Allison. "Ken is Karen Knight's cousin. I have no desire to deal with her questions if she finds out."

Her face scrunched with guilt, Emery's green eyes turned shiny with tears. "I'm so sorry, Allison. Ken ambushed me at my office with lunch earlier. He found me on my computer, re-watching the round-table YouTube videos Jay had posted, and it didn't occur to me to hide that you were seeing him."

Allison's pulse raced. She hoped Karen would honor their friend-ship over her love for scandal, but Fort Sunshine was a small town and news spread quickly.

"The last thing I need is that rumor reaching one of my hat-ers, like Wayne Nash." Allison groaned. "I can already imagine him boasting that the 'Triple B, man-hater' is lying to her readers and cli-ents about not needing a man."

Emery cringed. "I'm sorry, I promise I'll fix this. I'll talk to Ken and make sure he keeps quiet."

"But what worried me the most," Joy intervened, "is that Emery mentioned Ken seemed way too excited with the news. Why would he care?"

Allison considered it but was unable to come up with an answer.

"I can find that out too," Emery offered, eager to make up for her mistake. "Ken is constantly bothering me to go out with him and lis-ten to his version of the stripper incident. When he drinks, he often babbles about everything—even his confidential cases. I'm sure I can get him to tell me what that was about."

"I don't like this," Joy commented. "I'd hate for Ken to talk you into taking him back."

"Oh, please! I can handle the slug." Emery huffed and flicked a hand.

Allison was still trying to process it all when Fe's grandmother waved at them through the French doors.

"Okay!" Fe said. "Time to go back inside, Allison."

Still holding the phone, she followed Fe inside while pondering. *Why would Ken Carter care that I'm dating Jay?* She soon realized that was the least of her worries. She'd allowed herself to get lost in her dreamy world with Jay and lose sight of caution. Maybe it was time to pump the brakes.

Returning to the family room, Allison was surprised to find Liz and Gabriela playing alone. "Where's Gracie?"

"Her babysitter, Miranda, showed up to get her," Liz rushed to say. "Also, there was a guy waiting in a car—"

Fe covered Liz's mouth with her hand. "Okay, playdate's over. Let's clean up the toys!"

As Fe moved around the family room tossing dolls into a toy chest Allison scrutinized her. *Why is she so nervous?*

"Allison?" Joy said on the phone screen, reminding her of their call. "We have to go; Richard is here to pick me up."

Allison couldn't help rolling her eyes at the mention of Richard Fields. "Okay, girls. We'll talk later."

"Say hi to Jay for me," Joy said before disconnecting the call.

"I have lots of things I want to say to Jay," Fe grumbled while picking up toys. Her frown and lack of smile immediately alerted Allison.

"Fe, do you know something about Jay I don't know?"

The flash of guilt on Fe's face made Allison's stomach clench in apprehension. *Did Fe learn something about Jay she doesn't dare to tell me? Is this about Wednesday's mystery girl?*

"I honestly know nothing!" Fe avoided her eyes as she closed the toy chest. She then crossed her arms and tapped a foot on the floor. "But Shawn and I are going to have a talk. And the minute I learn something, you'll be the first to know."

Chapter 28

MOST FLIGHTS LEAVING THE FORT SUNSHINE AIRPORT HAD to stop in Atlanta. Having been there for the past few days, Jay booked the tickets so Allison would meet him at that connection and they would fly together to LA.

Already at the gate when she arrived, his face lit up when he saw her, and he rose from his chair to greet her with a kiss. After days apart, the long kiss felt wonderful, but it was more effusive than Allison thought appropriate for a public place.

"I missed you like hell," he whispered in her ear after they took a seat.

The middle-aged couple sitting in front of them threw half-amused, half-jealous glances at them.

They must think we're a couple newly in love—which, obviously, we're not.

Feeling the urge to bring herself back to reality, she cleared her throat and braced herself for the confrontation she'd been postponing. "So, what's going to happen to your Wednesday thing? *She* will be disappointed when you don't make it this week."

He tensed up. Slowly, he moved away from her ear and frowned at her. "What do you know about my Wednesdays?"

"I heard the rumor you see a 'female friend' those days. Is that true?"

His jaw dropped and his eyebrows shot up.

"Not that I'm jealous or anything," she continued. "I have no unrealistic expectations that—"

"You think that I'm seeing another woman?" He spoke so loud the couple sitting across from them jerked their heads to gape at them. Jay captured her face, almost yelling. "Allison, are you seeing other people besides me?"

Astounded, Allison nearly fell from her chair. "No! I'm only seeing you!"

Still keeping eye contact, he let go of her face. "How do you think I could put on a performance like that for you in bed and still have *anything* left for another woman?"

By now more passengers were staring at them. She shushed him and gestured for him to calm down.

He pierced her with his eyes, his hands on her shoulders. "You are the only woman I have and the only one I want." He paused; his fingers slowly slid from her shoulders down her arms until they held her hands. His next words seemed to come from another world. *"I love you."*

Allison's brain short-circuited. She could see the sparks flashing, smell the smoke, and feel the wheels stop turning. She vaguely knew she was expected to reciprocate by saying something nice, but she had no idea what.

His eyes darted away before returning to hers. "And I will tell you everything about my Wednesdays after this trip. I swear."

Allison's brain was still non-responsive. Luckily he didn't seem to be waiting for an answer. He exhaled sharply and then chuckled, shaking his head. "How could you think I'd cheat on you?" He took her hand, kissed it and tucked it into his chest. He then turned to the stunned couple eavesdropping in front of them and gave them a charming, apologetic simper. "I'm sorry, guys. She's my girlfriend, but, apparently, she doesn't know it yet."

Girlfriend. Allison's heart raced as the surreal word entered her ears and solidified in her consciousness.

* * *

In spite of the unconventional beginning, the flight to California was pleasant, catching up with Jay about their time apart.

With the help of the time difference, it was still early evening when they arrived in LA and picked up their rental convertible. He proposed going out for dinner, yet the moment they checked into their hotel room, it became clear they were more ravenous for each other than they were for food.

Allison fell asleep after their lovemaking, but Jay woke her up shortly so they could head out to see the city at night.

The pleasures of dating a manic man.

Yes, being with Jay was like being in a fun boot-camp run by a maniac. One pleasurable activity had to follow the next one with almost no time to breathe in between. After dinner, they spotted landmarks from the car, from The Dolby and TCL Chinese Theaters, to Rodeo Drive, to Venice Beach, then drove around aimlessly with the top down taking in the night energy of the city.

By the time they made it to bed it was 2:00 a.m., California time—5:00 a.m. for Allison—yet they were up four hours later for morning lovemaking, and then a run on the hotel gym's elliptical machines, before joining Matthew Hester for brunch. Sleep deprived and suffering from an excess of afterglow, Allison wasn't sure whether or not she was dreaming when she finally met the famous Hollywood actor. Jay introduced her as, "My girlfriend, but she doesn't know it yet."

After the early brunch, Hester took Jay to meet with some potential investors and Allison drove the rental car to the nearby Barnes & Noble where she had miraculously scored a short-notice book signing. With the recent attention generated by the boot camp, the attendance was greater than she expected. She had to sign so many books, chat with so many fans and pose for so many pictures she was exhausted by the end of the afternoon.

She hoped she could catch a nap before the premiere but barely made her appointment with the hotel salon to have her hair and makeup done—Fe would be proud of her.

Wearing the hotel terry-robe over her Spanx, her hair up in a few rollers to revitalize the waves, Allison worked on getting ready while Jay showered. She struggled with the stuck zipper of her garment bag when her phone rang with a FaceTime request from Karen.

She picked up. "Hi, Karen! You won't believe how many people showed up at my—"

"When were you planning to tell me that your book signing trip is an excuse to travel with your new boyfriend?" Karen interrupted her.

Shoot. How did she find out? Allison propped the phone on the dresser and removed her silver gown from the bag. "First of all, he's not my boyfriend. Second of all, I didn't think it was relevant to you." She slipped into the dress.

"Allison, how could you do this?" Karen wrinkled her nose. "Triple J is just planning to use you for sex for a short while. You're doing exactly what you warn your readers and clients against."

It's much more complicated than that. Jay's "I love you" at the airport, which she'd been trying to forget, returned to Allison's mind. Panic resurfaced inside her as she zipped up her dress.

"I couldn't believe it when your secretary told me you're planning to go to that premiere—the same one Triple J posted on his video-blog he's attending," Karen continued. "What if someone recognizes you two? This contradicts everything you're basing your career on. What will your readers think?"

You're preaching to the freaking choir. Allison's hands trembled mildly as she worked on removing the foam rollers from her hair. "Relax, Karen. We'll be invisible, next to a bunch of celebrities. It's not like we're walking the red carpet ourselves; we're going in through a side entrance."

Karen insisted. "But everyone will assume he's your boyfriend."

As she reached for the strappy silver sandals in her luggage, Allison grunted. "I told you, Karen, Jay is not my boyfriend." The more Allison said the words the less believable they became to herself. They were dating exclusively. They were on a trip together. He had just introduced her as his girlfriend to a famous actor, even if he was hiding behind a joke. Her pulse sped up.

Karen charged again. "So, if he's not your boyfriend, could you pass a lie detector on it?"

"Why do you ask?"

"Because you may need to. Do you know who's among the reporters covering that premiere Jay's attending? Wayne Nash."

Allison's heart dropped to the floor. She stopped fastening her sandal and snatched the phone. "What on earth is Nash doing here?"

"He got a press pass to cover that premiere for his next show because he's had a man-crush on Triple J since the roundtables. Nash has no idea you're there. Do you know what will happen when he finds you there hanging on Jay's arm? He'll destroy your credibility."

Feeling as if the AC had kicked into high gear, Allison shivered.

Karen moved her face closer to the screen. "Unless you can look Nash straight in the eye and swear that you and Jay have nothing going on but a weekend fling. Can you? And most importantly, will Jay answer the same?"

An alarm rang in Allison's mind. She was still processing the news that she and Jay were in an exclusive relationship—definitely not ready to admit it to the world. But she could feel the jet lag and the sleep deprivation taking a toll on her mental sharpness. She wasn't in a condition to face Nash tonight.

The bathroom door opened, and she heard Jay coming out.

"I'll get back to you later, Karen." Without waiting for her response, she disconnected the call.

Allison inhaled deeply, trying to calm herself down.

"Well. What do you think?" Jay asked behind her.

Slowly, she turned around to face him and lost her breath.

He looked stunning in his tuxedo, fingers running through his wet hair. It was a completely new—grown-up—image of him. The image of the man she would've fantasized about all her life if she'd ever cared about men.

From the shock on his face, she guessed he was impressed with her appearance too.

"Wow!" he said, slowly walking toward her. "You're… amazing. Gorgeous!" His eyes were filled with reverence as he removed one last roller from her hair and moved the golden curl away from her face. "I'm going to be the envy of every man in that place."

Her legs weakened at the sight of the spark in his eyes. As if she were struck by lightning, an epiphany hit her.

Who was she kidding? She was crazy about this man.

She was drooling, head over heels, flat on her face, hopelessly in love with him. So much, she was sure she had a neon sign on her face advertising it, and Wayne and every person in that party would know it the moment they saw her.

She was doomed.

Chuckling, he caressed her bare shoulder, exposed by the silver straps of the dress. "I must look fine if I've left you speechless! Are you ready?"

Mute and frozen in place she looked at her still untied sandal.

He followed the direction of her eyes and knelt on the carpeted floor to tie it. Mischief oozed from his lowered voice. "Do you notice anything strange? I'm cheating. My tie isn't really black; it's dark burgundy. I wonder if I can get away with no one noticing it."

A text on his phone got his attention as he finished tying the strap. "Oops. Our limo awaits. Are you ready?" As he got up from the floor, adoration filled his eyes. "I can't believe my luck! Look at my hot girlfriend!"

That did it.

"I'm not your girlfriend!" she snapped, taking a step back.

Startled, he flinched. "Darling, if it bothers you when I say—"

"I'm sorry, Jay, I can't do this!" Her breathing quickening, she shook her head.

Jay's jaw tightened and he took a step toward her. "What? What can't you do?"

She ran her fingers through her hair, messing it up as she backed away. "I can't go with you. I'm sorry. I'm really sorry."

She dashed into the bathroom, shut the door, and locked herself in.

Chapter 29

I T WAS PAST MIDNIGHT WHEN THE CLICK OF THE DOOR unlocking announced that Jay had returned from the after-party. Unable to sleep, Allison had just moved to the couch in the sitting area.

He seemed tired as he pushed the door open and walked in. His gaze moved from the empty bed to the couch where she sat, and their eyes met. The coldness in his stare stabbed her. He then averted his eyes and walked to the bathroom without a word, closing the door.

She let go of the breath she'd been holding and sank her face into her hands, dreading the confrontation and wanting to get it done.

A few minutes later, he returned wearing long silk pajama pants without a shirt. He stopped in front of the couch and locked eyes with her.

He spoke slowly. His voice wept of controlled anger. "This is not a drill and it's not a guilt trip. I'm so furious with you right now I feel like I want to hurt you."

His words terrified her for a second, but she could sense he was in control of himself. She stared at him in silence.

He continued, "And in case you missed it, I have *serious* issues with abandonment and rejection."

Allison felt her heart crack in pain, echoing the suffering in his eyes. At that moment he looked like a wounded little child.

"I'm going to need to process a whole lot of shit before I'm able to speak to you again," he concluded. "But I'm not sure if I'll ever be ready to forgive you. I trust you'll catch a flight back to Florida tomorrow."

She was still assimilating his words when he walked away from her to the bed.

* * *

Jay wasn't surprised when he couldn't fall asleep. He lay in bed in silence, on top of the blankets, his eyes fixed on the ceiling. The pain had moved beyond the sharp stage to numbness.

His mind whirled with memories. Memories of the shame in his father's eyes the day he showed up to pick him up from Port Popsicle. Memories of the long, silent ride to Chicago, feeling at the cellular level the embarrassment his father felt about bringing his bastard home.

He felt a presence near him; Allison knelt on the carpeted floor next to the bed.

"For what it's worth. I'm really sorry." Her voice was soft.

He kept looking away, without answering.

She moved in front of his face and searched for his gaze. "Is there anything I can do to make it up, so you would forgive me?"

He knew he came across like a little kid, sulking and pouting, but he couldn't get himself to reply.

"I'm desperate," she muttered. "What can I do to get you to talk to me again?"

He glowered at her. "There's nothing you can do to cheer me up after the horrible night I had."

She looked at him from under her eyelashes. "How about some angry sex?"

He froze, but then forced his eyes away. *I know what she's doing. She still believes men are hopeless single-minded creatures who can be manipulated with sex. I'm not falling for it.*

She pushed it further. "I'll let you blindfold me."

204

He tensed up. *Or maybe yes*? He turned his head to stare at her. "Would you also let me cuddle you?"

She winced, but then bobbed her head in agreement.

He felt something other than pain for the first time that evening.

"I'm going to take this offer for now, but don't get your hopes up that we are even. I'm still angry."

Holding her arms, he dragged her up from the floor on top of him and captured her mouth.

* * *

Allison had no idea how long she'd been asleep when the feeling of kisses on her neck awakened her. It must've been a short time, since it was still pitch-dark outside the window.

She felt Jay run his mouth down her neck, then slide up again until it reached her ear. He whispered, "I'm still mad."

She felt like a train had run over her, but also glowed in bliss. And if relinquishing some control had worked to break his silence, it was more than worth it. She gently scratched his back the way she knew he liked. As long as he was talking, it was progress. "Was it *that* bad having to be there alone?"

"You have no idea." He groaned. "It was the most boring and painful party I've attended in my life. And every five minutes someone would ask me where my date was. Even Nash was there."

She tensed. As much as she regretted having hurt his feelings, she'd made the right decision by not going. "What did you answer?"

"I kept repeating that my date got 'indisposed at the last minute.' It was humiliating."

She sat on the bed, back against the headrest, and coaxed his head into her lap while she caressed his hair. "Why was it painful?"

His long silence made her fear he'd slid back into silent treatment, but then he spoke. "I'll never forget the day my father showed up to pick me up after my mother died. What stuck with me wasn't the shock of hearing I had a living father, or meeting this man who looked so much like me. What I never forgot was the shame in his eyes."

He stopped talking. She felt tightness in her chest rise to her throat.

"At an intellectual level, I now know his shame wasn't directed at me," he resumed. "Confronting his bastard son, he was embarrassed of himself and his own cheating on his wife. Maybe even remorseful about having neglected me for eight years. But still, as a child I internalized that shame." He paused. "My last shrink said I've spent my life doing outrageous things to shock other people—because my biggest longing in the world is to feel loved in spite of being an embarrassment. I always said that shrink was crazy." He seemed to struggle for words. "Yet tonight I wonder if, deep inside, all I wanted from you was that—that you would not be ashamed of me."

She crumbled inside. Leaning forward, she kissed the scar over his eyebrow. "I'm so sorry that you had to go through that."

"But that wasn't the worst part." He pulled away from her hands and leaned against the headboard beside her. "The worst part was having to accept that you and I are in such different places in this relationship."

She couldn't answer.

"I've treated you pretty damn well these past few weeks, yet you still refuse to let me in." He drilled her with his eyes. "And it sucks to feel that I care for you far more than you care for me."

She wrapped her arms around him, leaning her face against his chest, and closed her eyes. "I do care for you. I want to trust you and let you in. I'm just not good at it."

He made no effort to hug her back. "You couldn't even stand the idea that someone would see you with me."

"Are you listening to yourself?" She sighed, releasing the embrace. "Any woman in the world would kill to be seen in public with you."

"But not you."

Because I just found out I love you and I'm terrified. "Because if my clients and readers see me smooching with a man, they'll say I'm a fraud. And I can't risk my career."

He recoiled as if she'd slapped him. "And I'm not worth that risk. And in the time we've been together I've done nothing to make you change your mind about men."

Darn it. In volatile moments like this, her best hope was keeping physical contact. She held his hand and kissed it, talking more to herself than to him. "I consider myself a scientist of mental health. Scientists conducting research on a new treatment don't talk about the results until they're final. This…" She pointed between them and spoke slowly. "This is so new for me it's like an experiment. No one knows how it will end. And until time confirms that this…" *This love thing.* "This trusting a man is safe, it would be irresponsible to advertise it to my clients, confusing them." She rubbed his strong arm. "If in a couple of years we're still together and happy, maybe then it makes sense to tell them, 'Forget everything I told you before. I found a better way.' In the meantime, all I ask is some discretion about… the ongoing experiment."

He didn't answer. He resembled that wounded kid again.

"All I ask is that we continue the way we've been: enjoying this happiness by ourselves, without advertising it to the rest of the world."

For a moment, he seemed moved. His hand reached for her face as if to caress it, but he changed his mind and dropped it. "That doesn't help me now, Allison. I'm still so angry at you."

He must be. It felt strange to hear him call her "Allison" instead of "darling."

"Okay. I deserve it." Sighing in resignation, she straightened up and held his face. "Listen to me, big kid. I *care* for you." She wished she could use the word love, but it still refused to leave her mouth. "I *do* care about what happens to us in the future, so pay attention now."

His eyes focused on her and she let go of his face. "In my career,

I've seen too many great couples drift apart because one of them made a mistake and the other one was unable to get past it. I refuse to let that happen to us. I'm going to give you a chance to get even with me so we can put this behind us."

"What do you mean?" he asked, frowning.

She took a deep breath. "Going with you to the premiere was supposed to be my way to do something scary, and I failed you. Now, you're going to choose something else—the most terrifying and horrendous thing you can come up with—as my punishment. I'm going to do it."

He raised his eyebrows.

"Don't hold back," she said, her newly discovered love giving her strange strength. "Bungee jumping, skydiving, kinky sex… Whatever it is, I'll do it. Then we're going to put this behind us and never mention it again. Agree?"

Slowly, he nodded. "But I've done all that. None of it is terrifying enough to be your punishment."

Allison froze at the sudden coldness in his tone. She always feared getting involved so quickly with someone she barely knew was dangerous.

Keeping her voice steady to hide her dread, she asked, "What do you have in mind?"

"What is the thing we both fear and despise the most in the world?" His eyes locked onto hers.

She squinted and pursed her lips. "Taxes?"

He shook his head. "Weddings."

The word was so surreal it didn't register in Allison's brain for several moments.

"Dr. Allison Connor, your worst nightmare is coming true: You're going to get married tonight."

Chapter 30

ALLISON COULD HARDLY BELIEVE SHE'D AGREED TO GO along with it. They drove the rental car to Las Vegas in record time and chose the cheesiest looking twenty-four-hour drive-through wedding chapel they could find—the one with the most neon bells on the sign. Jay's punishment for Allison had been clear: a Vegas wedding, three days as a married woman, then an annulment as soon as they returned to Florida.

The ceremony was short, and she felt numb through most of it. The hardest part was convincing the Elvis impersonator officiate not to up-sell them on a fancier package. The man finally gave up trying to sell his own professional video and agreed to take a few snaps with Jay's cell phone. Allison found herself giggling at the nonsense of posing for wedding pictures sitting in a convertible, wearing pajamas, a plastic tiara with a mosquito net veil, and fake wedding rings—Emery would faint.

After that, Jay drove the convertible to the nearest hospital and parked in front of the emergency room.

"What are we doing here?" she asked.

"Just a precaution. I've always thought that if I ever caved and got married, I would have a life-threatening allergic reaction or a stroke instantly." He placed his hands on his throat and faked hoarseness. "I think I feel it starting."

Allison laughed whole-heartedly while Jay faked symptoms of poisoning and neurological decline.

When neither of them had died after a while, they drove away from the hospital. Between the sleep deprivation and the recent emotional roller coaster, she felt like she was drugged or trapped in a dream. She wondered if that was why she'd agreed to the crazy idea of a Vegas wedding.

"Hopefully we're going to find a hotel and sleep now, instead of trying to drive back to LA immediately?" she commented, observing through the car window how less glamorous the city appeared in the morning with the lights off.

"Oh, yes, we're definitely going to a hotel. We have to consummate the marriage."

Allison burst into laughter again. "I think this 'marriage' has been pre-consummated plenty."

The hilarity didn't last long. He wasn't kidding. He jumped on her the minute they set foot in the hotel room, much more humble than their LA suite, and blew her mind in bed like never before.

She fell asleep immediately afterward and woke up four hours later. He brought her coffee and announced he'd booked them a flight to a surprise honeymoon destination. The flight would leave at 3:00 a.m., so they had a few hours in Las Vegas. Allison couldn't believe she was letting him take the lead like that. Finding out she was in love must've affected her brain.

"Let's go for dinner and catch a show," he begged, taking a seat next to her in bed. "And let's cash in the social rewards of marriage. Let's see if we can get special treatment everywhere by announcing we're newlyweds." He took a sip from his coffee. "But first, let's go to a drugstore and buy condoms—and make a big deal, bragging about it while we do."

"What?" She froze with the coffee cup halfway to her lips and gaped at him.

"Yes. Condoms and lube. As a married couple, we're legally entitled—even *obligated*—to have sex. We shouldn't have to whisper and feel self-conscious when buying those supplies."

She chuckled. "O-kay. I'll consider it part of my punishment." She gave him a small coffee-flavored kiss.

Maybe his previous therapist was onto something. If acting outrageous and not being rejected for it was Jay's way to feel loved, she'd gladly follow along.

* * *

Jay woke up wrapped around Allison in the hotel bed in Honolulu, Hawaii. Thanks to double jetlag, he had no idea what time it was—and he didn't care.

Her blond hair tickled his nose, but he didn't dare move lest he lose the privileged position of smelling her. What a wonderful smell, a mixture of her rose-scented soap with the cookie-dough scent her skin somehow held.

He noticed one of his arms draped over her shoulders and carefully moved it down to her waist, feeling thankful she hadn't found him in that forbidden position. His eyes caught a glimpse of the fake wedding ring on his hand, matching hers, and his heart jumped. One half of him wanted to run away, in panic.

The other half did too.

He still couldn't believe they'd gone through with it! The only thing more amazing than her agreeing was that he'd even proposed it in the first place.

"Are you awake?" she muttered.

He grunted in affirmation. "Retracing the day in my mind. I still can't believe we did it."

Her chest vibrated against his with giggles. She wiggled out of the tangle of their limbs and sat on the bed. Sometime during the night, she'd recovered her turquoise nightgown. "And you're still alive!"

"Amazingly!" he replied, grinning at the inside joke.

"The scariest moment was when the guy marrying us asked if I would take *Jacob James Johnson* as my husband. I had no idea who that was." She chuckled again. "I never knew until now what J.J. stood for."

Tensing, he reached for his wallet on the nightstand and retrieved his Atlanta driver's license. His heart speeding up, he handed it to her. "Yes. That's my real name; Jay is a nickname."

He held his breath as she studied the driver's license for what felt like an eternity. That was the first ID he'd gotten after his legal name change and the picture on it showed him before he'd lost the weight and shaven. Would she remember him? As much as he dreaded breaking this magic, he needed to start the conversation somehow about who he was.

She stared at something on the license. "Jay! We have the same birthday!" Her mouth fell open. "You said once that we shared our birthday. How did you know that?"

His pulse racing, he half-shrugged. "Maybe I wasn't kidding the day I told you I've been stalking you for years."

A flash of terror crossed Allison's face, then she burst into giggles. "You and your weird sense of humor!" She returned the ID to him.

Well, that didn't work.

Room service knocked on the door and her face lit up. "I woke up a little bit ago and ordered us breakfast before going back to sleep." She grabbed a robe from the floor and wrapped herself in it while staggering to the suite door.

He could hardly believe she'd kept her freaking organizational abilities through this haze. He found his pajama pants and slipped them back on.

"What is this?" he asked, surprised, while helping her set the trays on the room table.

After the server left, she went through the trays. "Faithful to my punishment, for the next two days, I'm behaving like the perfect little wife. I'll never be the woman who cooks for her man, but I can pick up the phone. I ordered your usual egg-white omelet and my eggs benedict—no hash browns anymore, but fresh fruit."

He was surprised she'd remembered his favorite breakfast omelet. He observed her while helping her sort the plates and the coffee. *Good thing this fake marriage isn't lasting long. Otherwise, I might get used to this.*

He accepted the mug of black coffee from her hand with a thank you and sipped the bitter drink while admiring the disheveled golden locks on her head.

Sipping her own coffee, she sat on her chair and crossed her legs—exposing a tempting, milky and soft thigh as her satin gown and robe rode up. Her voice was calm. "I'm proud of us! We took our contempt for marriage to the final frontier."

"Yes!" he agreed. "This sham marriage is the ultimate mockery of the institution." *Except married life feels pretty damn good so far.*

"And for the next forty-eight hours, we'll mock it to the last drop. So, tell me, bossy husband. What are we doing on the second day of our honeymoon? Hopefully touring the Island? I look forward to some nature for contrast."

"Sure. We'll do anything you want today." He took a sip of coffee. "Yesterday you were so patient with me and let me call all the shots—even coming to that drugstore to make a show about buying condoms."

She surprised him by sitting on his lap and circling his neck with her arms. Her eyes oozed with new warmth. "If it made you happy, I don't mind." She kissed him briefly on the lips.

He felt a clench in his chest. It was the closest thing to a declaration of love he'd ever gotten from her.

"And anyway." She shrugged. "In a few days it'll be over."

He held her hand and searched for her eyes. "Darling, maybe this is the best moment to make sure something is clear. When I said we'd end the marriage after returning to Florida, I never meant I wanted to end—" He stopped, afraid of scaring her with the word relationship, then moved his hand between them. "Us."

She swallowed hard and then nodded slowly.

"I don't know how we'll make things work considering you'd rather die than be seen in public with a man. I don't know how we'll manage things when I don't know what city I'll be living in." He paused. "All I know is that I want you in my life. Permanently."

She seemed as tense as a stretched rubber band. "There's no such thing as forever, you know. I've counseled too many heartbroken people over the years after their relationships go sour."

He kissed her hand. "Maybe that's our advantage. Most couples start full of illusion, and then half of them end up breaking their marriage. We'll be doing it the other way around. We're *starting* the relationship with a divorce—or an annulment. The worst thing that can happen will be behind us! Maybe getting that out of the way we'll have a better chance."

She rewarded him with the beautiful sound of her laughter. "That is just so crazy, wrong, and twisted, it kind of makes sense."

She kissed him on the cheek and returned to her chair. Watching her eat, a rumble of conflicted feelings mixed in his chest. *On second thought, this makes so much sense it would be crazy to end it.*

* * *

It took three flights to return from Honolulu to Fort Sunshine. Allison tried to sleep through the eight-hour transpacific flight, but her slumber wasn't restful and she felt exhausted. She had no idea how she'd face work the next day.

The sound of car doors and a trunk opening and closing woke Allison from a deep sleep. Only then did she realize she'd dozed off on the ride from the airport.

She stretched and yawned before opening her eyes. She'd assumed Jay was driving her home or to his hotel. Instead, they were in front of a house she didn't recognize. A whiff of ocean suggested they were near the beach.

"Where are we?" she asked, rubbing her eyes as Jay opened the car door for her.

Instead of answering, he scooped her up in his arms. Startled, she wrapped hers around his neck. By the time she realized what happened, he'd carried her into the house and across an unfurnished living room and deposited her onto a queen-sized bed.

"I'm sorry, I know you're opposed to the image of a man carrying a woman romance-novel style," he said while he worked on freeing her from her yoga pants—which she appreciated as they were cutting off her circulation. "But there was no way I was going to break tradition and let you walk over the threshold." He smiled. "Welcome home, Mrs. Johnson!"

She sat up on the bed. "This is not funny, Jay."

He lifted both hands. "Oops! My bad! Doctor Connor-hyphen-Johnson. Much better, right?" He removed her top, pulling it over her head, leaving her in her sports bra and comfy granny panties.

She groaned. "Jay, I'm too tired to joke—"

"Allison, have you looked at your hands?" he interrupted her.

That was the last thing she expected to hear. She examined her hands expecting to find blood on them or at least ink. She saw nothing but the plastic wedding band he'd given her in Vegas.

"I guess I forgot to take off the fake ring."

His lips twitched. "Are you sure that's all you see?"

She took a second look and noticed something different. The plastic ring she'd slipped on in Vegas was fake yellow gold. This one was a mixture of yellow and white gold. She touched it and realized it was a real ring. "Jay, what's this?"

He held his hand up to show a matching band while walking to the nearest window and tossing her clothes through it before closing it and locking it. "Don't you love them? I found them at a cute jewelry store in Honolulu. Mine fit perfectly off the rack, but yours may need some adjustment. It's just a tiny bit too small. Good thing you took that sleeping pill on the plane and it didn't seem to bother you when I used lotion to slide it on."

She tried to take the ring off, but it was stuck. Her hands must've swollen during travel. She grunted and groaned, struggling to remove it without success.

"Jay! This is not funny! Why are you doing this?"

"I changed my mind," he said, his eyes looking glassy. "I don't want a divorce."

Chapter 31

J AY'S WORDS SANK IN SLOWLY, AND IT TOOK ALLISON A FEW
moments to react.

"Jay, you're kidding again, aren't you?"

The seriousness in his expression answered even before his head-shake. "I decided I'm not signing any annulment papers."

A ripple of panic overtook Allison. Trembling, she got up from the bed—and only then understood why he had stripped her down to her underwear. Her eyes searched for her luggage. "Where are the rest of my clothes?"

"I hid them to make sure you can't run away."

"What?" She surveyed his face for a hint of a joke but found none.

"I also hid your wallet, your keys, and your cell phone. I had to make sure you at least listen to what I have to say."

Allison seriously considered marching out of the house in her underwear, yelling for help.

She backed away one step. "Give me my clothes right now! I'm getting out of here! Where are my car keys?"

He extended his hand. "Come on, beautiful, at least hear me out."

The tenderness in his expression softened her. He guided her to a reading chair while he sat on the bed.

"Allison, I'm not taking Matt's offer," he announced. "I'm not taking a job that forces me to move to LA, away from you."

She jerked in surprise. "But you said your current career will end

217

soon. What are you going to do then?"

"I'll get a real job, figure something out." He shrugged. "I've reinvented myself before; I can do it again."

Skeptical, she smiled. "Jay, I can't imagine you sticking with a 'real job,' no matter how well it pays." She stopped. "And the same goes for sticking with one woman."

"You don't think I can do it?" His eyes sought hers.

She leaned forward to run a finger down his face. "That inner child of yours is wonderful, but he's also a little dictator who refuses to do anything to break your glass ceiling of success. Or anything that requires long-term commitment."

With fake seriousness, he clicked his tongue. "Well, that's a problem. Maybe if I had a wife to reel me in and whip me into discipline... oh, wait!" With an exaggerated gasp, he lifted her from her chair and onto his lap. "I *do* have one!" Grinning, he gave her a small kiss on the lips.

She shook her head, but he didn't let her talk. "Imagine this. A friend of Ethan's is selling this house."—he pointed down—"and gave us first dibs before putting it on the market. You would love this house. Four bedrooms, three baths. We could have an office for each of us and one for... guests." He cleared his throat before continuing. "The house is a short walk from the beach. I even think we could see the ocean from the roof if we built a deck on it—"

"Jay, wait. Stop." Overwhelmed, she slid off his lap to sit back on her chair. "Jay, let's be real. Do you *realize* we barely know each other?"

He reached for her hand. "There are many things you still don't know about me. Most of them are good, some not so much. Some of them you're going to think they're bad when you learn about them. But trust me, they're not that bad if you just open your mind a little."

He wore such a grave expression she couldn't help chuckling nervously. "My goodness! I don't think I've ever seen you this serious!"

He kissed her hand. "I'm looking forward to you getting to know me better. But at this point, it almost doesn't matter what I get to learn about you."

"What do you mean?"

"I mean that every new fact and cool thing I learn about you is a pleasant surprise that adds another cherry on top of the sundae. But the truth is that the decision was already made at a deep level, and my brain had no say in it: You're the woman I want to be with. Period."

She was out of words, so she just repeated herself. "Jay, this is crazy. We barely know each other."

"Yet I've never been a stranger," he argued. "You know that we remember each other from somewhere—that our souls fit with each other."

Darn it. He was right. No way to explain it because it didn't come from the intellect. She just *knew* he was *it*.

"Please, don't reject the idea automatically. Just think about it," he asked. "You said in your third book people should date for at least a year or two before they decide if a marriage contract is a possibility. Well, we're already married, so maybe you need to give me at least a year or two before you decide I'm *not* husband material."

Speechless, she processed his words.

"If you don't want to commit to that much, let's take it one quarter at a time, like in a corporation," he insisted. "Give me three months. At the end of that time, we'll reevaluate things. If you still like me, we'll renew for three more months. If not, and if I can't convince you that I'm worth another chance, I'll sign the papers. That simple."

She tried to imagine what life would be like waking up next to him every morning. She tried to reconcile the two worlds that, until now, had been parallel: her routines and the heavenly time they spent together. The image was scarily appealing.

She covered his hand with hers. "Jay, I make no promises, except that I'll think about it." She stopped, her heart pounding. She never thought she'd be saying something like this. Hot flashes alternated with ice in her veins. "But no matter what my answer is, I want you to know I also want to be with you—" She stopped, surprised to realize the fear had dissipated and the words were flowing out of her mouth effortlessly. "I want you to know... I love you."

His breathing halted. The expression on his face seemed a mixture of grief and ecstasy. She caught a glimpse of the shine of tears in his eyes before he pulled her toward him abruptly, holding her in an embrace so tight her ribs ached. His body shuddered unevenly with each inhale.

With a suffocated voice, she mumbled. "Uh... Jay." She was having trouble breathing. "This is the part when you're supposed to say 'me too.'"

His voice was hoarse. "I will, don't worry. I'll get there." He kissed her head and the tightness of his embrace increased. "I've waited so long to hear this. Just let me enjoy this moment for a little longer."

Chapter 32

ALLISON'S MIND WAS IN A HAZE THAT EARLY MORNING WHEN she arrived back at her condo and got ready for work. Luckily, her first client wasn't booked until ten thirty and she had some extra time to organize her thoughts and remove the stuck wedding ring from her finger.

As she stowed the ring in her nightstand drawer, she mused. She couldn't believe she hadn't rejected Jay's proposal immediately—even less, that she was seriously considering it. Was she completely out of her mind?

Or was she crazy to hesitate?

Even her brain argued in his favor. Here was an up-and-coming celebrity with the potential to move to bigger and greater things—a ticket to the rich and famous.

Not to mention that small detail that she was crazy about him.

Darn it. Wasn't all this worth facing scandal in front of her readers? Reinventing her brand?

It was all too good. *Suspiciously* good. She had the nagging, burning worry that there was a piece of information she was missing. And through the craziness of the past few days, she'd completely forgotten to talk to him about his mysterious Wednesdays.

She was settling into the driver's seat when she remembered the battery of her phone had been dead since Vegas. She plugged the phone into the car charger, waited until the screen re-awakened and turned it on. As she drove away from her parking spot, she could hear the nonstop dinging of voicemails and lost text messages enter the phone. Shortly after, the phone rang.

She was about to send the call to voicemail when she noticed it was from her lawyer. She was probably answering the voicemail Allison had left her right before her phone died. She took the call. "Hi, Mercy?"

"What the hell! What were you thinking?"

Allison held the phone away from her ear until the worst of the loud reprimand in her heavy Southern accent was over, then put it on speakerphone and set it back on the dashboard holder. Mercy had probably been shocked to get that message from her from Vegas, asking for her help with a marriage annulment. "*Oh, and by the way, that's because I just got married.*"

"Were you drunk? Drugged? Under some form of intoxication?"

Changing lanes, Allison sighed. "No. We hadn't had anything to drink."

Mercy's interrogation continued. "Did he point a gun at you? Are you in danger right now?"

"No."

"I see! He's psychologically unstable and you're afraid that he may be eavesdropping. Should I FaceTime you so you can give me cues with your eyes?"

Allison groaned while taking the Highway US1. "Mercy, I know this doesn't sound like me, but for the thousandth time, I'm fine. I wasn't drugged, I wasn't drunk, and he didn't kidnap me against my will."

There was a long pause, then Mercy's voice acquired a cold and business-like tone. "Has the marriage been consummated yet?"

Allison blushed. "What kind of question is that? What century do you think this is?"

"I'll take that as a yes, and will also scratch the question about whether he's unable to perform his marital duties. The last item is: is he your blood relative?"

The strange question baffled Allison. "No! Why are you asking me that?"

"Well, dear." On the other side of the line, Mercy clicked her tongue. "I'm sorry to break it to you, but your marriage doesn't qualify for an annulment."

Allison almost rear-ended the car in front of her. "What?"

"I have the list of criteria for annulment in the state of Florida in front of me, and you don't fulfill any of them. There was no impairment of mental clarity, he didn't coerce you—"

"Wait. What are you saying?" Allison pulled into the parking lot of her work building and clasped the cell phone.

"An annulment won't do; you'll need to get an official divorce," Mercy summarized. "Please make an appointment with my secretary. I'll email you the list of documents I need from both of you, including financial affidavits."

Allison's heart dropped. "Wait, wait! Maybe I was wrong. Let's go over those questions again—"

"Too late!" Mercy cut her off. "I'm not the type of lawyer who lies on her documents. Get ready for a long process. This might take months."

Allison's insides twisted. Of all the lawyers in the city, she had to choose one with principles. "We can't wait for months until this stupid paperwork is done." *We have to do this quickly before he makes me change my mind.*

Mercy seemed amused by her dilemma. "Well, you should've thought about that before you did it. Some things in life are much easier to *do* than to *undo*. Marriage is a good example." She disconnected the call.

Allison considered heading to Mercy's office across the street to persuade her in person but decided against it. Mercy was one of Allison's readers who saw her as an inspiration for living happily as a single woman—and now Allison had betrayed her.

Shoot! Maybe she should go to another lawyer. She didn't want to bolster Jay's plans to boycott the annulment by prolonging the ordeal.

She accessed her office from the service elevator planning to use her secret back entrance and avoid the main lobby. As she stepped out of the elevator, she noticed the multitude of lost calls, voicemails and texts from her girlfriends. The last text message from Joy, begging her to call back, was written in all caps and labeled URGENT.

She hit dial and could hear Joy's ringtone—the annoying Abba song Dancing Queen—going off. Joy's office was just one floor below hers; she must be nearby.

"Allison! Finally! We're at your office. Are you on your way?"

The greeting surprised her. "We? You and who?" As Allison said the words, she opened her office door and found a small crowd inside. The first person she saw was Joy, with her phone still on her ear. Next to her was her annoying fiancé, Agent Fields. Sitting around were Fe, Hope, and Emery. All of them appeared deeply worried.

She had the feeling something very serious had happened. Stunned, she put her phone down and closed the door behind her. "What's going on?"

The brief silence that followed proved more worrisome than any words.

"You haven't listened to your messages?" Joy asked.

Dreading whatever she was about to hear, she shook her head.

After another short silence, Hope swallowed and stood up. "Sweetie. You better sit down."

* * *

Jay's brain raced as he sat in the brown room, waiting for Attorney Kind to finish a phone call so they could formally start a mediation session. Mercy Kind's law office, with its dark wood paneling on the walls, always made him think of chocolate. The lawyers babbled non-stop, and he made no effort to follow what they said.

He was surprised when Ken Carter showed up to the meeting

all quiet and nervous, avoiding his eyes. Apparently, he hadn't said anything yet to his sister about him dating Allison since nobody touched the subject. Maybe that was a good sign that the wind was in his favor.

Or maybe it was just a way to prolong his agony.

His plans to come clean on the flight back had gotten interrupted by his newer plans of cementing his marriage with Allison. At moments, he felt filled with hope because she hadn't immediately rejected his offer. But the rest of the time he was spiraling into despair, terrified of what would happen if she said no. Not to mention he still had to convince her to stick with him in spite of the inevitable scandal surrounding his identity. Carrie O'Brian's show was coming out this Friday and he better talk to Allison before that. He had to do it tonight.

Damn it. People were right after all; he was crazy and reckless and needed serious help.

"No," Tiffany blurted out, interrupting his lawyer mid-sentence. "I will not agree to anything that leaves me with less than full legal guardianship."

In the midst of his troubled thoughts, Jay felt like rolling his eyes at his sister. Gracie spent all day with Miranda and rarely saw her. Why would Tiffany insist so strongly on having the girl, except maybe as an occasional accessory?

As Attorney Kind took her seat, Ken Carter spoke to Jay's lawyer, Lewis Wall. "We strongly recommend that you take our offer of dropping your complaints about my client's mental stability in exchange for letting the girl visit her uncle for winter break and two weeks over summer break. Think like a judge would think. We're talking about a man with an unpredictable work schedule who travels constantly. Is he going to take his niece with him wherever he goes?"

"Yes," Jay answered. "I've traveled with her before and had her catch up with school work through online tutoring."

"Remember that we're talking about a girl here," Ken insisted.

"In a few short years, this girl will be a teenager. What kind of direction would she get without a maternal figure?"

There they go again. Carter's default argument was that he was a man, and therefore unlikely to offer the girl the guidance she needed. He knew what came next.

"And we also have to take into account that Mr. Johnson has been publicly open about his intention to remain single for the rest of his life," Ken added. "He will not be able, like my client, to offer the girl a steady family."

And, there they go again. Jay wanted to gag. Some steady family Tiffany had, even if she managed to save her current marriage. And what an irony that he was now married too, but couldn't rub it in their faces. On the contrary, when sooner than later they found out who he'd married—the same woman who was supposed to help Tiffany take his girl away from him—hell would break loose.

What a bad soap opera.

Why on earth was he putting himself through this?

Because I love that woman, damn it, and I'm not going down without a fight.

His phone rang, making him realize he'd forgotten to turn it off for the meeting. It was a call from Shawn and he remembered all the recent unheard voicemails and texts from his friend asking to call him urgently. He excused himself and took the call.

"Hey, Shawn, what's up?"

"I swear I didn't betray you. They pressured me, they tortured me. Richard used his scary FBI face. Fe threatened to withhold sex for the first time ever. But I would never—"

"Whoa. Slow down, man. What are you talking about?"

There was a silence on the other line. "You still don't know?"

"Know what?"

"Man, the girls found out everything somehow. They were on their way to Allison's office to catch her there since she wasn't answering her phone."

Fright clawed at Jay. "They're going to tell her?"

"If they didn't do it already! Man, if I were you I would rush and get to Allison before they do, to make sure she hears the story from you."

Jay caught a glimpse of flying papers, spinning chairs, and shocked looks as he left the meeting room and ran at top speed to Allison's office across the street.

Chapter 33

Joy had insisted on making Allison chamomile tea. Fe had insisted on rubbing her back "to help her relax before the news." It was taking forever to get to the point.

"Girls, what's going on? You're worrying me."

Fe took a seat and spoke first. "I'm so sorry. I swear I had no idea it was so serious. And even until the last minute, Shawn refused to talk."

"Talk about what?" Allison asked, growing more and more restless.

It must be the first time in her life Allison saw ultra-self-confident Hope nervous. "Liz commented on some things Gracie had told her that made me think."

"And then I talked to Ken," Emery intervened. "And he said a bunch of things, but I refused to believe it, so I asked Joy and Richard for help."

Richard intervened, "And knowing you'd been a witness for a drug-dealing case in another state in the past, I couldn't take any chances. I used FBI resources to research Jay. I confirmed he had changed his name legally in the past. And found other information that made me worried he's potentially dangerous."

Joy concluded, "Sweetie... Jay is—"

Every single hint and clue she'd previously overlooked jumped in front of Allison.

"*He goes by a different name now,*" Mercy had said.

"My last fight with my father before I left got kind of ugly," Jay had said.

"My uncle makes the best green beans in the world," Gracie had said.

"Jacob James Johnson," the Elvis impersonator marrying them had said.

The image of Jay's photo on his driver's license connected with an older memory of shaking a tall man's hand in a conference room.

Before Joy finished the sentence, Allison already knew. "Jacob Wetzel."

The cold realization hit Allison so abruptly she was in shock, unable to feel any pain.

Emery's face twisted with contrition. "Ken said Jay has been using you all this time and that all he wanted was to stop you from helping his sister. He said that all this was some form of revenge against his family—but that can't be true."

Before Allison could process those words, the door slammed open and Jay ran inside. "Allison! Wait, don't listen to them! Let me explain!"

Everything around Allison seemed to move in slow motion, like in a dream. She watched Agent Fields yell at Jay while blocking her with his body—but she couldn't understand any words. She watched Jay yelling back at Richard. Joy rushing to hold her. Fe, Hope, and Emery standing protectively beside her, staged like Charlie's Angels, ready to leap to her defense.

Jay's breathing was agitated. "Stay out of this, Fields. You think you know what's going on, but you don't!"

"Jay, you lied to me." Fe stepped forward, twirling an accusing finger.

He tried to take a step, but Richard contained him. "I never lied to you!"

Fe waved her hands in denial. "You did, and you lied to Allison too."

"Stop!"

Two security guards arrived out of somewhere and clasped Jay's arms, but his solid frame wouldn't budge.

"Allison! You have to listen to my side!" he kept yelling.

Agent Fields joined the guards' efforts and, between the three of them, they were finally able to muscle him out of the office.

"Where are they taking him?" Allison asked with a weak voice.

"To temporary detention until we can have a restraining order for you against him," answered Joy.

Allison's brain refused to understand. The shock had been so strong she felt faint. "Why? He hasn't done anything illegal, has he?"

Joy tightened the hold on her hand. "We still don't understand what's going on. When Shawn refused to talk, Richard went to Jay's therapist and subpoenaed him to break therapist-client privilege on behalf of law enforcement. The therapist confessed everything he knew. And then Richard got the FBI to hack into Jay's computers and phones and confirmed his obsessive activities."

"What obsessive activities?" Allison asked. She couldn't believe they'd managed to do so much in the few days they'd been gone.

Fe winced in concern as she placed her hand on Allison's shoulder. "I'm so sorry. I didn't know. Do you remember that woman I told you Jay had an unhealthy attachment to? The one he became obsessed with on and off to the point of stalking her?"

Allison nodded, but she wasn't sure she wanted to hear more.

It seemed like an eternity until Fe spoke again.

"Well… that woman is you."

Chapter 34

SUNKEN INTO HER DARKEST THOUGHTS, ALLISON WAITED IN the hallway until Richard and his team of men inspected every corner of her condo, making sure it was empty. Next to her, Joy clasped her arm and muttered soothing words, but her soul was impermeable to consolation.

It seemed like years since she'd been in her own home but it was just that morning. After the incident in her office, Richard and Joy had taken her to the police station to start the process of filing a restraining order against Jay. They'd then taken her for a late lunch/ early dinner while some of his contacts got the emergency court order. Even if Joy tactfully avoided any talk about the future, catastrophic thoughts overwhelmed Allison. Her career was in danger— the same career she'd claimed to hate. Now that seeing it end was a prospect, it was terrifying.

Not only had she gotten involved with a former client; she'd married him. And he was not just any client, but one who was seriously disturbed, using her for some incomprehensible revenge against his family. Even if she managed not to lose her license, the scandal would be unstoppable. She'd behaved like a reckless, immature woman.

It was already dark when they arrived to drop her at her place. Richard had arranged for someone to drop her car off in advance.

Richard emerged from the condo and held the door open. "It's safe; come in."

Mumbling a thank you, Allison dragged her feet into the place.

"I've alerted the building security and sent copies of the restraining order to the nearest police station," Richard said. "But if you still don't feel safe, I can arrange for an officer to stay here tonight."

"Or you can come and stay with us," Joy offered.

She shook her head. A corner of her mind knew she owed Richard a more formal thank you and an apology for how much she'd tortured him in the past—but right now she didn't have the energy.

Joy gave her one last, long hug and they left. She went straight to bed and lay in it fully dressed, knowing her chances of falling asleep were slim. Her physical safety was the least of her worries; her life had turned upside down.

Twenty-four hours ago she was the happiest woman in the world. She was in love. She was married to a man she was crazy about, one she admired and respected. She had a whole new life opening in front of her. Her biggest dilemma had been whether to keep her happiness hidden from her clients.

Now she wasn't even sure she had a job.

And she no longer had love.

Becoming a widow had to be better than falling from the cloud of love the way she had. At least a widow could treasure her memories. All Allison could do was wonder if her memories were even real, and if the man she loved had ever existed.

* * *

Allison did fall asleep and dreamed of being eight years old. She rode her pink bike, pedaling away from the house with the oak tree and the tire swing. Her hair flew in the wind, tears blowing away. She pedaled fast and cried, feeling the greatest pain she'd felt yet in her short life.

Back then she had no idea someone could hurt so much. A part of the little girl watched the event with detached attention, almost with the scientific interest of knowing she was discovering a new human experience.

A strong hand pinning both of her arms over her head woke Allison up. She opened her eyes but could see nothing in the pitch-dark room. She tried to scream, but another hand covered her mouth.

Her heart raced. She tried to hit the intruder, but his grip didn't budge. She tried to wiggle herself out of the restraint, but her knees were pressed down by something heavy—one of his legs.

This is it. She was sure she was going to die. Whether this person was a burglar or an assassin paid by Tiffany's family after finding out she'd married Jay, she had no escape.

A deep voice startled her. "I'm sorry. I am so sorry!"

She froze, recognizing Jay's voice. The night breeze hitting her suggested he'd climbed through a window.

In the darkness of the room, she couldn't see his face, but the sadness and remorse in his voice spoke volumes of the depth of his pain. "I'm so sorry," he repeated. "When I started this, I never intended to hurt your career. Never, in a million years could I have imagined things would get this far."

His apology sounded so sincere Allison's fear decreased. Having a better view of her face than she had of his, he seemed to notice it and released her from his hold.

She lowered her arms, feeling them tingle. Gosh, he was strong! It made her realize how vulnerable she'd been all this time. If he'd wanted to hurt her, she would've been helpless to fight him.

She finally found her voice. "You lied to me."

"I never did! I withheld some information from you; that's not the same as lying!"

Sliding on the bed edge, she sat as far from him as possible, leaning toward the headboard. "I'm your family's counselor! You're Tiffany's *brother*!"

"I didn't choose that."

She closed her eyes. "Do you realize that I've had five years to learn about the most disturbing details of your life? That I know everything about your violent tendencies, hurting your own father; about your drinking problem in college?"

"Everybody had a drinking problem in college!" He threaded a hand through his hair. "You have to consider your source. Chances are half of what you've heard is a lie or an exaggeration."

She spoke again. "You even managed to get me to marry you! Why was that? So no judge would ever believe what I said against you? To stop me from supporting Tiffany in court?"

"That's not what I was after! *Damn it!*"

He yelled so loudly it scared her. She reminded herself she was at the mercy of a psychologically unstable man and better keep her cool.

She finally gathered the courage to speak. "You were stalking me. The day we ran into each other at the beachside, did you plan it all along?"

A flash of guilt crossed his expression. "It was mostly coincidence."

"How long has this been going on?"

He seemed like a little boy being scolded. "On and off, about five years. Ever since I saw you at that family therapy session."

What have I done? I fell in love with an unstable man. I married an unstable man. "Oh, my God. You're completely crazy." She tried to bolt, but in a second he had pinned her down again, now holding each of her arms separately to the sides. His leg kept her knees from moving.

"I'm not crazy!"

She knew she shouldn't provoke him, but her pain was bigger than her self-preservation instinct. "It's the truth! Why else would you have stalked a complete stranger like me? Why else would you have gone to such lengths to seduce me and get me to trust you?"

"Grace."

It was just a whisper; still, she heard it clearly and it startled her to her core. "What did you just call me?"

His eyes pleaded for mercy. "Grace. It's me. It's Jake."

She stared at him blankly, unable to understand.

He softened the grip of his hands. "I'm Jake, from Port Popsicle, Wisconsin. From Ms. Zuckerman's second grade class. And before that, Ms. Smith's first grade class. And before that, Ms. Jones' kindergarten class. Don't you remember me?"

She was perplexed. It had been decades since she thought of those names.

He freed her legs and continued throwing facts at her. "I lived two blocks from you, in the old blue house with the giant oak tree and the tire swing in the front yard. We used to pretend that my attic was a spaceship and your basement was a submarine. You used to call me Cowlick. I had a brown and white Border collie that followed us everywhere…"

The last sentences clicked in her brain and a light switched on inside her. "Ginger!"

His face lit up and he let go of her hands. "Yes! My dog's name was Ginger! You remember!"

Hundreds of forgotten memories flooded Allison's mind. The two of them at the school playground, hanging from the monkey bars. Them, swimming in Lake Michigan together in the summer. It was them, building snowmen outside his house in the early winter. Them, catching fireflies in a glass jar at night. Them, hiding from their angry mothers inside the neighbor's barn after some mischief. Them, bringing cupcakes to school the same day because they shared a birthday.

And the day she went looking for him and Ginger at the tire swing to run away together—but he was gone.

Chapter 35

J AY WATCHED ALLISON SHAKE HER HEAD AGAIN AND AGAIN AS IF unable to understand his words.

"I couldn't believe it was you that day at the family therapy session," he began. Finally confessing his secret felt liberating. "Of course, I couldn't be sure it was you after so many years. But when you sneezed, I had a flashback of Ms. Jones calling the roll in kindergarten and saying your full name, 'Grace Allison Maxwell!' I stared at you the entire meeting, wondering if it was possible that I was in the same room with the first girl I fell in love with... And boy, what a gigantic crush I had on you back then!" He felt the blood rush to his face, reliving those old times. "You were the most beautiful thing I'd seen in my life! Yet, at first, you wouldn't give me the time of the day. The same way you ignored me in that therapy room."

Slowly, he sat on the edge of the bed and she sat too, keeping a distance from him.

He continued, "Finding you again felt miraculous. Happy scenes from childhood I'd completely forgotten about returned to me. I was more inspired than ever about getting back in shape. That night I went home and searched for you. I ordered your first book online. I've followed everything you've done ever since and read everything you've written.

"I couldn't believe my luck the day of Shawn and Fe's wedding when I ran into you—it was worth the risk of you running me over. At first, I thought that if I could just have you for a while, I'd finally humanize you and I'd move on. Many times after that I almost gave up, convinced that you were not the Grace I once knew."

"And then?" She sat an inch closer to him, absorbing the story.

Feeling powerless, he lifted his hands. "Then you danced and laughed the day you got the doll, and it was like being back in time with you. And I was hooked. I became addicted to that sound of delight, and all I wanted was to hear it again and again."

Growing hopeful by her more open attitude, he inched his hand closer to hers on the bed. "And I did see little Grace emerge again when we spent time together. But in between her appearances, I was getting to know *you*, Allison. And you blew me away—with your intelligence, with your soundness, with all that grounded maturity I lack. And every day it got better. And I couldn't stop."

He eased his hand closer. If he could get her to accept physical contact that would be the first step for reconnecting. "I knew that the moment I told you who I was I would need to explain how I'd found you. And that if you learned I was Jacob Wetzel, you'd push me away. Later on, I was sure I'd find a way to free you from your career, so we could be together." He moved his hand the last stretch and held hers.

An interminable silence fell in the room. If her face had always been inscrutable that day it became a mystery. His pulse raced as he awaited her next words, like a prisoner who awaits the verdict of a judge.

"You left me," she finally said in a whisper. "I went looking for you at the tire swing that morning."

He nodded. "We were supposed to run away, take Ginger with us to sniff our way into finding my mother." He chuckled at their clueless innocence back then but was also surprised by the sharp pain stabbing his chest and the tears threatening to spill from his eyes. "We still hadn't understood that she'd never be back; that she'd died."

"You left me," she repeated as if in a trance. "I never understood why you disappeared."

Sour sadness rising in him, he discreetly wiped moisture from a corner of his eye. "The last time we saw each other was the same night my father came to get me and took me to Chicago."

"Joy was right," she whispered. "I did have a big heartbreak in my life. *It was you.*" Covering her face with her free hand, she cried quietly.

Jay was dying to take her in his arms and console her, but not daring to, he limited himself to holding her hand. He felt like sobbing too, remembering his powerlessness back then. What different times those were, almost thirty years back, without Internet or cell phones to keep in touch.

Fortunately, strong as she was, Allison recomposed herself shortly. She wiped her eyes and her nose with the long sleeve of her business suit. "After two weeks searching for you everywhere and not finding you, I lost my temper and yelled at my stepfather. That was the day he hit me."

He froze, not knowing what to answer.

"I'm overwhelmed, and flooded with memories right now," she added. "Precisely the memories I fought all my life to bury."

"I... I'm sorry."

"I wish you'd never found me." She pulled her hand away from his.

He felt like he'd been punched in the stomach. "Allison."

She rose from the bed. "You're the symbol of the most difficult and confusing times of my life."

He wasn't expecting that. "Darling, but don't you remember? Those were also the happiest days of our childhood."

"Maybe *your* childhood," she interrupted. "I wish I could say, like you, that finding you again has brought me joy. But it didn't. And finding out you're a Wetzel, right after having allowed myself to trust you, is really hitting me hard. I'll never be able to let you in again."

If she'd lost her temper like she had so many times before, he'd have been less worried. But at this moment, the coldness in her voice chilled his bones. Never, in all the years he imagined his reunion with his Grace, could he have predicted she'd reject him. And until the last minute, he'd held on to the dumb illusion that remembering him from childhood would magically make Allison forgive him.

And then he realized something worse. Dr. Hazenberg had been right. He had lived his life under the delusion that if he could only find Grace, he'd undo the moment his father entered his life and would be able to return to the bliss of his early childhood. How stupid he had been.

But if he'd already lost Grace, he couldn't lose Allison too. "Darling, you can't push aside everything we've shared in the past months. I love you. And I know you love me too—you said it."

"I don't know you anymore."

He felt as if she had slapped his face. "We've known each other forever."

She stepped away. "I never knew you for real."

She walked out of the bedroom and into the living room. Confused, he followed her.

Opening the front door, she jerked her head toward it. "Get out of here."

Every bit of pain he'd ever repressed in his life clogged in his chest, choking him, while anger and frustration bubbled. "You can't leave me. You can't abandon *us*. I've spent my adult life searching for you—"

"Get out." Her voice was glacial.

The fire of anger replaced his sadness and rage simmered. "Allison, if you push me away now, I'll never forgive you."

They locked eyes. A subtle fluttering of her eyelids showed her hesitation before the mask of coldness took over again. "Out."

He plodded to the door. He stopped at the threshold and turned around to search her eyes, pleading for mercy.

She gave him a final push and slammed the door in his face.

Chapter 36

EVERY TIME ALLISON THOUGHT THE PAIN COULDN'T GET ANY worse, it did. Two days after their fight, she received an Express mail package from Jay, returning all her things. From her spare toothbrush to the clothes he'd kidnapped the day he asked her to give their marriage a trial, to the Christmas lights he'd hung for her in his hotel room. Opening the box had been like getting punched in the ribs. He wasn't kidding when he said he'd never forgive her.

Feeling too depressed to try to help anyone, she'd taken an indefinite leave of absence from work and spent the past two weeks hiding in her condo, writing. The last week, she'd shut down her phone to avoid calls from relentless reporters, asking to talk about her appearance on the Carrie O'Brian's special.

Worried about her silence, Joy, Hope, and Emery came to check on her. Unable to hold everything in anymore, she caught them up, starting with the events of the trip to LA.

When Allison concluded, Emery placed a hand on her chest and sighed. "This is the most romantic story I've ever heard!"

Allison shot her a baffled look. The labyrinths of that woman's brain were unconquerable for her. "Uh... *Romantic*? Are you talking about the creepy story of him stalking me for years? Or about our mock Vegas wedding when he wanted to punish me for standing him up?"

"Oh, come on!" Emery's expression was all serious, scientific interest. "Obviously, your unconscious remembered him from the past and that's the explanation for why you fell for him so quickly. And obviously, the only way you could get around your resistance to love was to create a situation like that."

Allison stared at her blankly. "*I created* this situation?"

"Use your therapist brain here!" Emery insisted. "For example, you probably caused that fight in LA as a way to fulfill your deepest secret wish of marrying him."

Allison glowered at Emery. "You analyze things too much. And this comes from someone who used to make a living analyzing people."

Hope was clearly fighting a smile. "I agree with Emery. You could've perfectly said no when he came up with the idea. You secretly wanted to marry him."

"For the hundredth time, my brain wasn't working well." With a grunt, Allison covered her eyes, wanting to disappear. "I was sleep-deprived; we'd been in a state of euphoria for days. I'm convinced he brainwashed me, the same way he brainwashes his boot camp participants."

Joy stroked her arm. "You have a point, sweetie. Studies show that sleep deprivation can impair the brain's functioning similar to alcohol."

Allison felt thankful for Joy's usual unconditional acceptance.

"How are you holding up?" Joy asked.

She didn't want to worry her friends telling them how she was living off her emergency savings. "I'm okay," she replied, not sounding convincing to herself. "I've been writing so much I haven't missed social interaction."

"So, is that a new book you're writing?"

She shrugged. "I don't know yet. I've written over fifty thousand words, but so far it's just a collection of random thoughts and memories from childhood." *And memories of Jay.*

Jay. Not Jake or Cowlick, the little boyfriend who broke her heart by standing her up that day at the tire swing. *Jay*, the man she'd fallen in love with. The man who'd helped her rediscover the joy of stomping in puddles, and chasing seagulls, and manufacturing rainbows from a prism and a beam of light.

And the joys of the flesh.

"Is there a common thread?" Joy asked. "Could it eventually become a book about healing from childhood?"

"It might, if it ever stopped hurting like hell every time I re-read the lines." Allison laid her arms on the dining table and rested her head on them. After decades of blocking the pain, she was still re-learning how to deal with it. "I'm a psychotherapist. Nobody knows more than me about confronting painful memories. Every minute that I'm not writing, I've been reading the psychological theories of healing your inner child. At an intellectual level, I know what's going on: I've just found my wounded inner child and she's desolate. Experts say now I have to rescue her. That I have to give little Grace the protection and the nurturing she didn't have before. Tell her that no one can hurt her anymore. But I don't know how. I can't reach her."

Silence fell. Joy caressed her back with tenderness and Allison felt like crying, remembering the time Jay had cradled her in his arms like a baby.

But she refused to feel sorry for herself. Composing herself, she straightened up. "Enough sulking. I have to think about the future. I have no idea if the Wetzels already know what's going on, or if they've filed an official complaint against my license."

"Ken didn't tell them," Emery intervened. "I warned him that if he said a word, he'd never see me again."

"Then maybe not all is lost," Hope said. "You can talk to them first and apologize. Explain that you didn't know anything. I'm sure they'll understand and agree not to report you."

Playing with her pink satin pajama buttons, Allison considered it. "I was already on the fence about continuing this career. Even if we could get Ken and Karen to keep the secret about my relationship with Jay, can I show up to work every day pretending nothing happened?"

"You have the argument of deceit, in order to get an annulment without Jay's cooperation," Hope argued, the eternal practical thinker. "Maybe we can still keep this marriage a secret and you can re-start your career where you left off."

Emery's phone rang with a FaceTime call and, sitting next to her, Allison noticed it was Karen.

"Hello. Karen?" Emery asked, obviously surprised to get a call from her.

"I know you're in Allison's house. She refuses to acknowledge my calls. Put her on the line NOW."

Eyes wide, Emery handed the phone to Allison.

On the screen, Karen scowled, her nostrils flaring. "I'm sorry, Karen. I'm not hiding from you; just from the whole world. I was—"

"Are you trying to commit career suicide? How could you do this?" Karen interrupted her.

Surprised by the abrupt statement, Allison went back in her mind, trying to remember their last conversation. "What are you talking about? I followed your advice. I never went to the premiere."

"Have you Googled yourself lately? The stupid video of your Vegas wedding has gone viral on YouTube! Everybody is talking about it on the whole freaking Internet!"

Allison's heart thudded. Emery jerked in her chair, Joy whipped her head toward her. With wide-open eyes, Hope turned to stare at Allison.

"That's not possible!" Allison whispered, feeling as if the walls of the room were closing in.

Karen gave her a killer look across the screen. "Your dream has come true. You're famous now!"

Trembling, Allison disconnected the call and opened her laptop, set on the table, to search her own name. Her friends moved behind her.

She found dozens of online articles posted over the past few days.

"Triple J elopes with mystery woman."

"The new Mrs. Legendary Heroes: The feminist in his Boot Camp."

"Triple J and the Triple B."

Hope bit her thumbnail. "I guess my suggestion of pretending the marriage never happened doesn't apply anymore."

Allison scanned over the articles, unable to believe her eyes. Somehow, Wayne Nash had found out about Jay's trip to Vegas, tracked down the Elvis impersonator officiant, and offered him money for the wedding pictures and video.

A feeling of impending doom fell over her. *And I thought I was in trouble before.*

* * *

Jay was having that dream again. He was eight. His little best friend held him in her surprisingly strong arms, and he felt just a bit less sad and scared.

"Everything's going to be okay," Grace mumbled, stroking his back. After the most confusing week he'd ever had it felt good to hold on to one thread of his life that was still unchanged.

"I'll tell you what we'll do, Cowlick," Grace declared with her usual self-confident voice, relaxing the hug and piercing him with her sky-blue eyes. "Tomorrow early morning, we'll give Ginger one of your mom's sweaters to smell, and she'll guide us to her."

His soul filled with hope. Grace was a genius! He knew that if someone could help him out of this mess and make things normal again, it was her. "Yes! Let's do that!" He answered with a feeble voice, holding her hands tightly.

Grace continued. "Grown-ups will try to stop us, so don't tell anybody. Pack a bag tonight and I'll come get you tomorrow morning at the tire swing."

Jay woke up slowly and the moment he was fully awake the little peace sleep had brought him was gone. He hated taking sleeping pills for the little effect they had, but he'd felt so depressed lately he feared what his brain could plan during his long nights of insomnia. He couldn't even make himself go to the gym—not even to vent his anger and frustration by working out to excruciating pain.

He lay in bed awake for the longest time, staring at the ceiling and processing the dream. He'd spent his adult life plastering a smile on his face, pushing through his root traumas of losing his mother and learning about his father's rejection. And the only thing that kept him going was the delusional hope that finding Grace would send him back to his life of childhood bliss, before his wounds.

And now that he'd found her, she'd pushed him away. He'd lost Grace *and* Allison at the same time.

If he ever thought he'd touched bottom in his life before, he knew nothing.

Now *this* was real depression.

He dragged himself out of bed and headed to the kitchen without even washing his face. There he found Ethan and Shawn sitting at the breakfast counter.

"Good morning," Jay mumbled and automatically reached for the coffee maker to pour himself a cup. The coffee he found inside was cold.

"It's actually seven in the evening, but that's okay," Ethan replied. "I'm glad you finally dozed off."

A corner of Jay's brain registered how much stronger his friend looked and how fast his brown hair was re-growing. But he felt no desire to make a comment. He took a long sip of the day-old cold black coffee. It tasted horrible, but he didn't care. "What are you doing here?" he asked Shawn.

"The usual." Shawn shrugged. "Making sure I don't have to medicate you. Making sure Ethan has the suicide hotline on speed dial."

"Oh, he *is* suicidal," Ethan commented, serious. "Yesterday I caught him staring at an egg like he was planning to—" He faked a gasp. "*Eat the yolk!*"

Taking a seat on the remaining barstool, Jay deadpanned, "Very funny."

There was sincere worry in Shawn's blue-green eyes. "Have I mentioned that I was *not* the one who told on you? That Richard threatened me with obstruction of justice charges, and Fe threatened me with a sex-strike, and I still didn't cave?"

"Yeah," Ethan nodded. "You've mentioned it a couple of hundred times."

"It's okay," Jay muttered. "Nothing matters now."

Shawn fidgeted in his seat. "I'm sorry, but I'm lost. You don't drink, you don't eat junk food, you don't follow real sports, and lately, you don't even want to go bike riding. I have no idea what to do to cheer you up."

"It's okay," Jay repeated. "You won't have to put up with my dark mood for much longer. I'm leaving."

Shawn and Ethan exchanged a puzzled look. Shawn recovered first. "Leaving for where?"

"I don't know yet. Climb a mountain, scuba dive somewhere. Anywhere I don't have to think."

"You're running away? You're giving up on Gracie?" Ethan asked, serious.

He drank the sour coffee to ease the knot in his throat. "She's better off with her grandparents—*real* adults."

"How about work?" Shawn asked.

Jay shrugged. "It's winding down. I always knew this spark of fame would come to an end sooner than later." The truth was, he hadn't updated his website or posted on his video blog for a month.

You're trying to sabotage your success again. He heard Allison's voice.

Damn it, Allison, get out of my head.

"Are you seriously leaving just like that?" Ethan asked scowling.

"With Gracie gone, and Allison breaking up with me, I have nothing to tie me here anymore."

Shawn crossed his arms and tilted his head. "You have to admit Allison didn't really 'break up' with you. You beat the crap out of her life, and she wasn't happy about it—who can blame her?"

"You're preaching to the choir!" Jay drank the remainder of the disgusting coffee as if to punish himself. "I was such an idiot. I've spent my life doing reckless things, always trusting that my good luck would catch me in the end. I can't believe I managed to practically… destroy her life."

"Haven't you tried to reach her?"

He groaned. "Nonstop for the past two weeks, ever since the news about our marriage exploded. She ignores my texts and calls." He dropped the empty cup in the sink. "Fe told me she's going through a rough patch, even financial strain now that she closed her practice. And it's killing me to know she's suffering and there's nothing I can do."

A long silence fell, broken by Ethan. "And do you really think that running away to climb a mountain is going to help her? You're her freaking husband. Support her."

Powerless, Jay lifted his hands. "Do you think she'll ever take money from me?"

"We'll never find out if you quit your damn job and don't have a dime to offer her, will we?" Ethan gave him a cynical grin.

Jay processed Ethan's words. He was right. He had a responsibility to help clean up the mess in Allison's life. And he couldn't do that by running away.

"But don't take crappy advice from me," Ethan added. "What would *she*, the ultimate therapist, tell you to do?"

It didn't take long to come up with the answer. "She'd tell me to stop sulking and pouting and sabotaging my success." He paused. "And she'd tell me it's time to take Matt's business offer."

It was decided. If he ever wanted to help Allison and have a chance to recover his niece Gracie, he needed to get himself a secure financial future. *It's time to grow up a little.* Just making the decision lifted his depression a notch.

Ethan added, "And what could *you*, the ultimate life coach, do to help Allison?"

Many answers crossed Jay's mind. One stronger answer emerged. "Help her find her joyful inner child again."

"Can you think of a way you could do that?"

It was like the sun slowly peeped out from behind the clouds as Jay remembered the box from his grandmother's attic. "I have an idea."

Chapter 37

"**A**LLISON! ALLISON!"

Emery's voice and the sound of loud banging on her door woke up Allison abruptly. She had no idea what time it was. Lately, she'd fallen into a reverse schedule of sleeping during the day and writing at night when the noises around were at the minimum. She lived in pajamas and couldn't remember the last time she'd washed her hair.

A glance at her phone told her it was 3:17 p.m. What day? It must be a weekend since Emery wasn't at the hospital.

She stumbled out of bed in her wrinkled pajamas and staggered to the door. There she found not only Emery but also Fe.

Yawning and rubbing her eyes she asked, "What's the matter?"

"You have to see this!" Fe held an iPad in front of Allison's face, almost shoving it down her nose. "Jay sent you a message through YouTube."

"What?" Allison's blood froze in her veins, but she soon had to retreat to avoid getting hit in the face by Fe's passionate hands.

"He emailed me two links and begged me to make sure you watch them. And to tell you to open the box he sent you while you do."

The day before, Allison had received another package from Jay in the mail and she hadn't bothered to open it, assuming it was another delivery of her things. "I can't, Fe. I know what he's going to say. He must be furious with me."

Emery shook her head adamantly. "One of them is a private video, so we didn't watch it without you, but the other one is public, so we did. He took responsibility for everything! He admits he developed an obsession with you. He says he tricked you into marrying him, he says you were an innocent bystander and asks you to forgive him for affecting your career."

A faint hope pulsated in Allison. "Did he say he wants me back?"

Emery's expressive eyes fluttered. "Uh, well... not *literally*."

Fe took over. "But he did say something important. He said his followers won't hear from him for a while because he'll be busy starting a new project in California. Allison, he's leaving for LA tomorrow. This message must be his way of giving you one last chance to stop him."

She felt as she'd been splashed with cold water. "He finally accepted Matthew Hester's offer. I'm happy for him."

"Please, Alli-gator!" Emery begged. "You have to watch the video he sent you. What if this is where he declares his love for you and asks you to meet him at midnight on top of the city's tallest building?"

Fe shot Emery a puzzled look. "I think that would be the hospital's tenth floor."

Bracing herself, Allison walked to the living room and dropped onto the white leather sofa. She was aware of the empty Chinese takeout cartons and dirty laundry on the floor. "What's the point of watching the video if he's leaving anyway and I'll never see him again? Masochism?"

"But... Allison!" Fe protested.

Still wrapping her arms around herself, she rocked back and forth. "If in that video he says he hates me, it'll break my heart. If he says he loves me, it'll hurt even worse. Because there's nothing he can say that can fix the fact that I can't be with him. I couldn't take it, girls. Not right now. Maybe tomorrow, or next week, when I gather some strength to face it."

"But... by then it may be too late!"

She lifted a hand. "I'm sorry, Fe. I can't."

Emery stamped her foot on the floor, startling Allison. "Grace Allison Connors-*Johnson!* Listen to me!" Her voice was thunder. Her angular green eyes seemed about to shoot lightning. "Do you remember the day you elbowed me in the face and gave me a black eye, a week before my wedding that never happened? Remember how you ruined my photo sessions?"

Shrinking back into the couch, Allison nodded.

"You owe me. And today I'm collecting. Watch the damn video. NOW!"

Allison had never seen Emery so serious. Weakly, she bobbed her head. Emery rushed to tap the link, pulled Fe by the arm, and they both left the house.

* * *

The moment Jay appeared on the iPad, Allison regretted agreeing to watch it. He'd made an effort to shave, but his hair was growing longer and showing gray on the temples, in that way he only let happen when he was under stress. His hazel eyes were loaded with grief and shaded by shadows. She could feel his pain through the screen.

"This message is not about us. It's about you," he said in the video.

Bad beginning.

"I'm not here to ask for forgiveness, or to beat a dead horse repeating that I love you. I'm here because I know you're suffering. Because you need to reinvent your life, and I'm an expert on that."

There was not a shred of pity in his reverent expression. "I've been there, darling. Everything you used to be is gone, but you haven't yet replaced it with something new. You think the pain will never go away, but it will. The reason it feels like you're dying is precisely because it's true. You're about to enter a new incarnation within this life. But before that happens, you have to die to your old self. And

251

that's never easy. Trust me, it will all be worth it in the end."

Tears brimmed in her eyes. She wished so much he could take her in his arms again.

"A life coach is not supposed to try to counsel a doctor in psychology." His playfulness on the screen lifted her soul. "But my impression is that you're too obsessed with your childhood wounds. Yes, you found your wounded inner child. Yes, it hurts… but you need to remind yourself that's not who you always were. You need to find the Grace before the fall. The one who was happy, joyful, innocent…"

She shook her head and talked to the iPad. "It's useless! I can't reach her."

"You were the most joyful little girl I've ever seen," he continued. "Your laughter is still recorded in my brain."

"I don't ever remember being like that," she whispered.

In the video, he lifted a box and placed it on the table in front of him. "Now open the last box I sent you."

Allison started in her seat. "The box. What did I do with the last box?"

She paused the video and, in a frenzy, searched her messy apartment until she found the unopened box hidden away in a linen closet. She used a kitchen knife to open it and a thrift store-like smell—mothballs and aging paper—hit her. The top of the box revealed a discolored school picture she immediately recognized as her kindergarten class.

As she searched the contents of the box, laughter and tears mixed. Jay must've taken a trip back to Wisconsin to rescue those things. Besides several school pictures, the box contained old toys, valentines she'd given him in school, and a long ancient dress she remembered finding in his grandma's attic.

A thousand flashbacks rushed through her mind. Christmas mornings opening presents, removing her first doll from its box, enjoying its plastic smell. Slipping on her favorite ladybug T-shirt, and little patent leather shoes with lacy socks. A hundred trips to the playground, riding her pink bike, to play with Cowlick.

She hit play on the video again. He went over the items in the box, reciting memories and quoting adventures they'd had together. Some of them she no longer recalled, but the rest she remembered so vividly she couldn't believe it. Blowing dandelions in the wind in the spring. Water fights in the lake during the summer. Jumping in the leaf piles in the fall. Winter sleigh rides they enjoyed so much they continued even after they fell and needed stitches—she under her chin, he over his right eyebrow.

"Do you remember this?" he asked and held up the dress she'd already pulled from the box. "You thought I was teasing you the day you almost ran me over, but it was true. A long time ago you wore this dress in my grandmother's attic. We danced together and then I kissed you. And the dress did get stuck over your head when you tried to take it off, and we guffawed, and fell on an old mattress as I freed you from it."

She laughed and cried, and laughed some more. Sitting on the carpeted floor, surrounded by toys and relics, absorbing his every word. For the first time in her life, she indulged in thinking about her childhood and not even once did she remember her stepfather.

"By second grade the other boys were teasing me for hanging out with a girl all the time," he said. "At once, they all decided that girls were disgusting. But, of course, this was no ordinary girl. This was *my Grace*, the coolest kid in the whole neighborhood." He smiled softly. "She was the brightest kid in class and could explain the lesson to me better than any teacher could. It's no wonder I was in love with her." He paused. "And it's no wonder I still am."

The video came to an end and Allison stared at the screen, processing it all.

We have to stop him! the little Grace inside her said. *You can't let him move away again*!

With a grunt, she climbed back on the couch and said aloud, "This gesture is beautiful, but it doesn't change anything. He's still the psychologically unstable man with known rage issues who stalked me for years. And I still can't be with him if I ever want to be a counselor again." The pain threatened to resurge in her soul, but the lingering bittersweet joy his video had brought her wouldn't let her fall back into despair. She straightened up in her seat. "But at least this does inspire me to stop sulking and pick up the pieces of my life again."

She knew she had to make amends with the people she'd unintentionally hurt. As much as she dreaded it, it was time to face the Wetzels.

Chapter 38

SITTING IN THE HUGE FORMAL LIVING ROOM AT THE WETZEL'S riverside mansion, Allison's chest tightened with anxiety. She hadn't expected them to say yes so quickly when she called yesterday requesting to see them.

Under different circumstances, she would've taken the time to appreciate the grand space they sat in. She'd been in that house many times, at various fundraiser galas they'd hosted. She'd always admired the cathedral ceilings, the crystal and gold chandeliers hanging from carved medallions, and the pristine hardwood floors, glossy enough to compete with the marble and jasper central fireplace—a beauty, though rarely used in Florida.

Across from her, on the antique furniture, sat a contrite-looking Conan and Regina Wetzel, along with a bored Tiffany browsing the web on her cell.

"Once again, I'm truly, deeply sorry about all this," Allison said. "I swear I had no idea that the Jay Johnson I was dating was Jacob Wetzel."

A long silence fell, increasing Allison's apprehension. She made an effort not to fidget in her seat. Behind her polite perfection, Allison guessed Regina Wetzel felt disturbed. It was impossible to know what Conan thought or felt.

Tiffany spoke first. "Why are you wasting my time making me listen to this generic apology to my family? You were *my* therapist. I am the one who was betrayed, and I should be getting a personal apology." She turned to her parents. "Would you give us some privacy, please?"

Conan reached for his cane to get up, but he wasn't fast enough for Tiffany's preference. "Never mind." With a huff, she stood up and signaled Allison to follow her.

Confused, Allison bowed her head in goodbye to Conan and Regina and followed Tiffany through a gigantic great room she knew was used as a dance floor during the fundraisers.

"Dr. Allison!"

Allison recognized the tiny voice as Gracie's. Before she could answer, the girl ran toward her and surprised her with a hug more effusive than she would've expected. Gracie then broke the embrace and looked at her with eagerness. "You're here! Does that mean we're still working on the mediation with Ms. Kind? Does that mean there's a hope I can see Uncle again?"

The desperation in the girl's eyes was moving. But it was also the first time Allison didn't feel sadness to see her face. "I... not really, sweetie. I don't work with your family anymore."

Disappointment filled Gracie's eyes. "Oh. I..."

"Excuse me, Gracie," Tiffany said, impatient. "We're busy here. Go with Miranda."

"But, Mom, I'm talking to Dr. Allison."

"Well, Dr. Allison and I have some things to talk about, okay?" Tiffany's voice rose on the last word with the petulance of a seven-year-old.

"Fine! I'm leaving." Gracie stomped away.

As the girl marched away, she turned and shot Allison one last look that seemed like a cry for help. Then, her little shoulders slumped, and she shuffled across the great room before disappearing through a door.

Allison felt the unreasonable urge to rescue that little girl as a symbol of rescuing herself at that age.

Tiffany guided Allison up a large, curved staircase and to a bedroom. Feeling awkward, she stopped at the threshold, but Tiffany insisted she come in.

Allison stepped into a room that seemed like a memorial. Every inch of the walls was covered with memorabilia from Tiffany's childhood show and posters of her from ages seven to twelve. Allison's inner therapist felt sorry for that woman, stuck in the only time of her life when her fame had matched her life expectations—the rest of her felt a little freaked out.

"I couldn't believe it when I heard the news," Tiffany said, frowning and bracing herself. "There I was, thinking you were my role model for what a strong, successful woman was supposed to be. And you were running around with my brother and acting so reckless as to… marry him? What were you thinking?"

Allison felt the blood rush to her face. "You're absolutely right. I owe you an apology for every time I reprimanded you for jumping into a new relationship too fast."

Tiffany seemed surprised as if she'd expected Allison to defend herself.

Allison went on, "I owe you an apology if I ever judged you or displayed any condescension toward you. This experience was a humbling lesson. Never again will I be harsh toward a woman who made an impulsive decision about her love life."

For a moment, Tiffany seemed moved.

Avoiding her eyes, Allison paced the room. "Without knowing it, I failed my ethical commitment as a therapist. I obviously can no longer be your counselor, but if there's anything I can do to compensate your family for my behavior, I would like to do it." She swallowed. "Except that I will have to recuse myself from Gracie's guardianship case. I'm sorry if this causes you to be deprived of your little girl's company."

"I don't want her company," Tiffany mumbled.

Allison was startled. "What did you just say?"

With a sigh, Tiffany looked up at the ceiling. "Do you think it's fun dealing night and day with a girl who looks so much like I used to look back then, the only time of my life when I was successful?" She walked to one of the posters on the walls. Allison could see the resemblance, but in her opinion, Gracie was a much prettier girl. "And can you imagine how it's going to be in ten years when I'm close to forty and she's eighteen?" Tiffany continued, "When my boobs are falling and hers are perkier than ever? When my skin starts sagging and she looks as gorgeous as I can only imagine she's going to look? I have no desire to go through that."

Allison made an effort to keep her face impassive. "Then why? Why did you insist on keeping her?"

Tiffany walked to a mini-bar in her room to serve herself a dry scotch. "Gracie's trust fund is more complicated than most people know."

"What?"

She took a long sip. "She not only has that Donovan Trust from her father's family I told you about, but Dad specifically wrote his will to screw me. He's leaving my share of his fortune to Grace. Bypassing me. He's not leaving *me* anything—I mean, just a miserable pension."

The wheels in Allison's brain started turning.

Tiffany took another sip. "His will's instructions spell out that the Wetzel Trust for Gracie will be administered by 'her legal guardian.' He didn't mention me by name, on purpose. Because he's never trusted me."

Allison understood. "That means that…"

"That means that if I lose her, I have nothing. The moment Dad is gone, I'm living on a budget."

She was perplexed. "Does Jay know that?"

"I doubt it." Tiffany snorted. "The sucker was willing to take over her without touching the Donovan Trust and without even asking for financial support from me."

Every bit of loyalty she had left for Tiffany disappeared. "Are you telling me that all the pain your family has gone through—the legal battle ripping your parents and your brother apart—all of which I thought was fueled by love for your daughter... has been about *money*?"

"Don't try to make me into the bad guy now." Tiffany rolled her eyes. "I've always felt like the third wheel, the betrayed woman in a triangle. My brother and Gracie have this... sickening puppy love for each other. He's been with her every Wednesday and visited her most holidays since she learned to walk. He wasn't going to stop seeing her, no matter what any judge said, so why sweat it."

Allison's heart wrenched, understanding things better now, and realizing for the first time the suffering Jay must've been going through being separated from his niece.

"And about this legal fight 'tearing apart' Jake and my parents," Tiffany argued. "The damage was done long ago. Dad exaggerated his hip injury and accused Jake of pushing him to take him to court when we all knew he'd messed up his hip long before that. And do you know why he did all that?" Allison was too shocked to respond, but Tiffany went on anyway. "To get him to come back from Atlanta and talk to him, damn it. Because he's the only one of all his children my father ever gave a damn about. That's why I hate him."

Allison wanted to cry. "I'm sorry," she muttered shaking her head. "The therapist in me would hold your hand right now and try to reassure you that those feelings are okay and you should not be ashamed of them. But, thank God, I can't be your therapist any longer. *I don't want to.*" She headed for the door. Once at the threshold, she stopped and turned around to add, "If you want to report me to the licensing agency, go ahead. I want no favors from your family. There's only one member among you who's decent and honest." She felt grief and regret clog in her throat. "And I was so stupid I pushed him away." Without waiting for an answer, she stomped out of the room.

Allison sped down the stairs, fighting tears. She wanted out of that house as soon as possible. She wanted nothing to do with those people ever again. She rushed across the expansive great room and had almost reached the door when a deep voice called her.

"Allison."

Recognizing Conan Wetzel's voice, she stopped in her tracks and pivoted to face him. For a moment, she considered giving him a piece of her mind for the way his family had been treating Jay. But the apologetic look in his eyes held her. His expression was of deep pain.

"Allison," he repeated, misery thick in his voice. "I... I have a confession to make."

Chapter 39

ALLISON SAT IN THE LIVING ROOM OF HER CONDO WITH HER four girlfriends.

"Wait, I'm having a hard time following," Hope said. "Jay's father caused all this *on purpose*?"

"Everything!" Allison rubbed her temples. "He knows Tiffany is fighting to keep Gracie just for the money. He could've just changed his freaking will and fixed it all. But he's terrified that if he lets Jay take Gracie, Jay will move somewhere far away with her and he'll never see either of them again. And all those acts of 'hate' Jay saw from his father: the lawsuit, taking away Gracie... they've all been desperate attempts to get his attention, to get him into the same room, so they could talk."

"Wow," Joy exclaimed, placing a hand on her chest. "So, the only way he gets to see his favorite son is if he drags him into court?"

Fe threw her hands in the air. "And I thought *my* family was dramatic."

With a sigh, Allison covered her eyes. "But the worst part was hearing from Tiffany that those horror stories they told me about Jacob Wetzel... I mean about Jay... They weren't true!" She dropped herself back on her seat. "God, I should've listened to him."

Emery's face went blank. Her eyelashes fluttered and her lips trembled. Her breath quickened and her hands shook, and Allison knew what was coming next.

"THAT'S WHAT I'VE BEEN SAYING FOR WEEKS! Didn't I tell you yesterday to go get him? Now he's gone and it's too late!"

Allison checked the time on her phone. "You're right. He's on his way to LA now."

"No, he's not!" Holding her phone, Hope raised a finger. "His flight is delayed! He might still be at the gate waiting to board!"

"Allison, you have to stop him! Call him!" Emery begged.

With fingers made clumsy by emotion, Allison dialed his number, but it went straight to voicemail. "He must've already switched his phone to airplane mode. It's too late!"

"It's not!" Emery insisted. "As long as the plane hasn't taken off, there's still hope."

"We can still make it!" Hope remarked. "The new departure time is in forty minutes, and it's only a twenty-minute drive to the airport. You can still sink that Titanic!"

Allison paced the room. "But they won't let me go through security without a ticket. By the time we get there the plane doors will be closed and no one will be allowed in."

"I know what would give us more time," Emery blurted out. "Let's fake call the airport saying there's a bomb on that plane!"

Allison resisted the urge to palm her face. "Emery, I have no patience for your wild imagination today."

"But what else do you suggest?" Emery asked, jittery. "What else would make the airport authorities stop that plane?"

A knock on the door was followed by Joy's fiancé entering. "Angel, you forgot your cell phone in the car again."

Hope lifted one eyebrow, and Allison could tell she was hatching a plan. "Do you know who the airport authorities always listen to? The FBI."

Her stomach knotted, Allison slowly turned to Richard, her long-term nemesis. "Agent Fields." She swallowed. "Would you be willing to set aside our issues and help me have a shot at happiness?"

A satisfied smirk crossed his face and Allison held her breath.

After what seemed like an eternity, he finally replied, "If you ask nicely."

* * *

Jay hated that flight from Fort Sunshine to Atlanta, his stop before heading to LA. His long legs always felt cramped in small planes without a business class. And on top of his flight delay, the plane had been stuck on the runway for half an hour, waiting for something. He hoped he didn't lose his connection.

But his low spirits went beyond that. He'd told himself he never expected Allison to reply to the video message he sent her, but maybe a part of him did. He'd been feeling lower than ever since yesterday when he didn't hear from her.

The intense surge of pain surprised him. He never thought he'd care about someone more than he cared about Grace. But Allison had done it. The woman she was now had stolen his heart even more than the little girl she'd once been.

Trying to distract himself, he searched his laptop carrier for wireless headphones when two male flight attendants approached. "Mr. Jacob James Johnson?"

Was it his imagination or did they both seem about to crap their pants? "Yes?"

The man who'd spoken swallowed. "We need you to come with us for a minute. It's a routine additional security check they forgot to do."

"Okay." He was starting to scoot out of the seat when the other man added, "We also need you to bring your carry-on luggage."

Confused, Jay put his business jacket back on, hung his laptop carrier strap diagonal across his chest and removed his rolling suitcase from the overhead compartment. Then, he followed the flight attendants through the narrow hallway under the attentive looks of all the other passengers.

At the plane door, two men in dark suits waited. The pit of his stomach fell when he recognized one as Agent Richard Fields. *What now?*

"Mr. Johnson?" Richard showed his ID. "FBI. We need you to come with us."

He trembled slightly as he wiped a sweaty palm on his suit pants. "What is this about now? Allison withdrew charges against me. I need to talk to my lawyer."

"You can come with us voluntarily, or you can come in handcuffs. Your choice." Agent Fields' glare left no room for negotiation.

His pulse sprinting, Jay followed the agents along the boarding tunnel and out to the terminal. They walked in silence through the security area and out to ground transportation where a black SUV awaited. Richard indicated that Jay should board.

"Is anyone going to tell me what this is about?" Jay asked once in the back seat.

"I'm sorry. I'm going to have to take some precautions." Richard handcuffed him to the car door.

Chapter 40

ALLISON HAD BRACED HERSELF FOR THE VIEW OF JAY'S SEXY arms in his usual gym outfit. But the stunning man standing at her condo door, dragging his carry-on luggage, wore a sharp business suit and a tie. He studied her with such intensity it made her forget everything she'd planned to say.

"Thank you, Agent Fields," she told Richard. "That will be it. I hope this doesn't cause you any trouble at work."

He gave a half shrug. "You know I'm kind of a sociopath who enjoys risking getting fired." Averting his eyes, Richard cleared his throat and scratched the back of his head. "So we're cool now? You forgive me for sending the FBI to hunt you down back then?"

She crossed her arms and shifted her weight. Her gaze darted away before she returned to him to give him a single nod. "And you forgive me for trying to break you up with Joy?"

"I guess the politically correct answer for that is yes, even if it's not true, right?" he mumbled, narrowing his eyes.

With a soft smile, she patted his shoulder. "You'll always be my Mycosis Fungoides."

He flashed Allison one last smirk before walking away, holding Joy by the hand.

Left alone with Jay, Allison returned her attention to him. Her pulse sped up.

"The FBI was hunting you?" he asked. She wished he weren't wearing that inscrutable expression.

"Long story," she replied. She eyed him from head to toe, then pointed at his tie. "Who died?"

He smiled at the inside joke. "Tiffany is going to, soon—but she doesn't know it yet."

She chuckled and then realized he was still standing at the door. "Would you like to sit down?"

"First, I'd like to know why I'm here," he replied.

Okay, this is it. Allison experienced again the unpleasant sensation of ice in her hands and fire in her face. The fluttering in her heart was only matched by the jumping in her stomach. There she was again, the teenage girl melting away at the sight of the boy she liked.

"Sorry for bringing you here this way, but you wouldn't answer your phone and I couldn't let you go to California without telling you something." She swallowed. "I will not be fighting for my counseling license. Now I know that I didn't do anything wrong. The man I married has nothing to do with the man I met that day at my office. And there's no point in me trying to explain it to the world."

Raising his eyebrows, he pulled the laptop strap over his head and off his shoulder and set it down.

She continued, "And one thing I will not do is apologize. Because falling in love with that man was the best thing that ever happened to me. I don't regret anything, because thanks to him I no longer see the world from inside a box. I want to get out, and be played with, and get scuffed and dirty, and make tons of memories."

His eyes darkened and she could tell she had his attention. Fighting tears, she continued, "And that man—I mean, *you* taught me many lessons, like, we all screw up sometimes and eat the pizza we shouldn't have had. But we don't use that as an excuse to throw away the diet." She trembled, and her voice threatened to crack. "You screwed up, and I screwed up. But, instead of throwing everything in the trash, if we decide to give each other grace, maybe we can still save—"

She couldn't finish the sentence because he took her in his arms

266

and kissed her.

She burst into tears and abandoned herself in his embrace. He cradled her head with one hand, deepening the kiss, and she delighted in the exquisite invasion of his mouth and the electrifying caress of his fingers, skimming over her body to find her favorite spots. Gently, as if in a slow dance, he walked her to the bedroom while shedding his jacket and tie on the way. Between kisses, he coaxed her into the bed and undid her clothing, making her whimper with longing, aching for his touch.

"Wait." She broke a kiss to say, "I still had three more pages of my speech."

He finished unbuttoning her shirt. "I'd love to hear them, darling—later. Much later." Then, the smoldering touch of his hands made her brain shut off and her body took over.

* * *

A trail of kisses down her neck woke Allison up. Had she fallen asleep?

The warmth of Jay's body was wonderful as he held her in his arms. His kisses had found their way to her ear and she heard him whisper, "God, I needed that so much!"

She giggled like an annoying woman in love. "Good. I needed you in a good mood for what comes next. I have a request."

"I hope it's something naughty and sexy," he said as he nibbled at her neck.

She held his face gently, making him look at her. "I need you to talk to your father."

His cheerfulness disappeared, and he stared at her in silence for a few moments. "I do not negotiate with terrorists." He sat on the bedside and started getting dressed.

She grabbed a terry robe from the floor and put it on. "Jay, listen to me. Your father is willing to help you."

"What?" He kept buttoning without looking at her.

She sat next to him on the bed edge. "The only reason your sister wants Gracie's custody is because your father skipped her in his will. If your father modifies his will and leaves Tiffany some money of her own, she would let you have her."

He sighed loudly. "This has been the story of my life. This is exactly the manipulating behavior typical of Conan—"

"Listen to me, stubborn child." She tugged on his arm to make him turn and look at her. "Would you put your resentments aside for one minute and see this guy the way he is now? He's old and sick and full of regrets. And he loves you."

A mixture of conflicting feelings crossed Jay's face. "He never loved me."

"He does, and he's desperate," she explained. "He said he's tried it all to get your attention. Taking you out of the will, adding you back, suing you for injury, sending you messages about his health. He admits he could've stopped this fight between you and Tiffany long ago. But he says this mediation was the only way to force you to talk to the family again."

When he didn't answer, she continued, "All he wants is one hour with you, a chance to ask for your forgiveness. If you grant him that, he'll support you in securing guardianship of Gracie. He hopes you'll let her visit with them, but he doesn't even put that as a condition."

He seemed hesitant, so she added, "And there's one more thing you need to know; you and I found each other again thanks to him."

"What?"

"Have you stopped to consider what a ridiculous coincidence it was that your family chose *me* as a therapist? Your father knew who I was. He'd heard you complain about having lost touch with me, he tracked me down, found out about my name change, and got involved as a donor in the Women's Shelter just to meet me."

To Jay's astonished look, she added, "That's how he learned about this city and ended up moving here. Conan had an agenda. He hoped that finding me, and bringing Tiffany and Gracie to live here would make you want to stay in this town, near him, instead of Atlanta."

As Jay processed her words, she charged again. "All I ask is for you to give him a chance to apologize. Then he'll help you get Gracie back."

After some time thinking, Jay met her gaze. "Do I get to bargain? Can I ask for something else?"

She considered it. "I don't see why not."

"All right." He narrowed his eyes. "Then here's my counter-offer. I also want my wife back."

Allison chuckled. "Jay, you're making no sense. You never really had a wife."

"My point exactly." He extended his open hands and only then did she realized he was still wearing the wedding ring. "Before all hell broke loose, you and I were negotiating a three-month contract, to be reviewed and renewed every quarter until one of the parties decided otherwise. I never got my three months."

Crossing her arms, she tried to shoot him her no-nonsense glare, but she was so overjoyed to have him back, she suspected she looked more crossed-eyed than anything. "I never made any promises. I told you the only logical thing to do was to annul this marriage and start fresh."

He traced her face with his finger, then slowly continued behind her ear and neck, triggering goose bumps on her skin. "If I agree, I'll never forgive myself for losing you a second time. You need to give me the chance to either make this work or prove it was a mistake."

With a groan, she uncrossed her arms. "Jay, I'm not wife material. I'm too set in my ways to live with anybody permanently—"

"Do you remember what I used to say in the boot camp about junk food?" he asked, kissing her shoulder.

She went back in her mind, but it was hard to concentrate when he was nibbling so deliciously above her collarbone.

Between love bites, he filled in, "The word permanently doesn't exist. You just give up donuts *today* for twenty-four hours. And then tomorrow you do it again. And then again." He stopped to look at her. "That's all I ask from you in this marriage, that you put up with me twenty-four hours at a time, and I promise I'll make it worth your while."

It was difficult to contradict him, so she pulled her ultimate argument. "Jay, I love you to death, but I'm pretty sure you'd make the worst husband in the world."

He gasped in mock horror, then chuckled. "And why is that?"

"You brag that 'you never do anything you don't want to do.'" She lifted her palms. "Isn't a matter of time until we start arguing about who's going to do the dishes or make the bed?"

"Darling, the best husband is the one who refuses to do what he doesn't want to do—because he'll never be resentful or ask for payback." He grabbed her hand to kiss her wrist. "And remember, you might never convince me to do anything I don't want to do, but you can always convince me *that I do want to do it*—that the long-term rewards outweigh the short-term comfort. Like you did with Matt's offer."

Allison's mood deflated. For a moment she'd forgotten that he was on his way to LA. "Oh, that's right. I guess you're moving to California now." She knew she would follow him wherever he went, but she would miss her friends terribly.

He shook his head. "I worked out a compromise with Matt. We're going to make Legendary Heroes Gyms a franchise. I'll be involved in opening the first gyms, flying back and forth to LA and training legions of trainers. But I hope to streamline the process enough that my presence is no longer needed, so I can eventually switch to a nine-to-five supervisory position."

She went speechless for a moment. "That's great. But are you going to be happy with that?"

"I'd better. I have a family to support now." He scooped her up to sit her on his lap and resumed kissing her neck. "And I want to make sure my wife can take her time figuring out what she wants to do, now that she's no longer a therapist."

She absorbed his words slowly. She'd never imagined she would see him that grounded. Maybe he did have a shot as a husband.

As if sensing she was weakening, he seized the chance. "We once said we'd help each other out of our comfort zones by taking risks together. You do that one thing that scares you—staying married to me for the next three months, then I'll do one thing that scares me—confronting my father."

From his lap, she reached for the nightstand drawer and found the wedding band she'd stowed there weeks ago. Jay's face lit up at the sight of it.

She placed it on her finger and, surprisingly, it slid on without a struggle.

"Okay." Her eyes fixed on him, she took a deep breath. "Three months, then we'll take it from there."

Chapter 41

J AY HAD TO ADMIT HE WAS MUCH MORE NERVOUS THAN HE expected. He hadn't seen his father in five years.

Allison seemed to sense his anxiety and kept holding his hand tightly as they walked across the long foyer and spacious great room, following Regina to his father's bedroom. There was no sign of Tiffany. He just wanted to get this done so he could see Gracie.

They arrived at the large master suite where Conan rested, not feeling well today. Wearing his blue robe over his plaid pajamas, he waited on a chair next to his bed. Jay couldn't believe how much older and frailer his father had become since the last time he'd seen him.

Jay braced himself for the moment they'd make eye contact. He expected the years of resentments and grief to make a come back full force.

Instead, he found a pair of pleading eyes. They were loaded with the same shame and regret they'd had thirty years ago. But this time, Jay understood the shame wasn't directed toward him. This time he could also see those eyes were oozing with love.

In a flash, the memory of the two of them playing with his action figures that one afternoon returned to him. He felt the inexplicable certainty that everything would be all right.

Epilogue

THE CAMERA LIGHTS THREATENED TO BLIND ALLISON EVERY time she looked up. But Carrie O'Brian's instructions had been clear: she had to keep packing her suitcase, ignoring the cameramen while they talked. She suspected that when Carrie suggested they'd bring the interview to her house, she did it not only to "show a slice of her life to her followers" but also to test the waters for some future reality show about her and Jay.

"Well, Allison." Carrie's face lit up. "Next month it will be a year since you made history by being the first woman to complete the Legendary Heroes Warriors Boot Camp. It's amazing how much a life can change in one year, isn't it?"

Folding clothes on her bed, Allison did her best not to look at the cameras. "It certainly is."

"Take your latest book," Carrie pointed out. "Your memoir, *I Married my Stalker*, promises to break records as an international bestseller. No wonder publishing houses started a bidding war the moment you announced you were writing it."

Allison cringed internally. "Ugh, I hate the name of that book. My new publisher insisted on it. But I see that memoir mostly as an instrument—the bait I used with publishing houses to make sure someone also picked up the other book I wrote this year, *Playing with Dolls: Healing your Inner Child*. That's the most successful self-help book I've written, and I'm proud of how it's been helping people since its release."

"I know! That book alone is launching your new career as a professional speaker and life coach. 'The woman who gave up her former life in the name of love.'"

Jay entered the bedroom in gym clothes, holding a box, and Allison lost her concentration. He kissed her briefly, waved at Carrie and the cameras, and kept going toward the bookshelf in the back of the room, where he was organizing his collection of action figures.

Allison still couldn't get used to having cameras focused on her instead of that hunk of a man. But as unbelievable as it felt, Carrie kept the attention on her. "So tell us about what we all want to hear." Carrie tilted her head on Jay's direction. "Your memoir ends with a three-month contract between you and Triple J. It has obviously been longer than that. What has happened since then?"

She returned her attention to the suitcase. "We were supposed to be revisiting the contract for the third time recently when I found myself pregnant, so that has automatically extended the deal at least an additional year."

Carrie clapped. "Pregnant? That's wonderful news, Allison, congratulations!"

Still digesting the news herself, Allison nodded while folding a nightgown. "It was a big surprise. I'd tried to get pregnant through IVF years ago and didn't succeed. I assumed I couldn't."

Jay wrapped his arms around Allison from the back and kissed her cheek before grinning at the camera. "And we're having triplets!"

"Is that true?" Carrie gawked at them.

Allison shook her head. "Jay has a crazy sense of humor; don't believe anything he says. I haven't had my first ultrasound yet."

Jay's expression was dead serious. "Oh, yes you did. Emery borrowed a machine and a tech from the hospital. You're such a heavy sleeper." Still hugging Allison, he lowered his voice and spoke to Carrie. "She didn't even wake up when we found the third heartbeat and Emery shrieked." He kissed Allison's cheek one more time and walked away.

"You're right; his sense of humor is something else." Carrie chuckled, then erased her smile. "He *is* kidding, isn't he?"

"I hope so," Allison mumbled. "Anyway, where were we?"

"I was congratulating you on the new baby—or babies," Carrie answered. "Though everyone knows Jay is nothing but a big kid. Aren't you worried he'll be zero help?"

"Actually, I've been pleasantly surprised," Allison answered. "He's a very involved father-like figure for his niece Gracie and does most of her care. As you might know, her mother and stepfather are in the Amazon rainforest, filming the Reality TV show, *Lost with the Stars*, so she's been staying with us indefinitely." Allison stuck to the official version of their arrangement with her sister-in-law. The truth was that they were in the process of legally adopting Gracie.

As if on cue—maybe the cameramen gave her a signal—Gracie entered the room. Allison wanted to laugh and also roll her eyes at the picture of "domestic perfection" the gorgeous blond girl made in her pink dress, holding a Border collie puppy in her arms while greeting her and Jay with hugs and kisses. Had Carrie staged that?

Nope. Apparently, this is my life now.

Becoming an adoptive mother barely weeks after settling into married life had been a scary prospect for Allison. Fortunately, Jay and Miranda were a well-oiled machine caring for Gracie, allowing Allison's interactions with the girl to be mostly fun-oriented. And there was something magical about seeing Gracie so happy now, free from her unstable mother. Allison almost felt as if she'd given her own childhood story an alternative ending.

"Uncle Jake, Aunt Allison, say bye to Ginger for now!" Gracie exclaimed, holding up the puppy.

Obviously moved, Carrie placed a hand on her chest. "You got a dog?"

"No," Allison rushed to correct. "This is my in-laws' new puppy."

"No, she's ours!" Gracie grinned.

Shaking her head with a smile, Allison scratched the puppy's head. "We've gone over this before, Gracie. We already have two cats. We were just keeping Ginger for a while until Grandma Regina recovered from her..." *Facelift.* "Procedure."

Carrie addressed Gracie. "So, you're coming on this trip to LA for the opening of the first Legendary Heroes Gym."

Gracie beamed. "And Miranda is coming with us to help watch me."

Carrie turned back to Allison. "It must be challenging to travel with a child. Wouldn't it have been easier for one of you to stay home?"

"Jay and I always travel together." She cleared her throat and confessed, "We don't do very well when we're apart." She then caressed Gracie's hair with tenderness. "But Gracie is a great traveler; she doesn't mind sleeping in hotel rooms and patiently waiting for hours in airports. She's only nine, yet she's one of the most mature and levelheaded people I've ever met—please do not ask me where she gets it from." Allison meant that. Gracie was single-handedly healing the relationship between Jay and Conan, lecturing them every day, manufacturing family gatherings and forcing them to spend time together.

"But now Miranda and I have to take Ginger to Grandma Regina's house so she can watch her until we come back," Gracie said.

Allison gave a tense smile. "She *is* Grandma Regina's puppy."

"Grandma Regina said I can keep her and Uncle said yes!" Gracie jumped up and down.

Allison shot Gracie and Jay alternating loving/warning looks.

"I only said we'd talk about it," Jay clarified from the bookshelf, raising his hands. "But it makes sense. We did the hardest part of the job already."

"What does he mean?" asked Carrie.

"It's quite handy having an insomniac for a spouse when you're taking care of a small puppy that cries all night and needs bottle feeds," Allison replied. "Jay took care of Ginger until she slept through the night."

Jay walked toward Gracie and took the puppy from her hands to pet it. "I loved it! After years tossing and turning in bed with nothing to do, I finally had a distraction. I can't wait to spend my nights changing diapers and burping babies." He signaled Carrie to come closer and whispered, "We really *are* having triplets, but Allison doesn't know it yet."

Ignoring what she hoped was another joke, Allison intervened, "And lately *he* is sleeping better than ever. The constant flying back and forth to California, and the demands of parenthood and dog care are finally catching up with him. Lately, he's so exhausted he *almost* seems like a normal person."

He snorted. "And I thought triathlons and weight lifting were tiring! Managing work and a family is like being on lithium."

As Gracie walked away with the dog to join Miranda in the car, Carrie addressed Jay. "Is it true that Allison is the one who wears the pants in the house? That much of your current success is due to her cracking the whip at you, and forcing you to do things you previously refused to do?"

"Oh, definitely. That's absolutely true." He took Allison in his arms and looked at her with adoration. "And I wouldn't have it any other way." He kissed her slowly and gently. Teasing with a deep kiss that only made her ravenous for more, knowing they couldn't overdo it in front of the cameras.

The interview came to an end and Allison exhaled in relief. After leading Carrie and her crew to the door with effusive goodbyes, they walked into the kitchen where Ethan was finishing fixing the sink for them. It was great counting on his handyman skills. And it was even greater seeing how healthy and strong he was now.

"You're a lifesaver, Ethan! I would've hated leaving this undone before our trip," she told him, kissing his cheek.

"You're welcome, pizza partner-in-crime," he answered, patting her back. He then gave her the under-the-eyelashes, puppy eyes she knew well. "You know I love to have an excuse to come over and interrogate you. Any updates on the life of the future mother of my children?" He grinned.

Rolling his eyes, Jay shook his head. "Have you checked the mirror lately, Ethan? It was one thing being obsessed with Emery when you were in the hospital all the time, looking like hell, and she was the only pretty woman around being nice to you. But you're back to yourself now."

"Yes. If you only tried, there would be plenty of other women to choose from," Allison added. She wasn't kidding. Ethan had turned into a very handsome man, with his full head of dark brown hair contrasting with striking blue eyes. But his good looks were nothing compared to his heart of gold.

Ethan offered a sad smile. "I know why you're trying to discourage me, guys. I heard she's dating that a-hole Ken Carter again. But don't worry. I broke them up once and I can break them up again."

Allison's jaw dropped as a memory hit her. "Wait a minute. We never found out who texted Emery that picture of Ken with the stripper. Was that *you*?"

Ethan suppressed a smirk. "Oh, not me personally. But I have friends and acquaintances working in every bar and restaurant in this town. And they're always willing to do anything I ask."

Jay crossed his arms and gave him a once-over. "And they never dare say no, because 'you had cancer.'"

Ethan beamed at him. "It still works."

With a fake exasperated huff that sounded more like a chortle, Jay pushed his shoulder to nudge him toward the door.

After saying goodbye to Ethan, Jay wrapped his arm around Allison's waist and strolled with her. "How's your next blog post going? I can't wait to read it."

"It's challenging," she replied. "Coming up with 'the three biggest lessons I learned in the past year' is proving harder than I thought."

"What do you have so far?"

As they walked to their bedroom, she put her thoughts in order. "Number one is: You know what? Men and women are NOT the same. Thank God for that! Their strengths compensate for our weaknesses—and vice versa."

"I'm honored." He moved the hair out of his face. "So you don't still think men are 'hairy, smelly creatures, slaves of our testosterone'?"

She tittered at the quote from her fourth book and pinched his bicep. "Thank God for testosterone!"

He chuckled. "What's the second one?"

Allison advanced to the wall of bookshelves in the back of the bedroom, displaying her growing doll collection next to his action figure collection. She grabbed the Barbie with the silver gown that started it all. "To never live in a box again. And the third one is to never lose touch with my inner child." She returned the doll to its honorary place. "And what would be yours?"

He considered it for a moment. "That the best play partner is the one who challenges you to climb the highest trees." He wrapped his arms around her waist and kissed her neck, then whispered in her ear. "And speaking of playing; we still have an hour before Miranda brings Gracie back from visiting her grandparents."

She ran her hands down the hard cords of his neck, his strong shoulders, his vast back, his powerful chest. "You know your body is my favorite playground."

He captured her mouth, and she was glad they didn't have to keep this kiss camera-appropriate.

Exclusive Bonus Scenes!

(Please don't forget to return here afterward, to read about other coming attractions, and to leave a book review)

Join my Newsletter to have access to exclusive bonus scenes:

<u>My Favorite Patient</u> (Ethan's last hospital admission): Ethan is convinced that he was just another patient for Dr. Love and she "barely knew he existed." Is he right? Exclusive Longing for Love teaser, only available to Newsletter subscribers.

<u>Deleted Scenes</u>: This novel went through dozens of revisions and many scenes didn't make it to the last cut. Find out more! (Includes scenes of Grace and Cowlick's childhood and censored scenes from Allison and Jay's first night together).

www.pichardo-johansson-md.com/grasping-for-grace-bonus-material

You will also gain access to:
-Opportunities to read future books for free.
-"Sexless in The Boondocks." The Series of Short Stories.
-Sneak-peeks of future releases.

Note from the Author

Dear Reader:

It is an honor to me that you took the time to read this story. I hope you've enjoyed it.

My goal is to write romance stories which are not only entertaining, but also enriching for the soul. Striking a balance between those two objectives is sometimes difficult, as it is to decide the right amount of sexy-spice to add into the mix.

I'd love to hear from you. What did you like in the story? What did you not like? What would you like to see more in future books? I would really appreciate if you could take the time and leave a review at Amazon, Goodreads, your blog or any other venue of your preference.

Please visit my website and sign for my email list for free short stories and sneak-peeks in future releases- http://www.pichardo-johansson-md.com/sign_up_form/

Please also feel free to email me at pichardojohanssonmd@gmail.com—I'm a busy lady, but I'll do my best to answer all emails.

Thank you again for reading me.

Love,
Diely

Other Books in This Series

Check my website www.pichardo-johansson-md.com/books for
more details.

And don't forget to join my e-mail list for further information about
these two and other upcoming books.
www.pichardo-johansson-md.com/sign_up_form

Love,
Diely

About the Author

Dr. Pichardo-Johansson is a Board Certified physician practicing in Florida. Her Romance specialty is "Connection of the minds and the souls, more than only the bodies." Her Mystery specialty is "How to murder someone and ensure a negative autopsy."

She's a firm believer in the body-mind-spirit link and the healing power of laughter. Her motto is that "The Best Health Booster Is Wanting to be Alive." For that reason, she only writes positive stories, uplifting for the heart.

She is a mother of four children, including twins and a child with special needs. She lives in Melbourne Beach, Florida with them and her Soulmate Husband, a reformed eternal bachelor turned into happy stepfather.

In spite of her busy life, she absolutely loves to get emails from readers and welcomes feedback. You can always email her at pichardojohanssonmd@gmail.com

For more information, and to learn about upcoming releases, visit her website at:
www.pichardo-johansson-md.com